Where She Went

B. E. Jones

Constable • London

CONSTABLE

First published in Great Britain in 2017 by Constable

1 3 5 7 9 10 8 6 4 2

Copyright © B. E. Jones, 2017

The moral right of the author has been asserted.

A CIP catalogue record for this book is available from the British Library.

ISBN: 978-1-47212-382-4

Typeset in Sabon by SX Composing DTP, Rayleigh, Essex
Printed and bound in Great Britain by Clays Ltd, St Ives plc

Papers used by Constable are from well-managed forests and
other responsible sources.

MIX
Paper from
responsible sources
FSC® C104740

For Kate, good sister

Chapter One

When I opened my eyes I knew right away I was not at home. I was somewhere I'd never been before and I didn't like the wallpaper, or the curtains.

Waking up was slow and treacly, like grasping for the edges of the morning after a late-night swallow of sleeping pills. I was groggy and light-blinded, though the snow floating past the open curtains of the bedroom window made the day dim enough.

I turned my head slowly. *Camera pan, 90 degrees left, then right. Start at the beginning. Establish the scene.*

Morning. Bedroom. Bed, window, wardrobe, twining yellow roses creeping up the walls, buttercream swagged curtains, faint scent of vanilla and linen; nothing threatening, nothing familiar. I sat up, carefully cracking each joint into place. Once semi-upright, supported on my elbows, I looked down at myself and considered the view. I was still wearing my work outfit: black skirt, pale grey blouse, black woollen coat, surprisingly dowdy lace-up leather shoes spoiling the ensemble, shedding grit and sand on the white bedcovers, my scarlet scarf still twined around my neck from last night.

Last night.

I shuddered seismically at the mosaic memory of splintering vision, pain and cold like an endlessly indrawn breath. Steeling myself, I reached up to my face, ran my fingers over my chin and cheekbones, then up and backwards, under the base of my skull, beneath my hair, feeling for questions, waiting to wince. My fingertips told me all was smooth, no blood, no bumps, no open, tender gashes but I still looked at my hands expecting to see a smear of hot red. My body was racing ahead of my mind – it was remembering before I could, or was trying to. But it was wrong apparently, misled, overexcited. My skin told no story of trauma or disarrangement. No clues were written there.

I took a long, slow breath and let it out. I gathered in my calm. I told myself, *I am not hurt. This is a safe place.* I find most things in life can be made fact by sheer effort of will, made solid by the saying of them. Most things.

So, where the hell was I? I'd been unconscious clearly, how else did I get into that room? Was it a hospital suite, perhaps? An expensive, private one styled to look like a home? No, the rose pattern on the walls, the dressing table with its neat rows of dainty glass jars and bottles meant this was a real bedroom, owned by someone who liked the Home Counties retro look, a woman. But there was a man lying next to me, sleeping, snoring slightly, the throaty rumble the only sound in the room.

His back was to me, his torso rising and falling steadily above the crisp, white bedcover wound at his waist. I didn't recognise him, or the curve of his neck, the close-cut dark hair, the faded scar from ear to collarbone, puckered slightly, silvery slick.

2

Had I met this guy somewhere last night? Had I been ragingly, roaringly drunk and come back to his place for a quick . . . what? What's your poison? What's your pleasure? Whatever? That seemed unlikely. Not that I was a nun or anything but it wasn't my style. Also, if some unexpected lapse of judgment had occurred and I'd trailed home with this mystery man, it didn't seem possible much could have happened between us on that pristine bed, fully dressed as I was. I patted my skirt, relieved to feel the elastic outline of my knickers beneath. Well, you never know. There are perverts about.

I tried to think back then, to remember, but the insides of my head revolved in slow circles around a void at the centre, torn pieces of pictures floating inside and outside, just out of reach, in the air above me – winter breath, laughter, liquid sounds, something dark and red like wine. Something about the scar on his neck? A slice in the skin, a slice in the sky? The smell of fish and chips. And salt. Then the golden morning aroma of toast wafted through the bedroom door, sending the fragments spiralling upwards, out of my reach under the ceiling. I realised there were sounds downstairs and heard a soft, squeaking tread on the stairs, coming closer.

Eve entered the room then. I know her now, of course, each part of her face is as familiar as my own; the grey underwater colour of her eyes, the fledgling frown line between them. But that morning she was just a pretty woman in her early thirties, with feathery bobbed black hair and a pink rosebud dressing gown. She was bringing a tray up to the bed bearing a pot of tea for one, a tray, judging by the careful way she carried it, made from eggshells and bird bones and infinitely breakable promises.

3

She hovered with the flowered pot, matching flowered china cup and saucer, strainer and tiny jug of milk over the bed. She didn't react to my presence, shoed and scarfed atop the bedcovers.

Okay then, I thought. *Scene established, partially – start the introduction because time's ticking by. Attention spans are short.*

'Hi,' I said. Always go for the oldies and the goodies. Tried and tested. 'This might sound odd, but where am I?'

She eased the tray on to the bedside table and stared at the man next to me for a moment, her face seizing into something uncomfortable – something that did not fit with the good china and starched bed linen. I'm adept enough at reading expressions to know that. The precise shade of this one would become clear to me in the weeks to come – something purplish and bruised? Something faded but tender? Something sorry?

But she still didn't answer me. Eventually she gave bed-man a little shake.

'Tea, Pete.'

He stirred, turned, stretched and smiled. And she smiled back, an eggshell, bird-boned, brittle smile, like something broken underfoot in soft earth. I smiled too, because I have to admit he had a nice smile and it was a way to quell the urge to laugh that was bubbling up in my throat. Because it was all so very weird and surreal, being there, like that, possibly the strangest thing that had ever happened to me, in fact. And it was not yet 8 a.m., still early in the day.

'Indian leaf tea, this morning?' asked Peter, running a hand through his hair as she poured carefully.

'Yes, of course, darling.'

'Well, that's a good start.'

She looked as if she was expecting him to say something else as she watched him stir in the milk and one level sugar.

'Everything go okay last night?'

'It was just work, Eve, I don't want to talk about work. But I know what I do want.'

He reached for her then, clasped a hand around her neck, pulled her in and kissed her, hard and long. When he drew back her smile had collapsed a little on one side. Flustered, she tried to twist away, to hide it.

'Hey! Hello,' I said, finally sparking with irritation, outrage igniting in my belly. I didn't know what kind of kinky game they were into but I don't care to be ignored. I don't like being on the back foot and not knowing exactly what is going on. I don't like being an observer.

'Nice to meet you,' I said, stretching out my hand for him to shake with exaggerated politeness, as if the formality could shatter the oddness of the scene and right-foot the askew morning world. 'Who are you and where am I, exactly?'

He cupped her breast through the thin robe. I could see her trying not to stiffen.

'Not now, Pete, Adam'll be up in a tick.'

'He's still dead to the world – I want you now.' Then he unwrapped the belt of her dressing gown, pulling her on top of him.

Christ – this is bizarre, I thought. I mean, I like to think of myself as fairly open-minded but . . . 'Look, what exactly is going on? And can you *stop* that? The joke's over.'

He slipped his hand into the dark shadow between her thighs. His morning hard-on reared up at full mast from the white wave of sheets.

Uh oh, dubious content, non-guideline, pan away. Cut/edit.

'Right, that's it.' I was off the bed and on my feet. 'Are you freaks or what?'

I stumbled to the door and on to the landing, brushing sand from my coat as she gave a tight gasp and he hushed her, rolling on top of her.

'That's my good girl,' he said.

Standing on the landing I took a deep breath and tried to clear the grains of sand from my head and lungs. An image flashed on to the back of my eyelids through the gloom. Dark water, ridged and rushing. Snow collecting on my eyelashes, grit on my tongue. I'd been on the beach. That's right. I was on the beach and then I was here. And I didn't know where here was.

Breaking news, ran the ticker text scrolling along the bottom of the screen inside my head. *You're a long way from home, girl.*

For a while I stood on the landing in the grey-snow light, trying to shake the confusion out of my head through my ears. I could hear squeaks and sighs through the bedroom door as I leaned against the stair rail. After the first few flashes the fog kept descending over the hours before my washing awake on the white shore of the bed. Something was slipping around in my head. I couldn't fix it back in place. Everything was edgeless. The house seemed to shimmer and undulate, or was that my vision?

The little sex bout on the other side of the door didn't seem likely to last long so I wandered downstairs looking for a phone. I needed my handbag, my great, big, something-for-every-emergency handbag with its reassuring bulk. I couldn't find it. But I didn't panic. *I* don't panic. There was no need for melodrama. I knew the situation would soon realign itself into a commonplace sequence of logical events and be sorted back into the proper narrative order. First, I needed to call home. But there didn't seem to be a landline. And then a great, grey dizziness overcame me and somehow I was sitting at the kitchen table, without having walked to the kitchen, or pulled out a chair, and Eve was standing opposite me, flushed, tousle-haired, a fresh plate of toast in her hand.

I've spent a lot of time in that kitchen with her since, lounging around the granite worktops while she kneads bread, bakes cakes, pokes things bubbling on the Aga – though she doesn't know it. You can learn a lot about someone from the way they keep their kitchen. And from watching them when they think they are alone.

It makes me smile now, to remember how calmly I tried to get the measure of her that morning, how I mulled over which approach might work best to get her to explain. At the thought of it my face flexes into something that feels like a smile, but is it still a smile if no one sees it?

'Hey, excuse me,' I said, 'I don't know if we've met before. I seem to be having trouble remembering. What exactly is going on?'

I tried to make my voice calm and coaxing in a 'girls together, you can let me in on the secret' way, but I suspect it came out pebbly and cold. And anyway, Eve just sat down in the chair opposite, trembling a little, rubbing her left wrist ringed with faint, looping red marks.

Fear fluttered inside me for the first time then, moth wings in my throat. It was an unexpected and new sensation. I didn't care for it. The morning was slipping from my grip.

'Tell me your name,' I said softly. 'Tell me what's happened?'

Because this is how it goes. These are the important questions – who and what. Who are you? What is your role? What has occurred? What did you see? What did you do? That, at least, was familiar and I clung to it. But there was more of a plea in the questions than I would have thought myself capable of twenty-four hours before my eyes opened on this woman's ceiling.

When she raised her head and stared straight into me, into and through me and away further than the eye could see, and said nothing, I felt the world start to slide to one side. The old ordering motions were not having the right effect – this story was making no sense. I tried waking myself then, willing myself out of sleep because I was obviously dreaming, some fucked up nightmare about being invisible and unseen and overlooked and unaccounted for. Isn't that how the nightmares of people like me always take shape? The fear that no one is actually watching or listening anymore, the fear of being caught in the moment when the lens closes, the screen goes dark and the channel changes?

'It's no big deal,' I told myself. 'Stay calm.'

I was always able to wake myself from a dream or nightmare if I really chose to. I just looked at the back of my own eyelids and imagined waking up in my bed. So I closed my eyes and looked hard. I said 'Wake up,' three times, in quick succession so the saying could make it so.

It didn't work that morning. Nor any of the mornings after, even later when I kept saying to myself, *There must be a way out of this. A way back.* I said it loudly and confidently that morning. But, when my eyes opened, I was still sitting opposite Eve and I realised a rumbling was approaching from above, making its way down the stairs. From the girth of the noise I expected a two-tonne rhinoceros to splinter its way into the kitchen, snorting and pawing. But it was just Adam – five years of enthusiasm in a smart school uniform, galumphing into her arms; a hot, breathless bundle, a single-sock and stick-up-hair boy with a sleepy grin.

Eve swept him high into her arms, seemingly intent on squeezing his ribs into shards until he struggled and tumbled free.

'Come on, little man, into your seat,' she said, tousling his hair and play-pinching his bare left foot. 'Where's your other sock? Never mind, Mummy'll find one. Sit up straight, now.'

She carefully positioned a fan of fresh toast on a large plate in the centre of the table and something spasmed in my stomach, stringy and tight, at the smell of the food. I wondered how long it'd been since I'd eaten. But I couldn't eat. I felt wrung out like a twisted rag, damp and clammy and gritty. I wondered briefly if I was meant to be on the late shift; at least that meant I wasn't already supposed to be on-air. I thought again about using the phone. If I was due on earlies I imagined the dozen frantic messages from whomever was producing, Sue or Sean or Tilly, piling up on my answerphone. 'Where are you?', 'Will you make it?' then maybe, 'I'm getting worried, call me ASAP.'

Then Peter strode into the kitchen to complete the little family picture, neat in a navy suit, tie in a Windsor knot beyond reproach. A blast of pain hit me as he sat at the table, sending me staggering back on to my chair. Somewhere inside, under my ribs, at the back, I felt the words *I know you, I know you, don't I know you?* forming out of the air.

But I didn't know him, not in any way that mattered. That was, and had been, the problem.

9

Chapter Two

Ishould tell you something about myself first, shouldn't I? Before we get to Peter and the rest of it? Because this is my story and also because that's how it's supposed to be done and it's important to have discipline. The first questions are always the same, or they should be if you know your job. Who am I? What is my role? What did I do? And I've broken the rules by not doing a proper introduction. I've just started in the middle, with the most interesting sound bites, the choice clips to get your attention, like all good journalists.

But I haven't given you any context so you know what to expect – tragedy, comedy, heartbreak, catharsis? First day at broadcast news class that's what you learn, the importance of structure. The introduction lets you know what sort of story you will see unfolding, then come the talking heads that offer opinions, then there's the sum-up and conclusion. Nice and neat. Nobody likes surprises. Here we go, then.

I am a reporter and my name is Melanie Black. When I met Peter I was thirty-three years old.

I never liked it, my name, I mean. I used to wonder if this christening gift was a cosmic joke or just the result of mild and wilful ignorance on my parents' part. You might not be aware that Melanie means black in Greek. And Black is just that, in English. My parents were neither English nor Greek. They were Welsh. They just liked the sound of it.

You could argue it has a certain ironic resonance now. Black by name, black by nature? I've wondered about this in the light of recent events, if my name made me black – black-headed, hearted, handed. Was the darkness there all along, waiting to leak out when an incision was made, when my fabric was torn, ready to spiral outwards like a reverse black hole that had been revolving under my skin all the while?

Would it, would I, would my story have been different if I'd been called Suky or Suzette, or Hope, or Poppy, names full of hot sugar and spring flowers? Or if I'd been called Eve, bearing the historic mantle of first woman, disobedient, desiring knowledge, eater of forbidden fruit; Christmas Eve, All Hallows Eve, something about to happen, *the eve of the war*. But then, how unlike my Eve are these promises of her name, with her dusters and mops and sensible shoes. The argument is probably flawed.

We should choose our own names.

I'd like to have been called Anne-Marie Loveday, the name of the second-best reporter on my training course, although it wouldn't really have suited me as well as it suited her. She looked like a girl in a 1950s crime noir novel: hourglass figure, upswept hair, the sort of 'broad' who'd perch on private investigator Humphrey Bogart's desk, blow a thin stream of smoke into his face and say, 'Here's the deal.'

It's true my name served as a nice hook during my early career, for every newsroom wanker who thought they were oh so funny and witty and therefore must have been engaging in a great form of wordplay they'd clearly invented.

'Isn't that the pot calling the kettle *black*, Mel?' Chuckle.

'My, my, am I in your *black* books.' Grin.

'Get him to talk, Mel. Work a little of your *black* magic.' Wink.

Snigger, self-congratulatory smile, shared smirk. *Give me a goddamn break!*

That *was* actually the name of my first radio show. *Black Magic*. The one I taped on the old voice-activated recording machine Dad filched for me from BBC Broadcasting House when he was still on the radio. It was my version of a current affairs and arts show like his. I was eleven years old.

My first guest was Lottie Borlotti. That was really her name, Charlotte Maria Borlotti, like the bean, small, smooth and white but with black Italian curls. And full of beans she was, and rainbow sprinkles and midget gems and pink unicorn rucksacks.

Lottie was my Brownie sixer. I interviewed her about badge acquirement and the gender role assigned to women by organisations like the Brownies and Guides. Surely in the twentieth century all girls secretly wanted to be Scouts? I posited, as my dad had suggested. I'd only joined the boring Brownies because Mum insisted I did something social and wholesome, and it was that or the church choir group. Lottie was lost on the topic of gender roles, but she had her uses – she knew a lot about making fairy cakes and got me through my cookery badge. She and Eve would have been famous pals. Mum loved her.

But the phrase 'black magic' couldn't easily be squeezed into the first news reports about me, the ones at 1.26 p.m. and 6.35 p.m. and 10.25 p.m., the ones with the reporters' serious faces, the police looking stern and someone usually crying. They had to stick to the old-school puns for those, retain the expected formality, show a little respect.

'A *black* cloud hangs over this quiet seaside community,' was how they phrased it, the first time I made the nightly news. *Tone – serious, ominous.*

Nice one, I thought, watching the bulletin from my perch on Peter's sofa, one of my colleagues standing suitably forlorn in the drizzly rain on the town quayside – it was the favourite haunt of suicide jumpers, clumsy drunken homeward-wanderers and now, just for me, a police scene and a live TV news team. The first of several.

They managed to get 'black day' and 'black night' into the reports before the end of that week. Once or twice I wondered if they'd had a bet on in the newsroom – you know, a tenner under the table for the one who slipped the most clichés into their report. (I once won £20 by managing to get the phrase 'up in arms' three times into a live report about unwelcome 'traveller' sites.)

It was only luck that I saw the news that evening really, three days after my unusual arrival on Peter's bed. By then I'd learned that he only permitted one hour of TV per evening and that night, instead of a documentary or a history show, he left the news on while he went to get some files from his study. Then, there I was, on the goggle box, the one-eyed god of the living room, the boob tube. Dun, dun, dun! went the familiar 10.25 music, *and tonight's top story . . .*

By then I had a pretty good idea of what was probably happening, unlike that first morning, or the ones immediately after, when time was topsy-turvy and passing strangely, in small spurts and great surges.

It's hard to explain, but I remember how on the first day at Peter's place there were parts of days and parts of nights all mixed together, and slivers of light and dark, day and night, and then whole oceans of it, inside, outside, the wind under the eaves and in the trees, snow falling across my vision. For moments, or much longer, time's seepage was vague and shadow-struck, and I know I sat for hours staring at the corner of the room. I only knew hours had passed because the long fingers of the garden trees lengthened across the floor, dozens of them interwoven, undulating as the clouds passed overhead. At other moments the world turned on a bead of water clinging to a leaf, falling for a lifetime on to the soft earth. But I was always there, when I returned to myself and my eyes opened – in Peter's house. Already part of the family.

But what sort of family? I asked myself from that first moment I sat opposite Eve at the table, watching her readying breakfast, seeing for the first time a routine I would come to know well.

First came the four-minute boiled eggs, perfectly placed in the flowered eggcups on the flowered plates, between the perfectly placed knives, forks, spoons. A tumbler of Michaelmas daisies in the centre of the table, smiling brightly, the newspaper folded cleanly to the right of what could only be Peter's seat.

'There,' she said to Adam, fidgeting in his seat. 'All nice for Daddy.'

His good girl, I thought, rolling my eyes, thinking of the minutes before on the upstairs bedcovers and her lopsided smile. In that instant I knew, without a doubt, that she was the sort of woman I usually made a point of disliking.

'School's open,' pronounced Peter, in residence at the head of the table, smiling at his wife and son. 'The roads have been gritted. I'll take the people carrier today. Nothing like a few inches of snow to bring the country to a standstill.'

So we all sat there at the table in a tea-and-toast-tinted silence that, in other circumstances, could have been companionable. Eve sipped her tea and Peter cut the top off his egg with a smile. Only when he took a thin finger of toast and broke the golden crown in the centre did Eve reach to decapitate Adam's and then her own and they began to eat. Peter popped a buttered finger in his mouth, chewed and then asked, 'So, has Mummy been good or bad today, Adam?'

They both looked at the boy and I recall quite clearly how Adam paused, a finger of toast frozen half way to his mouth. He glanced first at his mummy and then back at his daddy. His dark, raisin eyes were shrewd in his plump face, a globule of yolk collecting in the corner of his mouth. I could see he was a bright little thing, clearly thinking carefully about his answer in a way people forget children can. Fascinating things, children, from a distance.

'Good, Daddy?' he asked with hesitation.

Then Peter smiled, dipped another finger of toast into his yolk and inspected it. 'Yes, I believe so, Mummy's been good.' He ran his tongue over his lips in a way that hinted at the morning's upstairs activity rather than the exemplary egg. 'Yes, very good. Two toasts for Mummy, then.'

Adam smiled, teeth and dimples combining in relief, the first challenge of the morning complete.

Eve wiped her son's mouth with a napkin and reached for the butter dish, but Adam's pudgy fingers rested on top of it and he pulled it away.

'No, Mummy, jam only,' said Adam, a little too loudly, looking to Peter for approval.

'Why, Adam?' asked Peter, a smile hovering behind his napkin as he patted his mouth.

'Cos Mummy's getting fat.'

'Good boy,' said Peter. He ruffled Adam's head and unfolded his newspaper, revealing a beatific smile straight from a toothpaste advert. Shiny white. Whiter than white. A perfect smile for Peter Perfect. Adam smiled, too.

Eve withdrew her hand from the butter dish and looked down into her lap. She crunched on her jam consolation prize, sipped her tea and then, after a moment, adopted the very definition of forced cheer.

'So who do you want to be for Book Day next week, Adam? You said Aladdin from the story.'

'What story?' asked Peter. 'I thought we agreed, Peter Rabbit. I was going to pick up the costume today.'

'Yes,' said Eve, carefully. 'But the boys like to be something more exciting.'

'You like Peter Rabbit, don't you, Adam Ant?' said Peter.

Adam looked at his mummy again, another challenge to navigate, then nodded at his daddy.

Eve said, 'I can make it myself, the costume, from the stuff in my box – all the mums make them now, better than buying those nylon things from the supermarket. They always look . . .' her words were carefully chosen, ' . . . a little cheap.'

'Yes, of course. All right then, funny bunny,' said Peter, 'Aladdin, just this once,' and he leaned over to tickle Adam.

'Thank you, Daddy,' said Adam with a grin.

'My good boy. We must get you a lamp so you can rub it and the genie will grant you three wishes.'

I only need one, said a voice, sharp as a razor's edge, sliding through the morning light. I remember actually looking around to see the source of it, expecting to see another person standing silently in the room. But no one had spoken.

'I wish I knew what was going on,' I said aloud.

'If wishes were fishes we'd all cast nets,' said Eve, brushing some crumbs from the corner of Adam's mouth. I thought for a moment she'd finally heard me, but her eyes were still fixed on the tablecloth, a small tea stain on the white expanse.

'Come on then, Adam Ant,' said Peter. 'You'll be late for school, little man.'

Then Eve was on her feet with Adam's small rucksack, ready packed, Peter's car keys and his packed lunch in hand. Peter handed her a phone from his jacket pocket and planted a precise kiss on her cheek.

As she stood, waving for a moment on the doorstep as the car started up, I had my first glimpse of my new community: a shady avenue with trees, a prosperous street with cared-for cars and gardens sleeping under snow. Then the front door closed as they pulled off down the drive and everything contracted once more to the size of the house.

I watched Eve walk back to the kitchen. I was trying to decide what to do next. I recall I didn't feel all that well but I remember thinking, *I might as well just play along, my alarm clock will go off any second now and I'll roll out of bed, through the shower and kitchen and into the studio as I do every day.* So I watched with pale, shivery detachment as Eve came back to the kitchen and leaned into the table, seemingly stabilising herself against the roiling floor. She dry-heaved just once and then sat down as if every last bone in her legs had crumbled to dust.

17

She put the mobile phone Peter had just given her down on the table and poked it further away with one finger, as if it might be booby-trapped. She clearly didn't want to use it because, instead, she went to the flour tin on the worktop and took out another mobile phone. It was in a plastic re-sealable sandwich bag.

Sitting opposite her at the table, in the strange dream I couldn't wake from, this didn't seem particularly weird, although it was an odd place to keep a spare mobile. I immediately thought she was probably calling a 'fancy man', as my mum might say, a lover, or maybe a drug dealer – so many mummies self-medicate now, with Valium and so on. It's pretty much the equivalent of cupcake shells and brie on the shopping list. But even when I'd known her all of twenty minutes I realised these clichés would probably be too much for Eve, for someone who had just hosted the perfect 1960s breakfast. I can usually hand-sort people in five seconds flat, like a Las Vegas card dealer, sifting Kings from Queens and Jacks – Eve wasn't interesting enough to have secrets. I'd already decided she was somewhere in the middle of a suit, easily ignored, easily sacrificed.

Queasily I watched as Eve hit speed-dial and said, 'Hi, it's me – how're you?' The forced cheer was present again, the edges of her voice glittering like diamonds. 'Lots better today?' She looked relieved. 'Good, good. Yes, Mair stayed. She was fine. He was fine. It was fine. No, no, don't say anything. Yes I came straight back, of course, the roads were clear. Look, I'll try and come when I can but I can't say for sure. I love you.'

The effort of the call made her face turn as grey as the light filling the kitchen. She turned off the phone, slid it into the bag and placed it back in the flour tin, taking care to cover it over once more.

And that turned out to be the main event of my first day with Eve. Of course, elsewhere, outside the house, other things were happening, slowly at first and then with more haste; phone calls were being made, voices were raised, reluctant orders were given over radios and numbers finally allocated to a police file. But that was not part of my world at Peter's house. Eve's wife-and-mother bubble was mine and nothing broke the quiet domesticity of it.

She didn't even listen to the radio or turn on the TV. (I didn't notice at the time that it was because the TV cabinet was locked, like the upstairs wardrobes.) But even if she had it would have been too soon for the news to jog my memory – that part of my story was in production and being assembled ready for broadcast.

So I dogged her steps while she set about her chores. I stood close to her as she took some trainers out of the cupboard under the stairs and cleaned them, brushed the grit and muck into the kitchen bin, put them by the front door. I looked over her shoulder as she made a cake, two cakes – one chocolate, one lemon drizzle.

I followed in her footsteps as she cleaned the rest of the house as thoroughly as if expecting royalty, moving from room to room with a vast pedlar-like basket of cleaning products full of bottles and sprays, dusters and chamois pads.

Why was I watching her do these things? Because at no point had my alarm clock sounded. Eventually, when I'd tried to open the front door of the house to go home nausea had gushed through me, like the worst twenty-four-hour bug I'd ever had, roiling like acid up the pipes of my chest, dissolving my lungs. Each time I tried the door handle the sickness got worse. I vomited for a few seconds, a gush of black liquid sluicing up, pooling on the immaculately lint-free hall carpet before vanishing inexplicably into the plush pile.

I wanted to cry then, but I didn't. *I* don't cry. Instead I jumped up and down in the hall. I beat my hands on the wall until they should have been pulped and bloody. But not even a crack appeared in the plaster walls or the family portrait glass. I called, I cursed, I screamed indigo-tinged oaths until I should have been blue in the face, until my throat should have been stripped and raked raw. But the curtains didn't even shiver nor did the little collections of carefully dusted angel figurines on the mantelpiece shudder in their prayers. Nothing.

As I stood in Eve's face, inches from her nose, and screamed and screamed she just carried on dusting the picture frames.

In the end I had to stop screaming.

That was a long day. It was punctuated only occasionally by the ringing of the phone Eve kept in her trouser pocket. It rang once at 11 a.m., then again at 2 p.m., then at 4 p.m., shrilling its way into every corner of the quiet and composed house. Each time Eve answered, her face turned that floury colour but her voice was bright like polished glass.

'Yes, of course, darling. Everything's fine. No, darling, how could I forget the parents evening? Yes, lemon and chocolate. No, I'll be ready.'

And she was ready, and waiting, as the winter darkness closed around the house once more and Peter came home with Adam in tow, pink-cheeked and snow-dusted. She'd dressed in the black jumper and white pearls that had been laid out for her on the bed upstairs since that morning's eggy breakfast. A pair of cream pumps had also been left for her but she hadn't put them on.

'May I have the black patent shoes instead?' Eve asked Peter, as he combed his sleek head of hair in front of the bedroom mirror, inspecting his angular reflection with satisfaction. I stood behind him, over his shoulder, waving my arms, but he didn't notice.

'I think the cream pumps are more appropriate for the chairman's wife, don't you?' he said to Eve. 'Got to make the right impression.'

'Yes but, darling, look, the heel is loose,' she said, wiggling the low block back and forth. 'I don't know when that happened. I'll have to get it mended.'

'Hmmm, yes of course. You could be a bit more careful, Eve. First those torn trousers, now this.'

That was the first time I saw him take the little bunch of keys out of his trouser pocket and open the big cupboard lined with pairs of shoes in two neat racks. He selected some black ones as Eve waited.

'Give them a little polish,' he said, handing them to her.

'Of course, darling,' said Eve, though I could almost see her face in them from across the room where I was sitting on the bed.

Then they were ready to leave, every inch the handsome, middle-class, professional couple, with the afternoon's fresh lemon cake in a tin under Peter's arm. Adam was swinging from Peter's hand and Eve was singing 'When You Wish Upon a Star', tickling his ribs.

Panic finally threatened to choke me when Peter grabbed his car keys from the hook and fumbled in his coat pockets by the hall table. I was somehow afraid of them leaving me all alone in that house, still kicking and struggling through my confusion, through my incomprehension, through my slowly crystallising suspicions.

'My gloves, what have you done with my gloves, Eve?' Peter demanded, oblivious to my attempt to tug on his coat sleeve, to put myself between him and the door. 'The black leather ones? The ones you gave me? Why aren't they here on the table where they always are? I always keep them here.'

'Haven't seen them, sweetheart,' said Eve smiling, a tightness around her mouth.

Peter cast his gaze around the darkened hall as if expecting to see his gloves appear, as if I was not demanding, in the darkness at his side, that he stop and take his coat off and tell me what was happening.

'Shall I check upstairs?' asked Eve.

'Oh for goodness sake, don't fuss,' said Peter, fiddling with his scarf. 'We're late enough already.'

Then, despite my protests, they were going, going, gone.

I tried to follow them but the nausea drove me back from the doorstep. The front door clicked shut and the sound of the engine reached me through the glass panes. I was alone and the world went away for a while as I sat on a chair in the hall, staring at the door, waiting. I felt as if I should do something, anything. I had to act, to take control of what was happening. But I was so very weak and sleepy. I meant to just rest a while on the chair.

'That was lovely,' said Peter, flicking on the hall light as my eyes flicked open.

How long had they been gone? Hours? Days? Centuries? All of the above?

'Went very well, I thought,' said Peter. 'The PTA can be such imbeciles. You looked very pretty tonight, darling.' Then he took Eve into the crook of his shoulder, Adam asleep in the nook of his other arm, chubby legs dangling. They looked for a moment like a sculpture of family-hood. Peter at the centre, her strength, her pillar, the innocent child in his arms, the tender kiss on her brow.

I almost showered them with more black water then but at the last minute I managed to aim for the ground between us as my insides came out.

'I'll take the little man up,' said Peter. 'You can pour us some wine as a treat, the Cabernet Sauvignon, I think.'

When he returned we all sat on the sofa together. I didn't know what else to do, at the end of that first and infinitely strange day. Their red wine pulsed in the TV flicker, like two excised but still beating hearts in glass globes on long stems. We watched the news and Eve's eyes flickered eagerly across the TV screen, as if the reports of casualties in Afghanistan were news to her, as if a Welsh Assembly member caught drink-driving, and a charity dog-grooming contest in Llangollen, were riveting pieces of reportage, instead of Jack's usual workman-like court report and Polly's familiar, sentimental filler.

'What a nice story,' said Peter, as the little Welsh corgi got its rosette, and a big cheque was paraded. Eve looked relieved to see him smile as the weather forecast came up. The afternoon snow was passing over but the house still creaked and groaned under the weight of winter.

'Tired, sweetheart?' asked Peter. 'We should go up. Lovely

cake tonight. Maybe just a little too much lemon essence in the sponge, but lovely.'

And that was it – the epic nature of my introduction to Peter's kingdom.

As he got to his feet and led Eve by the hand to the stairs I yelled in his face once more, 'I know you! I know you! Don't I know you?' But all he did was frown. Just a suggestion of a frown really, and only for a second but it was a start. It was there. I grew to know that frown over time. I learned to dig my nails in around the corners of his brow, slide my teeth across his peace of mind and summon it, those three lines on his forehead. *Tip, tap – I am here, right inside. Nowhere to hide.*

You see, Peter was a thing of my making and I of his, and I knew that right at the start, in some creased and folded and put-away part of me waiting to be opened, waiting to remember, waiting to understand. I knew we were connected, because of what he had done and what I would need to do.

So there we were, our little family. Peter and Eve and Adam and me. In our little house. On a February night. On the day I was born.

Chapter Three

The first time I saw Peter, I thought he was handsome. It took me only a second to think, *yeah, I probably would.* You know what I mean. If you say you don't you're *that* sort of woman, or a liar, or both. Because we all do it – we judge and grade people as soon as we set eyes on them. We score them and weigh them and balance them against ourselves, place them in or out of proximity, even if, technically, we never intend to act. No harm in looking.

What I noticed right away, from across the room, was his shiny hair and a gym-polished physique. But he was lean like a runner, not bulked up with six-packs and four-packs and a neck like roped oak. I liked that. He had a razor-advert, shaved smoothness about him, three-bladed and clean – an office professional, a family man, a dream catch. I imagine that veneer was what must once have made Eve look into his eyes and feel safe. And there, down the side of his neck, visible when he turned his head, between his hair and collar, was the silver skein of a scar, suggesting a slight mystery perhaps: a childhood accident, a crashed car, an encounter with violence, a moment of peril or bravery? Well, anything to keep the mind occupied during the usual, boring, council event with networking and buffet.

How Peter stood out among the usual crowd, from the morass of boring middle-aged men, grey in nature and disposition, padding out the room with their expanding auras of feared irrelevance. A tinge of off-whiteness had settled on their sagging suits and thinning hair long ago, lifetimes probably. I'd have bet a year's wages that, even in their youth, they'd never pulsed with Technicolor enthusiasm or drunkenly screwed ponytailed girls after running barefoot on beaches. Not *those* men. They stood up extra straight at the buffet line to compensate for their colourlessness. They sipped their free drinks slowly because they didn't want anyone to think they were immoderate or taking their ease at the taxpayer's expense. And glaring out of the middle, tall and straight and alive, was Peter.

There'd been a touch of something flinty in his eyes though, as he stood surveying the room, *his colleagues*, drink in hand, from the edge of the bar. There was something coiled in his cool-scented, shower-fresh muscles, ready to lash out. Wasn't there? I suppose it's hard to say now if that was then or later. I suppose I should try not to add little editorial touches if I can, not too soon anyway.

There was certainly a tentative circle of space surrounding him at the bar – the eyes of women around the room eagerly crossing it, over that no man's land of empty chairs, gauging their approach. The defence field of his detachment buzzed across the synthetic fibres of the corporate carpet making them hesitate and look for excuses to advance.

I was thinking the same thing. *What's my 'in' with him?* because I was bored and toying with the idea of saying hello. I could summon electricity of my own if needed, spark up a winning smile, a one-liner. But I hesitated, too. He bothered me a little. I was at odds with what I could see under his skin. I couldn't verbalise what troubled me exactly, only that I recognised it in him because it was in me, shifting like flocks of blood-born birds around my insides, at the sight of these people, these mediocre, time-tired people, clad in bad suits and Old Spice and apology.

Peter's right hand curled around his wine glass, the other affected to hang casually from his trouser pocket. He had smooth, office hands but it turned out they were very strong, startlingly so, the one time he laid them on me, some months later. When it happened I remember I was too surprised to react, too winded to speak. If women are lucky they never really encounter that moment when male muscle is turned against them. I assure you it's not like wrestling your boy-friend over the remote control on a Sunday evening on the sofa, when you end up pinned to the floor, giggling, ready for more complicated body contact. It's hard. It hurts.

By the time I realised how outmatched I was the countdown to my last breath had already begun.

That was later of course, long after I left the council meeting without ever speaking to him because Tilly rang and said they needed me out at an arson in Killay. But I wish that, later, when there had still been a moment to walk away, still a choice that was mine, I had remembered how he'd looked that night, at his fellows and at the women who would've liked to be at his side. I've had plenty of time since to look and learn and remember.

Later, in those first weeks after I joined Peter's family, I paid close attention. I watched him constantly, ready to learn, willing myself to remember the sequence of events that had thrown us together and placed me there at his side. At that point my memory was still returning in prods and shoves, reassembling awkwardly, pieces of coloured glass and shells of images sticking into a picture that was unclear. Except, there, in the centre, was Peter's face. Always. That's what I held on to and focused upon.

I rarely let him out of my sight. I watched him at breakfast each day, over sticky toast soldiers. I stared at him during dinner, ignoring the appearance and removal of plates of food that revolved around him like a magic whirlwind but was called Eve. At weekends I watched him reading the paper or using his special sharp scissors to cut thin crescents of fingernail into always-emptied wastepaper bins. I leaned over his shoulder as he attended to his files and paperwork.

I watched.

Under my gaze a domestic drama unfolded with all the excitement of the world's worst reality TV show, the sort I'd once have stapled my eyes shut to avoid watching. But somehow I'd become the viewer who couldn't change the channel.

In the mornings I watched him brush his perfect teeth and dress in his perfectly pressed suits. In the evenings I watched him shower, steam rising from his torso as he towelled the long planes of his thighs and the hard flank of his chest. It was curiosity rather than desire that made me sit and watch him undress. I thought perhaps naked he would reveal something human, something fragile, something childlike about himself, that would help me understand him. But he was just skin and hair and the angle of bones meeting joints.

It wasn't intimate. Even when he was wanking over the magazines in his media room, where Eve could only go by strict invitation, or watching a porno on the 42-inch flat-screen TV, it didn't seem intimate.

The first time I spotted him thumbing his collection of DVDs, popping one in the player and undoing his trousers, I expected to at least see some sado-masochistic bondage, women bound and submissive, panting and pleading. But it was dull really, almost prim. I'm no connoisseur of porn but in my line of work I've seen stuff that made Peter's fancies look like Mills & Boon – lots of soft focus and white underwear.

I was tempted to touch his cock once or twice, just out of curiosity, to see if he could feel it. It would have been easy to brush against it with my hand, slide up and down its length, see if it would rise to the challenge. But wouldn't that feel like a favour, the legitimate no-strings-attached fuck?

No, at first I only observed. I was within touching distance but did not.

I watched Adam, too, playing on the living room rug or bedroom floor with his old-fashioned toy soldiers and train set, or I sat with him at the table while he crayoned cute garden animals in waistcoats and dungarees on fat pads of paper. I learned his favourite foods were sausages and chocolate mousse and seedless green grapes. I learned he was always singing one little song or another. I saw the tiny frown form between his eyes, a miniature squint, like his father's, when Monday morning came and school shoes and shirt had to be put on.

And in those first days, as I came to acquaint myself with Peter and his son, I began to despise Eve.

I'd already had the pleasure of observing her unfailing domestic routine, which told me pretty much everything I needed to know about her. Just as well, as she didn't say a great deal. In addition I soon learned that, on Mondays and Fridays, Peter took Adam to school, she the days in between. On Tuesdays and Fridays she went to the supermarket with seven, crisp £10 notes that Peter left for her on the kitchen table and where she placed any change. I didn't go with her at first, shopping. I didn't know I could then. She just left in the silver Corsa at 1 p.m. and came home at 3 p.m. with an armful of bags, usually precisely the same items – variety was not the spice of her life. The receipts were pinned religiously to the fridge under the Thomas the Tank Engine magnet so Peter could double-check them later.

House cleaning was a precise ritual that started in the bathroom and progressed to all the other rooms in a neat cycle as reliable as the turning seasons, death and taxes. In the times in between, if chores were done, Eve sometimes did some yoga in the living room with the rug rolled back, following the prompts from a scratched CD played on Adam's mini stereo (presumably to earn back some extra toast in the mornings, though she was far from 'getting fat'). Now and then she sketched in a little pad, with coloured pencils, at the kitchen table, pictures of Adam, characters from children's stories, some of which were on the walls of Adam's bedroom – Peter Pan with a cutlass, Thomas the Tank Engine smiling vacantly, Peter Rabbit.

Little occurred to break the house-proud monotony of those days. Sometimes people called, a neighbour, a charity collector, but mostly not, except for frizzy-haired Mair, with her bad skin and fondness for brightly coloured, logo-plastered hooded tops, who came by once a week for a quick coffee.

Occasionally there was a play date for Adam and a friend would appear at the front door. Usually it was Charles with his cool blonde curls and cruel green eyes, so pale he reminded me of a Midwich Cuckoo. Occasionally it was polite Benedict with his constantly drippy nose and nasal whine. Kyle came for tea once, but only once.

On these occasions Eve ministered tea and cake to the attendant mums and sat with a tight smile while they complimented her cooking and lovely home. Their shoes, boys' and mums', big and small, were always lined up on the mat by the door and Eve would be wearing pink slippers. Often a mum would say how lovely Peter was, how authoritatively he'd spoken at the parents' evening or how helpful he'd been at the school fundraiser.

'What a catch,' they said, twirling their perfect hair, like parodies of moony 1950s teenagers in a family sitcom. I couldn't believe any grown woman would actually use such phrases. I, sitting next to the mum, would snort and Eve's lips would tighten further, into a thin smile, and make the words, 'indeed' and 'oh yes', and 'I'm very lucky'.

Each day the phone rang at 11 a.m. and 4 p.m., sometimes in between. Eve kept the phone in her pocket at all times. She made an effort to answer by the third ring or Peter would ask why it had taken her so long to pick up. I couldn't imagine what he was expecting to learn each day by checking in. *Breaking news* – the meringue collapsed! *Newsflash* – the toilet duck has run out!

Every afternoon, about ten minutes before Peter was due to return from work, Eve would run a comb through the black waves of her hair, rub some blusher on her cheeks, apply coloured balm to her lips, spritz herself with Chanel No 5, the frustrated housewife's favourite, as if she could atomise on a little Audrey Hepburn-ness, a little chic and adorableness, at the press of a nozzle.

'That's it, fix yourself up for him, sort out your hair and make-up like a good little wife,' I sneered. It was easy to sneer at Eve. It wasn't long before the sight of her was enough to make my lip start to curl all on its own.

What did I do in those days if both she and Peter were out? It's hard to say. I think I was still settling somehow, into the house – perhaps finding a level, like sediment in a cloudy glass, sinking down. Like I said, time seemed disjointed, elastic, unreliable.

If Peter was at work, and then Eve went out, I felt myself starting to become thin and pulled apart, like those fake spiderwebs you buy at Halloween to decorate a haunted house – oddly appropriate, now I come to think of it. It made me think of the story of the old gods of Ancient Greece who'd lived so long on Mount Olympus, and grew so tired, that they spread themselves out on to the winds and soon were no more. I always found that story sad – to be godlike and yet still, in the end, so weary of everything.

Never one to be idle, I began to experiment with my new existence, stretching its boundaries and possibilities. For example, I quickly learned I couldn't imagine myself any-where else by force of will. I couldn't, for example, teleport to my flat, back to my mum's house or into the studio to see Bron the editor dissecting the 6.30 bulletin with pre-cision sarcasm. I couldn't click my heels and go home. I wasn't in Kansas anymore. I was over some sort of rainbow boundary but one that had landed me back in Swansea on the South Wales coast, in a nice detached house with fairly rich people, a few miles from where I used to live, within smell of the sea.

I didn't need to be a genius to know things were certainly not as they had been. Most days it felt as if the interior of the house was merely a TV set, or a film sound stage. I spent hours running my fingers over things, chairs, tables, crockery, clothes, but they all felt insubstantial. Sometimes the edges of things wobbled – not back and forth but in and out. Sometimes I thought I could see tiny cracks and joins where the scenery and props had been assembled. Everything was a little unreal. Of course, it was me that was unreal but that took time to accept. It's not something the mind can easily accommodate, you know. Especially not one like mine, primed for facts and figures and proper structure.

I couldn't grab or grip anything as such. And, no, before you start thinking it, I couldn't make items hover in the air or fly across the room either. I did try. I tried with Eve's white porcelain figurine of the Angel Gabriel, trumpet aloft, but I couldn't make him rise from the mantelpiece and hover over the sofa. I couldn't walk through walls either. Perhaps I could have if I'd tried long enough, but it just seemed undignified, and I was afraid I'd get stuck in the middle of the bricks and plaster, a set of legs and arms waving on each side, my head canted on one or the other, like a fairground funhouse mirror trick. Instead I stuck to the familiar and conventional, open doors and so on, to make my way around.

I didn't moan or wail at night either. When I tried, when I screamed and groaned, no one seemed to be able to hear me and that was tiring, not to mention depressing.

Overall, I was confused and frustrated. What was the point of it all? Being this way? Surely there had to be some upside to my new existence that would ease the, well, the boredom? If I could just find it. Otherwise, what was the purpose of being there at all? How come no one tells you that the next bit, after the last ever bit, might actually just be more of the same, grinding along day by day in a routine groove that includes stocking the fridge and washing-up. I'd never been big on theology, but I remember thinking, around the end of the first month, *no wonder the vicars and bishops keep it to themselves. No wonder they gloss over and stick the true nature of what's in store for us under their silly hats and up their copious sleeves – if they're in on it, that is. Unless they don't know either, in which case they're in for a treat!*

Maybe it's all down to your own personal perspective. Steve used to say he liked to think that heaven might be a lovely meal with family and friends that never ended, while hell was waiting in a restaurant for a waiter to come and take your order, but he or she never came and your date never showed up. So you just sat there, getting more and more hungry, unpeeling endless paper tubes of breadsticks, while other people were served and looked at you with pity.

Steve, bless him. He was always impatient in restaurants, always hungry, and I was always late.

At Peter's place dinner was always on time and the service impeccable, but there was a constant gravelly feeling in my stomach. It could have been a hunger of sorts, though a hunger for what was not clear. Obviously I had no need to eat.

So what did I do? I watched and I waited and let the hours pass.

34

It was very different to my old life, where every beat of the day had been broken down into tick-tock slices of stopwatches and cues and autocues and word-filled, picture-covered news packages preceded by the red light that said 'on-air'. But time didn't have that crucial role anymore. It had become an irrelevance. It's not as if there was anywhere else I needed to be. And I always looked the same – clothes, hair, make-up.

I worked it out in the end, just as you have by now.

I no longer had a body. I had only my memory of it. Without the idea of myself how would I make sense of the space I had come to inhabit and stay separate from it? Work skirt, work blouse, coat, red scarf, those last-minute sensible shoes. Me. The usual.

For a long time I studied myself, this veneer of the old me, in mirrors, to see if I was still solid and the answer was, not always. Sometimes I thought I could see a little of the furniture behind me, like an old double-exposure photo print, even sometimes, the bones beneath my skin, a shiny white skull, the X-rayed roots of my teeth in my jaw. Mostly, I concentrated hard and saw the same version of me that had walked abroad for the last time, that night. An oval face, crisp blue eyes, pale, blade-straight blonde hair, slick pink lips; at my throat, the necklace – gold with tiny red stones, Venetian in look, old, antique. I had worn it for him, that night. My scarlet scarf and black coat.

But before long, looking at myself became a bit like saying a certain word over and over again, you know the one I mean by now. It begins with 'gh' and ends in a 'ost'. I'm not going to say it – *to make it so*. Anyway, like all words, the more you say it the less meaning it has, until it's just a jumble of gibberish – sound and fury, signifying nothing, right? Like good old Shakespeare said, the human performance in a nutshell, when all's said and done, nothing but a last breath, leaving. Close the door, turn out the lights.

So I was still me. But I wasn't. I thought a lot about that, about who I'd once been and would not now become. Because of Peter.

I would never be the girl who married her lover. No 'happy couple' picture montage, flowers and fingers of dark, iced cake for me. I wouldn't be a smiling wife, wed in white or otherwise. Nor would I be a newsreader in London when my time in the BBC Cardiff studio was up. I wouldn't be the one, groomed and Jaeger-jacketed, saying at 10 p.m., 'Good evening. Tonight's top story, explosions kill three in Basra.'

That was the worst thing, somehow. I'd lived every minute of every day of my life since I turned ten years old to make it to network news. To have my chance to tell the big, beautiful, bloody stories; my words carrying weight, my voice sonorous with the authority of truth.

That would not happen. Though, as it happened, I did make it on to the national news many times in the weeks and months to come – in the ominous-toned news reports featuring my photograph. Funny how things turn out, isn't it? Hilarious, absolutely hilarious. But I suppose you have to have a sense of humour about these things.

Who was it that said, 'Be careful what you wish for?'

Know-it-all bastard!

Chapter Four

It just had to be that total bitch Polly Wilcox! It had to be her eventually 'breaking the news' – holding it up and cracking it in half on air for all to see – live on screen, microphone in hand, doing my bloody job with my old crew.

'Three days after the disappearance of our reporter Melanie Black, hopes of finding the thirty-four year old alive are fading fast . . . ' she intoned.

'I'm only thirty-three, you silly cow!' I spat at the screen. 'And I don't look it! And well done for getting cliché number five in right at the start.'

Good old hopes, eh? They always start out high, apple pie, up in the sky and then 'fade fast' into the second half of the week, just like communities are at first 'shocked' and then occasionally go 'up in arms' for a bit, and then slide into 'an air of mourning' – it's the order of the TV world. You just never think such bland, verbal shorthand will ever apply to you because you're special.

'The police continue to search but as the days progress this small and close community is asking, "Where is our Melanie?"' continued Polly.

Our Melanie? Nice touch that, I thought, well, a bit too US network big-haired, anchorwoman for South Wales, but nice. How intimate it seemed, when she said it that way, her serious voice on, one register down for doom and gloom. As if I belonged in the caring bosom of the city 'community' and they really wanted me back – those few who would know who I was and the fewer still who might actually care as they watched the bulletin and tucked into their evening meal.

I sat down then, plopped into the plump cushions on the upstairs sofa. Something sucked the strength out of my remembered legs as I watched the predictable montage of uniformed police officers in high-visibility fluorescent jackets poking bits of shrubbery with sticks.

Polly ran through the facts efficiently enough. She said I'd last been seen on my way to The Gowerton Hotel (of course, I hadn't gone there. I was never going there. But they weren't to know that). Polly described what I'd been wearing, my height and hair colour and so on, and did a quick appeal clip with an uncomfortable-looking detective from Swansea Central nick while an incident room number scrolled across the screen. Then she cued into her video piece.

They'd pulled out all the stops (or at least rummaged the archives) for a montage of my greatest screen hits over the past six years; the landfill enquiry, power station accident inquest, river pollution exposé. No fluff pieces or dog fashion shows there, all TV-clip shorthand for seeker of truths, pursuer of justice. Implication? *This is a serious career woman we are talking about, not some pissed up bimbo in a short skirt with a penchant for pork scratchings and a pint of Brain's Dark. Pay attention! This one matters!*

Then they covered the human interest one, with its attendant suggestion of softness and affection – Melanie Black, see her here – daughter, girlfriend, friend.

There was a nice picture of me, smiling, looking surprisingly approachable. Mum must have given it to them.

Oh God, poor Mum! I thought, for the first time, as I stared at the TV. How distraught she'd be, how embarrassed to see me on the news this way, as if she hadn't hated my job enough to make sure she never caught sight of me on air each day dealing with all that 'gloom and doom'. And the people from the town council would see it, the women from the church roof fundraiser, that old busybody from the bookshop with the pencilled on eyebrows. *Sorry, Mum.*

And Steve. *Poor Steve.* Forced now to deal with the uncertainty and the questions and the fascist police and the fascist media scrum that would no doubt be disturbing him at his flat and during his quiet lunchtime, laptop-fiddling coffee sessions in Verdi's on the Prom, for comment and reaction. *Sorry, hun.*

How awful for them both.

I wasn't the only one who was distressed. When Peter saw the screen, the police, my picture, his eyes grew wide, his whole body stiffened. Sitting next to him on the sofa I thought, *How can you look so surprised? What did you think would happen next?* And in the exact second Peter's hand tightened on the arm of the chair I realised I'd just remembered it all. It returned in the pop of the photographers' news-conferences flashes, like the pop of my ears on an aeroplane. Everything was stereo clear. I knew.

Breaking news, Melly: You're screwed, girl!

Okay. So I'd been in denial until that first TV report laid

out the facts of my disappearance in bones so bare they were indecent and un-ignorable. Until then I'd been clinging to the cliché that maybe I was really in a coma somewhere and having an out-of-body experience, like that story I did once, from the hospital bed of the rugby flanker who'd been in a coma for six months. He'd woken up on the day of the Wales v England international to the sound of the national anthem. Yeah, I still think he was full of shit. He'd been about to get dropped from the squad and probably needed the money from selling his 'miracle recovery' story. Dafydd the flanker, faking wanker.

But at that stage I thought maybe it was possible that *I* might still wake up that way, perhaps to the tune of Amy Winehouse's 'Back to Black' on the radio at my Swansea General Hospital bed, not because I like the song, but because it would have been a great news hook and Polly had always said it could be my theme tune. She'd play it for me at the hospital bed, naturally, probably on camera with a radio mic on the bed to catch the action, and I'd wake up and raise my eyelids long enough to smile for the lens then stick a biro in her eye.

But there she was, on screen, mic in hand, undeniably 'live', whereas I was otherwise. And if that wasn't enough, there was Eliot, at the desk in the studio, picking up from Polly's link. It was not his usual night to read, but they would've wanted someone with gravitas for this story. Someone who could look sympathetic and not too smarmy – someone sincere to suggest the gravity of the situation, one of their own, a missing person they were actually missing themselves. Eliot Masters was that man.

It felt as if I hadn't seen him for decades, centuries, not just three days, and at the sight of him a great black, wordless wail poured out of my head, unbidden. It cleared the sofa with one exhalation and reverberated round the walls like thunder trapped in a snow-strung mountain range. I thought I saw the ceiling-sky darken above me.

Eliot, my beloved. How I loved you. How we would have had a life together. How I longed to hold him again with an ache that rattled my bones so hard I think I saw them shimmer beneath my sleeves and skirt.

He was ashen-faced, too much direct light. I'd told Tilly about that more than once – she never listened. His mic was crackling or maybe it was his voice, saying the news team was in deep shock

Under the lights of the studio I could see it was hard for him to remain detached and professional. His mouth was too rigid, his delivery too precise. Between shots he'd be taking a sip of water and swallowing loudly. I'd sat in the dark director's booth opposite him often enough, while he read reports, under the on-air sign, scanning the monitors, counting him in, cueing him out on the earpiece mic when I was helping out producing. I had been the familiar voice in his head or on the end of the mic.

Now he was throwing questions back and forth to Polly, looking suitably sombre in her *take me seriously* beige trench coat but I thought I could detect a crackle of glee in her eyes. Her first live, outside broadcast – thanks, Mel! Opportunity knocks and Polly's always on hand to answer.

Interviewing your own reporters is lazy cliché number one, but I know they had to milk it for all it was worth. I know I would have. If it'd been Polly that was missing and me reporting on it, I'd have had her chuckling baby photos up on screen in five seconds flat.

That first TV appeal was six months after I first told Eliot I loved him. Six wonderfully tortuous months since we'd fallen into bed in his room in The Pengelly Arms, after a day of OBs (that's outside broadcasts to you) from a scene where three generations of the same family of seven had been killed in a suspicious gas explosion.

Four live slots that day, two for Regional and two for Network. He on camera, me doing the legwork behind, sending the video packages to Cardiff and London down the live line; a little taste of what it could be like when we got to the city together. Then we shared two long evenings in a cramped hotel room with fish and chips for supper and each other for dessert, among the blankets, listening to the radio and the rain and the beat of his heart soothed by whisky and kisses.

It had been more than two years since we'd started working together. It'd taken us that long to admit how we felt. Twenty-three months and twenty-four days of three-second glances across monitors and two-second finger-brushes disguised as cappuccino excuses to touch; leaning in a little too close in the rush-fuss mania of the editing suite on deadline, offering silent-eyed support at morning news conference, a symphony of patience and denial.

I'd always said I'd never mix work with pleasure. It was such a cliché and sex makes things messy. If I'd wanted to get laid there would have been plenty of opportunity. Newsrooms are full of confident cocks in swaggering Ralph Lauren shirts, and bookish, sensitive producers who really want to be making documentaries or indie movies. But today's tosser is tomorrow's executive producer and, if it ends badly, there goes your promotion. It's an old story but, even in the twenty-first century, it's never the guy who zips up his flies and packs his briefcase, is it?

But Eliot was different. I knew that when I watched him reporting, before I even joined the news team. His square, honest face and honest voice on local stories, then presenting the weekend bulletins, filling the daily lunch spots; slow and steady, on the greasy pole of advancement, he appeared grease-proof, shine free.

Trustworthy, sincere – these were the words that Eliot inspired. That was his *brand*. They say once you can fake sincerity you're made. But he didn't fake it. Or didn't seem to. Eliot was Eliot. Strategy-free, open-agenda, perfectly structured, orderly Eliot.

Fucking Polly Wilcox obviously thought so, too, from the first day she turned up at the newsroom in her cherry-red, retro Mary Janes and little black suit. Even back when she used to write the entertainment columns at *The Evening Post* she was always hanging around in the background of his live broadcasts, spiral notepad in hand, scribbling. I should've known then she'd be a royal pain in the arse. Never more so than the moment she started playing the stoic reporter, reading out a police phone number saying, 'Anyone with any information about Miss Black's whereabouts is asked to call the police immediately.'

Shame I couldn't pick up the phone and call in. What a lot I would have had to say.

Chapter Five

In the days that rolled out after that first missing person's report Peter kept a close eye on the news. Usually he followed the headlines on the TV in his 'media' room where Eve would not see it. The TV cupboard downstairs was mostly locked because he didn't want Adam to 'be exposed to populist rubbish, sex and violence', as he reminded Eve every week if Adam wanted to watch CBeebies. What Eve wanted to watch didn't seem to be an issue.

I sat alongside him on those evenings and it was plain from the outset that the police were looking for me in the wrong place. They were searching the area around The Gowerton Hotel, at the east end of town, and the round-table function I was supposed to have attended that night, 21 February – the night of the Big Snow.

Council members and investors would have been there as usual, JPs and local pundits, the familiar round of self-important morons with sweaty handshakes accompanied by cheap, warm wine and plates of E. coli-laced prawn sandwiches. But I'd had somewhere better to be. Or so I'd thought.

The police had searched the hotel, its grounds and car park, and questioned the guests. Pretty Polly was on hand for most of this, looking more carefully preened and calculatedly wistful each day, and sounding more confident. She'd clearly been having some voice training – she'd lost a little of that occasional *Caardiff*, brought up in the shadow of the *Aaaarmms Paaark*, twang that used to make me snigger, and not try too hard to hide it.

Then the police searched the surrounding streets and choppy harbour for signs of me. They searched under bushes and in drains, with men and women at first then the dogs, the cadaver dogs, although we don't use that word on air because of the unsavoury connotations. No one can hear the word cadaver and not immediately think of a rotting corpse. And people don't want to think of that while they eat their morning porridge or evening egg and chips. People love the dogs though, always got good pictures with the dogs.

Later, when the spaniels, with their chocolate-button noses and willing, waggy tails failed to find me, not a sniff, not a sign, they searched CCTV, interviewing staff and taxi drivers with Polly elucidating in her helpful commentary. *My movements were unconfirmed. My car was still missing . . . police talking to drivers . . . No sign of Melanie Black . . .*

Cut, exit cue, black screen.

I'd vanished from the outside world only to reappear in high-quality digital news format, twice daily. In many ways I was bigger, better and brighter than I had been in the flesh. When Polly reiterated that the police incident room had received calls but no useful leads, I knew I wasn't going to leave Peter's side any time soon. I didn't know how exactly, but it was clear that Peter had brought me home somehow.

Or I'd followed him, like a stray cat. I had nosed at an open window crack, snuck inside and I was trapped, pawing at the door. It would be a while before I started to scratch and spit.

But to begin with I was a model house guest at number 31 Rosemary Close; the one who's quiet, never complains that the heating is on too high, and never eats the final Jaffa Cake and puts the empty box back in the cupboard. Slowly I adapted to family life, imposing structure on the days because structure is the illusion of order and order is the illusion of control.

Old habits die hard and, while shadowing Eve in her chores, I passed the time by laying down an imaginary voiceover, like one of those stick-up-your-arse women on that show *How Clean is Your House?*

'Missed a speck there, Eve, love,' I'd say. 'Yes, I know that bicarbonate of soda makes an environmentally friendly surface cleaner but how much polishing is too much? Have you ever thought of just killing yourself now and getting it over with?'

Or I'd run a news commentary: 'Yes, Huw, the UN will be pleased to know that today, the cupboard under the stairs has been invaded and the outdoor shoes forced into a détente with the vacuum and steam cleaners. Negotiations continue, situation stable.'

Or I'd lie on the living-room floor next to Adam as he re-enacted scenes from made-up stories that always involved toys hiding in various places then jumping out and punching each other in the head.

Don't tell anyone I said it, but Adam was rather endearing – being the least pathetic member of my new extended family, having a wrinkly and cute smile, and a tendency to blow snot bubbles through his nose when overexcited and then laugh.

At dinner I sat opposite Peter and pulled faces at him when he pronounced on topics of domestic and national import in his pompous 'head of the family' voice. I ran a commentary for him, too, 'Yes, Huw, tonight's headlines, Peter is a colossal wanker. Sources once more confirm he knows fuck all about Afghanistan or the Palestinian–Israeli conflict. But in other news, the wet-dishcloth wife is enduring the criticism of her pot-roast with admirable aplomb.'

Then, at the end of those days I'd follow Eve upstairs when she was putting Adam to bed. I liked Adam's room better than the cosy girl-nest of the rest of the house. A relic of the 1960s, it had shiny enamel toy cars on the windowsills and painted model planes on strings above his bed; a little sprinkle of glow-in-the-dark stars pulsed on the ceiling above his pillow and a mobile of the solar system wobbled above his feet. There was no TV, but there were lots of books: fairy stories, Beatrix Potter and a couple of Disney favourites and *Thomas the Tank Engine*.

The books on the shelves were well-thumbed Enid Blytons – Noddy, *The Magic Faraway Tree* and *The Famous Five*. Just my luck, I thought, watching Eve take down *The Wishing-Chair*, the happy homemaker's taste in reading material is as evolved as her self-esteem. I'm trapped in the middle of *Five Go Quietly Bored Out of Their Minds. Noddy Goes Doolally in Toyland.*

How different those tales were to my own bedtime stories. Dad had preferred the Grimm ones, in name and nature. In their version of *Cinderella* the ugly sisters cut off their own toes to try and fit their fat feet into the glass slipper, to impress the prince. For this display of dedication they had their eyes pecked out by doves. I bet most women can relate to this in one way or another. As a kid it scared me shitless.

Adam's bedtime routine was military, where mine had been easy-going. Peter issued orders, keeping everything running whip-smart and on schedule. At 7 p.m. precisely, bath. At 7.15 p.m., towel-dry, glass of milk, kiss for Daddy. Once Adam was in his Thomas the Tank Engine pyjamas, and the red-and-white toadstool nightlight was switched on, Peter would return to his work and Eve would read Adam a story. Lying next to him on the bed, propped up on cushions with Old Lamby, the cuddle-ragged fluff-bundle of Adam's choice, and Soft Peter (Rabbit) between them, the tightness and forced cheer evaporated from Eve. Her breath, usually high and tight in her chest, slowed and Adam became unguarded and giggly.

As the stories ended, Adam's eyes would become gummy, his face peaceful and Eve would sing 'Baa Baa Black Sheep', Lamby's favourite, then 'When You Wish Upon a Star' for Soft Peter. Then not-so-soft Peter would put his head round the door at 8 p.m. and smile at Eve and his own slack-faced sleeping lamb.

After they had both left I began to make a habit of lying down next to Adam. Somehow his snuffing ball of chocolate smell was sugary and comforting. I couldn't feel him exactly, not his pink skin, his hot breath, it was just an idea of him, chubby and warm and I think sometimes I wanted to cry. For myself, for both of us, dead to the world in our different ways. But I wasn't sure how to start, how to charm the drops of water out of my eyes. What's that they say about old dogs and new tricks?

I'm ashamed to admit it but I felt sorry for myself then. I spent many a night like that, wondering what I'd done to make my worst nightmare come true. To be there and not there, where no one could hear my voice or see me, in that house, for all intents and purposes a g-word. I had unfinished business obviously and had to address it before I could move on to . . . where . . . where?

I suspected I should have felt anger, vengeful and hot, and many a night I looked for my righteous indignation, inside, under my ribs and in the pit of my stomach. In life my temper had been legendary, hot and spitting and wont to poke like a heated darning needle into people's soft places, then curl out into the world in tongues of cold fire. As the dark thing I had evidently become, trapped in the night hours with my own thoughts, should not maelstroms have whirled twice as fierce and fast?

So I rummaged around for a spark of that rage but came up only with cobwebby corners.

I would've liked to at least rattle pots and pans and chains or something, poltergeist-like and unseen, in those long winter evenings. But how could I if I couldn't touch or be heard?

Some nights I thought maybe I should just let go, let myself go, accept the truth of my situation. More than once I said to myself, in my best chapel minister voice, there is a time to live and a time to, *you know* . . . a time to rage and a time to sit with soft toys and watch cakes rise. Then there's a time to move on.

I said it earnestly, but I just couldn't think about it too deeply because, eventually, it could only give rise to a potent and terrifying question. If I let go, unhooked my fingers and toes from their clinging, lay back on the air around me like the ancients of Olympus, would I float off into a bright and benevolent light? Or would I slide down a dark and slippery chute in the bedroom floor to be swallowed up by somewhere else?

Where, oh where will Melly go? Up above, or down below?

Either way I wasn't ready to leave on such uncertain terms – not on Peter's terms. I wanted him to pay first. I knew that much. That was the undisputed and unbeating heart of the matter. In a cold place in the night, I felt myself deepen and sharpen and fill with black water and icy clarity and sometimes I longed to tear a hole in the night and reach through and drag Peter to me kicking and screaming on to my side.

But how could I do it? What words would make it so?

There was a poem I thought about a lot, from a picture above my dad's desk in his study. He had a lot of William Blake illustrations and my favourite was *A Poison Tree*, about a man who takes his anger towards his enemy and plants it as a seed that grows into a great tree. And he waits and watches and waters and tends it until it's ready. And an apple grows. And the taste of it is deadly.

I used to stare at the picture when Dad was on-air, down at the studio, soothing his audience through hours of easy listening and easier chat. I'd follow the whorls of the hand-drawn branches, listening to his easy, afternoon, tea-and-biscuit voice coming from the Roberts radio on the windowsill. I liked the poem because it was a bit immoral and not a warning about forgiving but of the sugary sweetness of revenge, and the biding of secret time.

So in the deep hours of the silent morning, when things are said to walk abroad that no one should see, I curled up on the bed next to Adam, or squatted at the bed foot, beneath the warm glow of his toadstool nightlight and watched him breathing. Sometimes I sang softly the lines from 'When You Wish Upon a Star', crooning, making the motion of stroking his hair.

Then I watched Peter and Eve sleeping, standing for a long time at the foot of their shared bed, hidden in the patterns of the shifting night, before lying down next to Peter and talking to him.

Peter was listening. He didn't know he was, to whom he was, and he didn't know why. He didn't even hear me, really, not the first time at least. But I was there nevertheless. And I'd talked for a living once. I saw no reason to stop. In fact, I thought it was a good time to start up again. Old habits die hard. Old dogs have old tricks.

And I had lots of time to kill.

Chapter Six

On a brisk Tuesday in March, when the initial TV appeals were finally cooling and the police slowly winding up their search for me, I went to work with Peter for the first time.

It wasn't just a whim that made me risk leaving the house. I'd decided it was time to stop wallowing in self-pity and carry out some proper research. If I was going to make Peter pay I had to find the right way to do it and that meant knowing more about him than the man he was at home. I had to see what else there was to him besides the husband and father and master of all he surveyed between the four walls of Rosemary Close.

No one is the same person at all times – to observe Peter in other habitats would help me see him more completely, all the better to slide the hot needle into his weak spots when the moment came.

It wasn't easy at first, leaving the house. The nausea came, at the threshold of the front door. The black water bubbled up, overflowed and everything went gauzy, dissolving the gravel drive and the mock-Tudor houses opposite and threatening to fold me to my knees. But I was determined. I ground my nails into my palms and fixed myself to Peter's side, to the shape of his sleeve through my closed eyelids. I pulled myself upright and set one foot in front of the other as his feet hit the path and he opened the car door.

By the time I was in the passenger seat next to him the urge to vomit had faded. I felt hungover and a bit faint. Fainthearted, perhaps? What if I became sick again and faded out of existence on the Fabian Way dual carriageway, or round by the super Tesco? What if I couldn't think my way back home to the house or to Peter's side? Would I then have to haunt the shopping centre or ribbon of bike track along Swansea Bay for the rest of my days? Some forlorn spectre of a TV reporter, wild haired, grubby fingered, microphone in hand, endlessly searching for her last exclusive?

But Dad used to say, 'Faint heart never won fair maiden,' or by extension a shot at a fair fight.

Come on, girl, I said. *Iron spine time,* Dad's pre-exam, pre-job interview, pre-first broadcast courage mantra. I pulled up my shoulders, held my head high and opened my eyes on the outside world, on the wide expanse of cloud-puffed sky, the watery sunshine, the fat, pecking gulls and puddle-shiny streets that striped by the car windows. I was almost in a good mood, until Peter switched on Radio Two and turned the volume up. Well, come on, I might have been, well, *you know,* but I wasn't a geriatric.

He made me sit through some Neil Diamond song first. Then 'Those Were the Days', for God's sake. After two minutes of that my teeth were so on edge I started to make a high-pitched whistling sound between them, the one I used to make when people pissed me off, or when I was bored, or sometimes just to unsettle people. After all, there's only so much Mary Hopkin a girl can take, I don't care if she is Welsh.

That's when a weird thing happened. The reception on the radio started to become crackly and was replaced by a feedback whine. I stopped whistling for a moment and the signal returned. So I whistled again and the music became distant once more, as if through a static storm.

Peter frowned and flipped the channels back and forth until the radio settled itself on some thrash rock station and refused to budge. By chance it was Nine Inch Nails' singer Trent Reznor screaming anguished lines about getting what you deserve. I recognised the track as 'Head Like a Hole', not that I'd had a great deal of time for hard rock but they were Steve's go-to band in his anti-establishment moments so I know the words well.

I took great pleasure in singing along at the top of my lungs as we slid through the traffic, smiling as Peter stabbed at the stubborn channel button that now refused to flip. And all the while I wailed like a banshee Peter rubbed the bridge of his nose with his left hand, wincing, as if someone was sticking an ice-pick in there and twisting it around.

By the time we reached work I was grinning.

When we pulled in through the main gates of the council offices and up to the car park I wasn't surprised to see that Peter had his own parking space – his name was written on the white plate on the railing next to a row of others. Number six – Peter Albright – Deputy Finance Director.

Albright, of course. He'd told me his last name when he'd eventually introduced himself but I'd forgotten it. I ran the two words round my mouth, back and forth, testing the sound. Peter Albright.

Albright on the night. Peter Albright, he's always right. Peter Albright, he's full of spite.

But it wasn't spite that came off him in waves that morning, as he locked his car and stared up at the 1970s edifice of local government. There was a different vibration, resonating around him at something like the level of dread. And that wasn't just because such places seem built to generate exactly these feelings, and I should know, I'd reported from outside the building often enough on council tax rises, school bus route cuts, Welsh language provision. The nuts and bolts of news, of living and learning and paying your dues. I sensed it was something waiting for him inside – behind the larger windows of the second floor – that was at the bottom of it.

He did a good job of hiding it though, as he strode through reception and along the corridors, tilting his head like a returning Caesar. Various underlings nodded deferentially or exchanged pleasantries with him as he passed, taking his swagger at face value.

'Morning, Peter.'

'Morning, Jack.'

'Morning, Peter.'

'Morning, Lucy.'

'Morning, Councillor Wilbert.'

'Morning, Mr Albright.'

The women all flexed the same shy smile as he passed, trailing aftershave and self-possession. You know the one I mean, the one where they're trying to pretend they're not self-conscious and flustered but they are, because, fair play to Peter, whatever was coiling around his chest on the inside, he was six foot two of great physique and monumental jawline in a world of bald patches and paunches. It's hard, in that sort of soft-carpeted, tight smile, sign-here environment not to be swayed by a surge of walking testosterone with sparkly blue eyes. And why wouldn't you want to be?

Peter's second-floor office was nice enough, with a big window and an expensive-looking 'breakout corner', with bucket seats for those highly invigorating mini-meetings, no doubt. He had his own PA, pretty and young, sitting outside wearing too much mascara and not enough lipstick. She was clearly the sort of girl who didn't mind making the tea and popping out to buy his family birthday cards, her adoration tinkling in her breathy, 'Morning, Peter,' and the ready chink of china. How predictable.

Then I met the woman who proved the exception to the Peter-worship rule.

'Morning, Julienne,' said Peter, as a tall blonde in her early forties stuck her head round the door. 'Still settling in okay with the quarterly budgets?'

'A word, please,' she said. It wasn't a request and she didn't wait for his reply, striding away to *her* office next door, with a nameplate on the door that read 'Julienne Henry, Head of Finance'.

Her room had *two* large windows, a breakout area with bucket chairs *and* an expensive boardroom table with a view of the ornamental lake on the landscaped grass below. She stood by that window, seemingly mesmerised by the spitting fountains but really just letting Peter know she was only giving him the meagre attention she could spare after she'd completed the important task of admiring the bathing ducks. I liked her.

She was perhaps six feet tall in her heels, with nicely cut ash blonde hair, dark blue suit, grey blouse. She might have been ten years older than me but the resemblance, or the impression of it, was striking. Tall, tailored, sharp-edged, here was a woman who knew how to play the game and played no games – offered no excuses. My mantra had always been 'never apologise, never explain'. I think Ms Henry would have approved of that.

She motioned to Peter to sit and then leaned against her massive desk and handed him a report.

'Very . . . ' she let the pause stretch out ' . . . imaginative.'

'Thank you,' said Peter, though he didn't smile.

'It's not what I asked for though, is it?'

Peter sighed. 'I know that, Julienne, but if you take a minute to look at the highlighted figures . . . '

'Which part of 14 per cent reduction did you not understand, Peter?'

'I appreciate that, Julienne, but if you look at the figures I've underlined . . . '

'What you've detailed here is a 12 per cent reduction, but only after an initial outlay of £35,000. Help me out here. Maybe my maths isn't what it used to be? I ask for reductions and you offer me further expenditure.' She paused for a moment to throw a perfectly arched eyebrow a little higher up her forehead and narrow her eyes at her deputy.

'These are difficult times, Peter,' she said, as he opened his mouth to speak. 'As I'm sure you know. People love their swimming pools when they're under threat of closure but they don't use them. Find three of the worst performing within the borough. Close them. Get me the 14 per cent. Not 12 per cent, 14 per cent.'

'But with the initial outlay we can maintain at least one.'

'Get the figures back to me before the meeting tomorrow. Thank you.'

She turned back to the window and fixed her gaze in the direction of the lawn again. Peter sat for a moment longer, his hands tightening on the report, before acknowledging his dismissal.

I couldn't hear his thoughts precisely, not the exact words, but I caught the sense of them inside his skull, exploding like a flare in radiant waves of white rage.

The voice in his head was full of fists. He wanted to leap up from his chair, across the table, grab his boss's neck, his *boss* for Christ's sake, just a year or two older than him, in a suit three times as expensive, and throw her backwards, snapping her spine over her massive desk, to feel the vertebrae snap. He wanted to fuck her first. He wanted to bend her forwards, then and there, hitch up her tight skirt and ram home a lesson in manners. And maths. Hopefully while she whimpered. Possibly while she was choking on the report he would feed page by annotated page, underlined figures notwithstanding, down her elegant throat.

The images were jagged and bright under his skin and behind his eyes. I saw them and felt them and I thought, *I see you now, Mr Albright. I see you where and who you really are. Under your suit and beneath your smile. In that hot place, behind the closed door. I am there, too.*

After a moment Peter got to his feet, sighed again. 'Of course, Julienne. I'll see what I can do.'

Of course, Peter, I thought.

He left, closing the door quietly, and I couldn't fight the urge to skip beside him as he strode his rage out onto the tiled floor. The morning had turned out surprisingly well. Not ten minutes in the office and I'd already learned something of value I would surely be able to use to my advantage. I realised I was enjoying myself for the first time in a long time. How predictable he was. How obedient, here. Not so Perfect Peter. Soft Peter, after all. *Peter Albright, what a sight. Peter, Peter, total shit eater*, I whispered with polished glee, skip, skip beside him. And in that second, I believe my sharp seed went into his soft ear and landed where there was light and water, and enough room to lay roots. Peter scratched his ear, as if he felt it, too, then strode into his office, shut the door and told his PA not to disturb him for the rest of the morning.

He was still scratching his ear at home time, walking to his car with me beside him, after seven hours of boring budget revisions ending with the 14 per cent reduction Julienne had insisted upon. The report was now in her inbox, ready for the morning. She hadn't deigned to open it yet, the read-receipt had not returned to him. He knew he'd probably find out what she had to say about it in the meeting, in front of all the senior managers.

Preoccupied with this thought he didn't notice the woman I later came to know as Marilyn hovering by the badge-activated foot-gate, breathless and eager. She was the deputy panel chair for the Culture and Tourism working group, and one of those 'proving the rule' women, always waiting for an excuse to engage him in conversation. She always parked her car quite near his every day, on purpose, knowing they would be likely to leave at the same time each night, giving her the perfect 'random' opportunity to speak to him. It continues to take me by surprise that fairly stupid people can have the capacity for unexpected cunning.

Peter was already wise to her, though. I felt habitual contempt rattle his bones as soon as he saw her approaching, briefcase ostentatiously tucked under her arm, carrying a box of promotional tourist leaflets. *Fucking old trout! Fuck off!* were the words under his breath, on the back of his tongue.

'Phew, five-thirty, another day in the salt mines over,' said Marilyn, with an unnecessary laugh. By way of answer Peter waved her through the turnstile ahead him with cool chivalry and a glacial smile.

'Mystery about that girl isn't it – the reporter girl?' continued Marilyn, as if she'd been discussing the latest titbits all day in the office but was still keen to give them another airing and get his hallowed opinion.

'What?' asked Peter, making a point of not looking at her. He couldn't bear the sight of her dark roots, the wide strip along the honey blonde parting or the fact she always had lipstick on her teeth.

'You remember,' she said. 'That girl who came to the full council meeting last December and the vote count, last elections. Melanie Black – handsome woman, don't usually use that word, handsome, for women but she was handsome, and tall.' She gave another unnecessary laugh. 'Surely you remember? Sort of a no-nonsense type. It's worrying, isn't it? If a girl like that can't look after herself . . . they're winding up the search, the police, for now. The news said so, at lunchtime.'

The whole time she was speaking Peter kept walking steadily towards his car, making noncommittal bobs with his head, which Marilyn took as licence to continue.

'My Moira . . . you know, my daughter. She's a community support officer, down at Central Police Station, and she says there's no sign of her – just vanished off the face of the earth. Poof! You wouldn't think that was possible, would you, in this day and age, all the CCTV and mobile phones and so on?'

'This is me, Ms Metcalf,' said Peter with a polite smile, pointedly readying his car keys.

'*Marilyn*, please. I've said before. Bit old for Ms Metcalf,' she giggled, fishing for a compliment. Though she might only have been in her late-forties the faint sunbed crow's feet at her eyes would not tempt Peter to a fake demurral.

'They've been searching her flat, you know,' she said, after a moment, realising she had failed to hook him. 'Nothing untoward . . . no struggle, no blood, Moira said. Weird, isn't it? But Moira says there might be something else to perk up the appeal tomorrow. *A development.*'

She leaned in a little close, causing Peter to draw back slightly as she mock-whispered, 'I'll find out tonight, I expect. I get the inside info on everything she does. She rings me every night, does Moira. She's a good girl.'

For a moment Peter met Marilyn's eye, possibly for the first time ever in the years they had worked in the same building. Marilyn herself was surprised. She began to blush beetroot under the scrutiny of his council ladies-room-famous, storm-blue eyes. For a moment Peter seemed about to ask her something but then to think better of it. Instead he scratched his ear with irritation, looked down at his jacket sleeves. He put his hand on the right one, above the cuff as if expecting to see something there, brushing at it absently so his car keys tinkled.

'Best leave it to the police, I think, Marilyn,' he said, after a moment, moving to unlock his car.

'Yes, of course,' said Marilyn, clearly disappointed. 'Well, night then, Mr A. I'm over here.' She gestured to her silver estate. 'Let's hope there isn't some maniac out there prowling the streets. *That* would be terrible for the summer tourism push. See you tomorrow,' she added, when Peter didn't smile.

On the drive home, while I sat cheerfully humming beside him, birds fluttered beneath Peter's skin. I could feel their wings in motion. They took flight en masse as we approached The Gowerton Hotel, past the sagging search-area tape and police teams by the harbour. Some of the officers were flopped on the bench, drinking tea, feeding a biscuit to one of the dogs, evidently winding up the search as Marilyn had suggested. But what caught Peter's eye, made his head crane round, was Polly. She was standing with a couple of other reporters in a tight, fidgety huddle, her cherry-red shoes splashed against the twilight pavement like blood.

A shiver of anticipation ran through the assembled group as one of the police inspectors got out of a parked car and walked purposefully towards them. Nice guy – something Murphy, I'd dealt with him a few times. Both me and Peter could see he had a piece of paper in his hand, most likely a press release to read, before our car turned the corner on a green light and we lost sight of them. Peter was wondering if Marilyn already knew what was in it, or would as soon as her daughter rang later.

When we got home Peter called to Eve as his key turned in the door, before he'd even pulled off his trench coat or discarded his shoes.

'Eve, where's my black mackintosh? You know, the one I wore during the Big Snow? What have you done with it?'

It took only a second for Eve to open the kitchen door and appear with the usual tea towel stapled to her hand. The smell of roasting lamb seeped ahead of her and I thought I caught a flicker of apprehension in her face when she saw his impatience. But her voice was set at 'solicitous', as per normal.

'Hello, darling. I think I took it to the dry-cleaner's with your other suit. The trouser hems were dirty from the snow and there was something on the coat sleeve, oil or paint, or something, so I put it in, too. Actually I forgot to pick them up. I can do it first thing tomorrow if you need it.'

He looked at her very hard then, the house humming with the smell of meat fat and uncertainty. Eve returned his gaze steadily before saying, 'What is it, darling? Do you need it tonight? It's late but they might still be open?'

She seemed relieved when he kissed the tip of her nose tenderly and gave her a hard hug.

'No, that's okay. Thank you, Eve. I forgot to ask you to get it cleaned. But obviously I didn't need to. You read my mind. What would I do without you?'

She smiled again before returning to the kitchen but I didn't. My lip curled as I said to Eve's back, 'That's my job, now, sweetheart, reading his mind,' as I followed Peter upstairs.

Chapter Seven

The next morning the police announced that they'd found my missing car. It was parked in Chapel Street, on the hill above the seafront.

Peter was already tired and tetchy before he heard the update. He hadn't slept well. I knew he'd been worrying about what the police were going to say, after we'd driven past the clutch of eager media on the way home. He'd been wondering what was on that piece of paper in the Inspector's hand. They must have embargoed the news or it would have been everywhere long before we all woke to another drizzle-soaked day in Wales.

The headlines rolled into Peter's study through the radio as he packed his briefcase. He paused for a moment as the announcer said, 'Breaking news, missing reporter's car recovered, police appeal for information following what could be a significant development in the search for Melanie Black. More, just after the hour.'

From that moment a great frown creased Peter's face. It didn't help that nothing was quite right with his breakfast. The tea was wrong for starters, only Tetley not fair-trade

Indian leaf because Eve had forgotten to pick up some teabags at the shops. And his eggs were too hard, overcooked. They resisted the onslaught of the soldiers.

'Has Mummy been good today, Adam Ant?' asked Peter, crumpling his napkin with calm deliberation. I heard Eve's breath quicken a little as she stared rather miserably at the boiled, decapitated eggs.

'No, Daddy?' asked Adam, looking at his own egg, across at his mummy, then over at his father.

'I don't think so either. No toast for Mummy, then.' He curled his forefinger and, evidently well trained, Adam passed the toast plate to his dad. Then, in one smooth and unexpected motion, Peter swept the toast and plate to the floor beside him where it rolled round and round against the tiles as if fulfilling an ambition to participate in a Greek wedding.

It made an appalling clatter in the still kitchen. Adam jumped about a foot off his chair and his lip started to tremble. He didn't cry though, just stared at the plate on the floor, at his mummy, then back at his egg.

'Whoops, aren't I a clumsy daddy today,' said Peter, taking a sip of tea.

Eve, startled at first, looked back at her cup and concentrated on her tea. Peter unfolded and read his paper. He kept scratching at his ear, the one I'd whispered in all night. Something was itching inside, where he couldn't reach, something prickly and growing, pushing upwards. Five minutes later he got to his feet, without having his usual second cup of tea, and only then did Eve finally move to retrieve the plate from the floor. But this was not the right thing to do because Peter grabbed her wrist, hard enough to make her wince.

'Not now, for God's sake! Do it later. Adam's late already. Smarten yourself up. Get your son to school on time. See if you can at least do that single thing properly.'

Her hand went through her hair, through the usual motions; the blush on the cheeks, the gloss on the lips, the Chanel No 5 spritzed out in a cloud. Peter gave a curt nod of approval and handed her a £10 note from his wallet.

'Get some proper bloody tea. Is that too much to ask? And make some fresh cake.' He gestured to the one in the tin on the sideboard. 'That one tastes like three-day-old wallpaper paste for Christ's sake.'

Then he handed her the Corsa keys, wrote the date and the words 'school run' in the margin of the blue notebook he kept on the hall table, noted the mileage.

After Eve returned from the school run that morning, and had cleaned up the toast plate still abandoned on the floor, she made a cake as directed – a date and walnut cream sponge. The radio was on while she cooked, Swansea Sound, and the bump of chart hits filled the sugary kitchen. While she weighed and sieved and mixed I did a little dance around the table to Bon Jovi's 'Livin' on a Prayer'. I was singing and playing a bit of air guitar because I was pleased with the effect my little night of whisperings had obviously had on Peter's mood.

Eve did not sing nor swing in time, though. She didn't appear to register it when Polly's full news package came on the radio saying my car had been found, locked and lonely, parked up in the street behind The Rising Sun pub on Chapel Street in Mumbles. I stopped dancing to listen, as Polly described how police forensic teams were 'combing it for clues', ever the one for clichés, and trying to determine why it might be parked there at the other end of town where they had not expected it to be.

Polly went on to explain that some nosey old biddy (she used the phrase 'concerned resident') had called the police ten days ago to complain about the blue Vauxhall Vectra still parked in her dedicated disabled parking space and covered in parking tickets. It had been there since the night of the Big Snow. The police declined to comment on why the report hadn't been followed up sooner, Polly said, implying someone had clearly been careless and was in for an arse-kicking from the top brass.

Not that the ten days would have made any difference to me, nor the ministrations of the CID officers, no doubt already prying open the door of my car and poking around inside, under the gaze of the Chapel Street residents. It was highly unlikely to be a 'significant development' of any kind. They wouldn't find anything useful in there or indeed anything distasteful. I wasn't one of those reporters who insulated their footwells with used coffee cups, burger wrappers and receipts, papered their back seats with old scripts and notebooks or had tampons and hairspray shoved in the glove box. I always preferred a nice controlled environment. It saved time in the long run, everything in its place where it could be found the moment there was a call to action.

The same thing applied to my second-floor, one-bed flat, which I knew the police would already have searched thoroughly by that point. That didn't bother me either, really. Not that I liked the idea of my privacy being violated by some chin-stubbled PC rifling through my pants and socks, snickering at the sight of my vibrator in the bedside drawer, but at least I didn't have to worry about them sniffing through old, unwashed knickers or turning up their nose at gummy bottles on the bathroom shelf. My flat was also the image of order – a neat blank canvas of neutral blue and cream, devoid of clutter and gossip fodder. Well, they say a home reflects its owner.

Polly was winding up then, saying that the search area was widening dramatically and door-to-door questioning would be extended to encompass the Mumbles area. Eve still didn't appear to be listening though, and why should she? She was lost in her own emergency – the eggs were almost curdling and that would be very bad. Her wooden spoon beat harder at the mixture, a sheen of cool sweat on her forehead. She rubbed her friction-red wrist a little every time she took a break from folding the mixture.

'Breaking news, sweetie,' I said, 'it could be a cake fit for a king but it'll never be good enough for Saint Peter.'

'I'm sorry, I'm sorry, I'm sorry' she muttered into the eggs and flour.

'You certainly are,' I whispered, then resumed my dancing.

'I'm sorry, baby,' said Peter when he arrived home that night, and he actually looked like he meant it. 'I was tired this morning.'

He seated himself at the kitchen table, took the cup of tea Eve had put out ready for him, took a sip, nodded in approval. 'I've been so tired lately. I've not been sleeping well and, well, the office, you know, *Julienne*, the budget report was today. I've been under a lot of pressure.'

I can't deny it, he could be charmingly hangdog when feeling sorry for himself. Eve seemed to think so. She stood next to him and took his hand.

'I'm sorry, too, honey,' she said. 'You work so hard. The least I can do is get you a proper breakfast.'

You're both about the sorriest fucking people I've ever known, I thought as she smoothed her hand through her hair once more, placing a fat slice of walnut cake, frosted with buttercream in front of him. He took a bite. She waited for the verdict.

'Delicious, darling,' he said, and she smiled.

I hated her then. I couldn't bear to look at her a moment longer, at her simpering face, desperate for approval, standing like a waitress in her own kitchen, waiting for his next order. It typified everything I despised about fucking desperate housewives and their majestic Holy-Mary motherhood martyrdom.

'No change in the Albright house tonight, Huw,' I sneered. 'I'll update you as soon as Eve grows a sprig of backbone or the Le Creuset tableware takes another tumble. One side-plate down, five to go. Cake stops play.'

I followed Peter upstairs after dinner, so as not to have to be around Eve for a bit. Wednesday night was Adam and Daddy night and I always went up to watch that. I'd realised by then that it was Peter who'd chosen the books and old-school paraphernalia for Adam's bedroom. And I can't lie, well, I shouldn't, I should try to be dispassionate and detached, shouldn't I? There was something marginally warmer about Peter when he was in that room with his son. It was as if a thaw set in when he was helping Adam add a new section of track to the railway set snaking round the table, using his announcer voice to say, 'Thomas the Tank Engine approaches platform two,' or pretending to fly the planes on their strings in a wide circle to make Adam laugh.

The rushing under his skin slowed, the blood-birds ceased to flock and roosted quietly.

If Peter had a sound then it was a delicate hum, like electricity gathering, instead of the snap-crackle-buzz of the day. When he ran his fingertips over the old cars, gently rearranging the station master on the train platform, I realised they were probably his old toys, or if not the exact ones, ones very like them. I knew very little about Peter of course, nothing at all before the day we met, and I often found myself wondering what kind of daddy Peter had had; perhaps a kick-about-in-the-park, handy-with-his-hands, model-making man by the feel of the warm colours that pulsed in Peter when he thought the word *father* and tried to be one.

There was a black-and-white photo of Peter's dad in a frame in the master bedroom, on the dresser, with a sharp side-parting and moustache, leaning on the bonnet of an old Austin Allegro. When Peter looked at it a memory surfaced from inside him, one suffused with rushing steam and the clank of wheels on track, a man's voice saying, 'All aboard!' and a small hand in a larger one.

And Peter's mother? Had she perhaps been a doting, cake-making sort of Enid Blyton aunty, always in the kitchen? Never too tired to read little Peterkins a story? There were no photos of her in the house, not that I had seen. The colour of her in Peter's head was harder to interpret than his father's, the images were pushed down deeper, bound up more tightly. I couldn't pick them free and unravel them.

'What story would you like tonight then, Adam Ant?' Peter always asked, settling in on the bed beside him.

'You could try *The Gruffalo*,' said Eve, standing in the

doorway, her voice bright and shiny as ever. 'Benedict's mum brought it round today. Benedict likes it. It's the one all the kids like. You'd like it, for a change, wouldn't you, Adam Ant?'

'Yes, we have him in school. I want Gruffalo pyjamas,' grinned Adam, adding a little roar.

No sooner were the words out of his mouth than he saw Daddy's face and added, 'but I like Daddy's old stories best.'

Eve's mouth tightened in response. In some ways it amazed me there was any give left in her, the way she just kept winding in and tying off a bit more of herself day by day, biting back any criticism, any contrary opinion. If you plucked her surely she'd emit the high twang of a violin's E string.

Adam saw the look though. He knew somehow that he'd just betrayed his mummy, though he couldn't voice it in those words – he knew he'd taken his daddy's side. But it had made Daddy happy because he was smiling, so Mummy would be happy, too. And that was a good thing. To my surprise I heard this sequence of Adam's thoughts, clear as a bell, bundling out in a ball from under the bedcovers. Not in words exactly, but the essence of them in five-year-old form, finger-paint splodges of colour and sound frothing in the front of my head.

How quickly they learn, I thought in fascination. How quickly they learn to be afraid. Before they know what the word really means, and can come to mean, and why. And how quickly they learn to please because to please is to be loved.

'Yes, Adam, good boy,' said Peter. 'A nice old-fashioned family tale, like my mummy used to read to me when I was a little boy.'

'Like fuck!' said a voice in the room, sharp like a whetted knife through the air, the sound shimmering. But Peter didn't glance up from the book and Adam didn't seem to notice. When I looked around it appeared, once again, that no one had spoken.

'Your mummy was my granny, who went to be with the angels when she was still too young?' said Adam as if he'd recited this many times before, from memory. And to my surprise Peter looked as if he might break open into two halves right there.

'That's right. Clever boy. My boy.'

Seeing Peter's face then, the love in his eyes, caused a gash to zipper open inside me. The jagged halves of my chest parted and blackness sloshed around and pooled out on to the carpet. I thought of my own mum, sitting perhaps in my old bedroom, in the low-ceilinged, bread-smelling farmhouse where I'd grown up, holding my own Soft Peter called Cheeky Charlie, a fat wise owl with specky glasses, blue dungarees and an opinion on everything.

And then I thought of Eliot. What was he doing right then? Was he lying on a rumpled bed thinking of me? Of how I felt in his arms, long and smooth and hard-limbed? Of my mouth on his, tight and hot? No one would look at me like that again, like he had, full of wonder at the cool, bright thing he had caught, electricity cracking in my fingertips and the ends of my hair as we moved together, for him alone. Eliot would feel this loss now, in a dampened night room, alone.

As Peter sang the usual verses of 'Baa Baa Black Sheep' and 'When You Wish Upon a Star', Old Lamby and Soft Peter tucked under Adam's arms, I lay next to them. I made my breathing, or memory of it, match Adam's but, try as I might I could not match the glow inside his chest that was happy and warm. Instead I began to understand how fragile everything about a child is, of the easy damage you can do to one without ever laying a finger on them. I could sense the imprint of Peter on Adam, invisible finger marks already beneath his skin.

The crown of Adam's head smelled like a memory of baby shampoo and talcum powder, yellow and sweet. The skin of his neck was so delicate I could see the blood pulse in the vein beneath it. I remembered the throb of blood in my own veins when Eliot touched me, deep into the skin, down to the bone, painful and welcome. Peter had taken that from me. Taken the thing I loved so I could never feel him again, or the pads of his fingers playing along my collarbone in a strip-lit corridor in the 6 a.m. studio silence. He could never give that back to me.

Adam shifted beneath my hand then, hugging Old Lamby, abandoning Soft Peter to the sheets. All at once I was in need, I wanted something warm to fill the space as empty as the aeons ahead in my chest. And when my Peter left the room and closed the door, a longing came down over my eyes, swelling coldly in my mouth, and I sang to Adam to keep it inside and unspoken. I sang a tune from my silent throat like the tune of a flute that once lured children from the village of Hamelin in my father's picture-book stories. My voice said, don't be afraid. Just listen. For now just learn to follow and find me. I will tell you better tales than your father's tainted ones.

At last, hours later, when Adam's eyes were flitting with flying dreams, I went into Peter and Eve's room. I lay down next to sleeping Peter on the bed, cupped my hand round his neck and whispered to him, raked the furrows of his brain, turned my fingers in the soil of his thoughts.

I sang him a little tune: 'Melly, Melly, quite contrary, How does your garden grow?' I knew my fingers were not terribly green but time was on my side. And inside Peter's head I heard a young shoot prick upwards from the surface of his brain and strain around for the light.

Chapter Eight

Four weeks later, one smiley kitchen morning of golden sunrise eggs and crisp toast, I heard Eliot's voice on the radio, clear and true as if he were standing next to me. He said my body had been found.

The words hovered over the plates of peeled shells and cooling cups and for a moment no one moved or spoke. Not even me. Because what was there to say once those words were spoken? I knew what they meant. I had known all along but the saying made it so. Not just in the house and in my head but in the world outside that, all the while, had kept on turning.

As the report continued, Peter's hands tightened around his butter knife and his head made a roaring sound only I could hear. Spotting the reaction, without really knowing what had caused it, but knowing only too well what it might mean, Eve's hands tightened on her cup. Perhaps she was thinking of the lifespan of another plate. The words settled on the tabletop, waiting for someone to pick them up and speak about them, to hand them on.

Stupid Bitch! said Peter's head-voice, clear and sharp across the ditzy-print tablecloth.

Dear God! It can't be true! said that invisible voice in the room, unseen but closer and louder than before.

'It's so sad,' said Eve, putting down her cup. 'I feel so sorry for her family.'

Then she brushed the remnants of Eliot's words off the table and into her hand with the crumbs of a surprise cinnamon Danish.

'Why? It's not as if you know them,' said Peter. 'Why should you care? Why are we listening to this at breakfast anyway? Why isn't Radio Two on as usual?'

He got up and changed the station with a pointed look at Eve.

'Please don't play with my radio, Eve, for God's sake, how many times do I have to say it.'

He sat back down.

'Another bloody stupid woman,' he said after a moment, stabbing his egg with his spoon. 'Getting herself into trouble. They're all the same these *career girls*.'

His sneer slid across the morning. We'd heard this speech before, many times, the one Peter liked to make about the true value of a woman being a mother and raising a family. For once Eve looked at him with something like reproach in her eyes.

'You don't know that, Peter,' she said. 'You didn't know her, that girl.' There was a touch of defiance in her eyes, just a flicker. For a moment I thought she was going to say something else, something in my defence, perhaps.

'You didn't know her either, Eve,' said Peter with quiet menace. 'She was probably just another one of those sluts. Her sort attracts this sort of thing.'

Eve shot a pointed look at Adam, obliviously munching

on his last bit of pastry, but Peter continued. 'You don't know what young women are like today, Eve – I'm the one who has to work with them. Honestly, the way they conduct themselves. The way they speak and dress. What do they expect?'

He held Eve's gaze until she let it fall to her plate. He seemed satisfied with the last word.

At that moment I hated Eve more than ever, for just sitting there, listening to Pontificating Peter, staying silent when she had a choice, to retort or retaliate, to yell, 'You don't know that, you don't know anything about her, who she really was or what happened to her or how!' Or at the very least, 'I'll listen to whatever radio station I choose, you fucking control freak!' She could even send the butter dish spinning into his smug, complacent face, if she wanted to. Well, that's what *I* wanted to say and do, but my hands could only itch impotently and my tongue shrivel.

For the millionth time I wondered why she didn't just say 'fuck this' to Peter and his fucking loose leaf tea and his weird routines and locked cupboards and little, quiet, bullying games. Did she have no self-respect at all? She could get up right now and pack a bag, take Adam away, somewhere, anywhere, out of this constrained existence of locked wardrobes, cream pumps, mileage notes and daily phone check-ins.

If she just had the guts.

That was it, I suppose. Why I felt the wheels of my rage start to turn for her that morning, faster and faster, clanking and steaming. I wanted to hurt her then. I really did. Because she had a choice, to stay or leave, whereas I did not. I wanted to break open the charade in front of her, the one she maintained with such care each day, shored up by the Cath Kidston china and Habitat home furnishings, the perfect jammy sponges, the pink slippers. I wanted to whip back those Laura Ashley curtains exposing her primrose-coloured, vanilla-scented existence for the twisted sham it was.

She had allowed it to be made. She had chosen Peter – consequences came. But she still had options.

It didn't take much effort on my part to do it. To intervene for just a second, in that fiery moment when the slash of her quiet pity for me, for a woman she'd never even known, was more than I could bear. That was the moment the nights of whispering to Peter paid off.

What had I been whispering to him every night in his bed, as close as a lover, closer than a wife?

'Wake up, Peter the not so fucking great. Newsflash! You're a total arsehole, Peter my boy. You have a small cock. She doesn't love you. She's fucking the milkman' (even though they didn't have a milkman). 'She steals from your wallet. The guys at work think you're a wanker. And hey, Mr Floppy, where'd your wood go? Soft Peter, Mr Floppy Peter Rabbit – can't even get it up to stab it. You're getting grey. Peter Pan, you're a sad old man. Peter Piper, nobody likes ya! You're getting fat, Peter, Peter pumpkin eater.'

And I sang. I sang to him a lot, that Nine Inch Nails song he'd hated so much in the car, and others from the repertoire of Steve's CDs I could remember.

I'd been diligent in my practice but, up until that morning, the results had been inconsistent; the troubled sleep, irritation, short temper, were fun to produce but weren't really *useful*. On that breakfast morning, hearing beloved Eliot's voice on the radio, and Eve's empty and gutless condolences, I didn't even think about it. I just said in Peter's ear, cold and sharp as a needle – 'Look in the flour barrel.' I drove the thought between his eyes like a lightning bolt across the table. I looked at Eve and waited.

Peter probably couldn't have told you what possessed him to do it, to walk over and open a kitchen container he'd never thought to look in before, to sift the white dust through his fingers until he found the edge of the plastic bag. By the time Eve realised what he was doing it was too late. Her face was an absolute picture, an award-winning still, poignant and raw – fear, guilt, horror – all of the above?

Peter found the phone, the one she'd been making the secret calls on when he was out. When he pulled it out in a cloud of soft talcum white his eyes grew glassy and blank. The colour drained out of Eve's face until it matched the flour that dusted his fingers. He didn't break her wrist when she tried to snatch it from him, when he sent Adam upstairs and demanded to know what was going on. Who the hell was she calling? Some man? Some fancy man? Was she just like all the others? Did she think she could make a fool of him again?

He flung the phone with enough force to smash it against the wall. He didn't break her wrist but he twisted it into the next best thing with those strong hands of his, a sprain that she later dressed with a tube bandage under a long-sleeved shirt. And the bruise on her neck, where he grabbed her and demanded she bring up the list of calls and show him who this fucking other man was, meant she had to wear a scarf for a week afterwards.

'It was for emergencies,' she pleaded, hands up to ward off his anger and then, predictably, 'I'm sorry, I'm sorry.'

We've already established that, I thought, smiling. But a recap never hurts.

Because I was pleased to see her cry, even as Adam sat frozen at the foot of the stairs, little fingers splayed over his ears as Peter banged out of the house. I was pleased for another reason, too. It meant my influence over Peter was finally sharpening behind the little lines between his eyes where I had been wiggling my invisible ice-pick.

On that day Eve's tears were my gift, to myself. A little treat. I felt I deserved it. It was something just for me, something I'd earned while I was forced to watch and wait silently, while the radio and then the TV told the rest of the world about my sodden corpse.

Chapter Nine

I know I must have been a particularly bloated and insect-riddled dead body. I couldn't have been nice to look at. Shame really, I'd spent a lot of time in the gym over the years, keeping my body trim, the cardio-burst sessions, the spin classes – not to mention all the sit-ups and bicep curls in the living room while watching *Newsnight*, the burning squats while blow-drying my hair. All gone to waste, corrupted and decayed.

It turned out I was even further away from home than anyone had realised, in Weston-super-Mare, on the broad, brown sand beach, across the English Channel. The kids who'd literally stumbled across me would no doubt have nightmares for weeks, well the younger one would. The two cute ginger things, brothers, nine and twelve, appeared on the late bulletin, their aghast parents huddled behind them in crackly anoraks as the camera focused in on the boys' freckles.

They hadn't needed a cadaver dog to find me – the smell would have been its own red flag. Nine weeks in wind and water and winter rains . . .

'It was 'im,' said the older one, gesturing to his brother.
'We were lookin' for crabs and 'e fell over something, like, a
sack, only it weren't a sack, it was a lady. It was like something on TV, wern it, Ross?'

He was just a kid, no doubt raised on video-game slaughter
and carnage, so I couldn't really blame him for the almost
excited look in his eye. Ross just sniffed and looked tearful.

'Like something on TV, was it, boys?' There was a certain
irony in that. Like something that had once been real and
now was not.

The reporters made the most of it, naturally; the *black day*
for the kids and family who'd trodden unexpectedly on my
rotting limbs, the *black clouds* over the tourism community
and so on. I'd developed my own stubborn weather systems
over the elapsed weeks, generated dark skies that had spread
across the Severn Estuary into the West Country on the
reporters' eager clouds of breath.

The little white SOCO tent was the focus of the news
footage, families tramping the windswept sand in a wide
circumference around it, gawping through wind-slitted eyes.
They'd gathered the usual vox pops; the talking heads.

'Not what you expect, is it?' – Woman in headscarf, with
scraggy Lurcher.

'Not the sort of thing that 'appens round 'ere.' – Man
with yappy collie.

Never is, lovelies, I thought, from my perch on the arm
of Peter's media room wing-backed chair; on both counts,
unless you're one of us, the producers, instead of one of you,
the consumers. Then it's every day and always, somewhere
or other, never expected.

In all the reports it was carefully phrased that a formal ID had not yet been carried out, but the implication was clear. 'A woman's body found on a Somerset beach is believed to be that of missing journalist Melanie Black . . . ' It was too early to tell if the cause was 'suspicious', but I was fully clothed, said Polly pointedly, so the implication was that sexual assault seemed unlikely. Nor were there any visible signs of restraint or ligature marks or anything kinky – she didn't say kinky, of course, she said 'untoward'.

There'd be a long process of forensics to powder, print and pick through before the police could reach a definitive conclusion, but the reporters could, and did, say that the body was found wearing what I had been last seen wearing – a black skirt, light blouse, black coat, red scarf.

Mesmerised, I stared at the TV screen, at the snatched footage of Inspector something Murphy ushering my mum and Steve into Swansea Central Police Station, blinking and bemused. One of them would have had to ID my belongings, if they hadn't been claimed by the sea or rotted beyond recognition. Poor Mum; I could see her being led into the alien environment of a tiled hospital corridor, waiting for a DC to meet her, looking uncharacteristically precise in a smart two-piece suit. Might she have her cashmere scarf around her neck, or the pink one with flowers wound round her head like a grieving Hitchcock movie widow?

Would she raise her hand, her perfectly French-manicured hand, to the cool barrier of a separating pane of glass beyond which was a shape under a sheet, leaving faint moist marks when she raised them, distraught, to her mouth?

When I was still a little girl she used to paint my fingernails with pale pink varnish, to match hers, Peony Poesy or Pretty Princess, for a treat, then become impatient when I fidgeted and smudged them before they could dry. I fancied I could smell acetone and Oil of Olay. Pink smells for pink moments with no place in a hall of unexpected death.

I was so lost in thought that I actually jumped when Peter made a fist and detonated it towards the arm of the chair I was sitting on. I'd almost forgotten he was there, watching the bulletin. The story made a longish piece on the national news that followed, too. Once, twice, Peter pounded the frame, cursed at the screen then got up, staring at the fist and the reddening skin before flicking off the TV and going to bed.

It was a strange feeling, sitting in the media room alone that night, in the grip of the dark, moving my hand back and forth in the moonlight streaming through the window. I was thinking of myself lying on a coroner's cold table – a replica hand, arm, leg and foot, still as marble. Neatly cut nails, grimed and torn.

I knew my family wouldn't be allowed to see me – for their sakes. There'd be no farewell kiss of a brow or stroke of a hand that would bear little resemblance to the one, moving white and wand-like, through the air in front of me. The last chance of human contact had long passed – dissolved into the Bristol Channel and the places of memory.

Yet I could still feel the way Eliot had felt next to me, arms touching at our desks, a prickle of heat and indrawn breath. How he'd felt beside me and inside me, in the wet heat of the bed. How I'd loved watching him in the dark from inside the director's booth, even though he couldn't see me, because then I'd felt less alone. And I'd been alone a great deal in my life, I realised that then, even under the gaze of the newsroom cameras and in the square of world view in your living room, I was largely unknown, untouched.

It probably wouldn't have seemed that way, to anyone watching, when the hours and days and minutes and seconds had still been flying by. I'd often been in company, the centre of a newsroom conversation, sharp-witted and sharp-tongued, smiling and bestowing barbed praise. I'd worn my self-reliance as a virtue, donned it like a bullet-proof vest. It hadn't seemed a sacrifice but rather a necessary statement that said, 'Stand off, don't presume, wait to be invited,' or you might get a nip of my teeth.

I didn't start out that way. As a child I'd been the very picture of a good little girl, like the nursery rhyme maids in Adam's stories, Miss Muffet-sunny and Little Bo Peep-sweet. Dressed in pretty candy-cotton frocks chosen by my mum people naturally fussed and petted me.

It turned out Mum had actually named me after a character in *Gone With the Wind*, her favourite movie. Melanie Wilkes – good-hearted Melanie – self-sacrificing, pure and patient. Melanie was my name and Mum wanted me to be Melanie by nature so we both tried to make it so. But by the age of seven, despite my pale Scandinavian hair, pixie blue eyes and high cheekbones inherited from my father's ancestors, I disliked the things of girls. I scorned pinafores and frills. I hated French pleats and pink hairslides.

Friends like Lottie the Bean might inexplicably find bubblegum in *their* perfect hair if they were spiteful to me at break time or laughed at my proclamation that one day I'd be 'on the telly'. Once I sawed seven inches off my own blonde mane after a hair-pulling bout with Susie Francis, forcing my mum to trim it into the sharp elfin bob I'd demanded for months.

'There's a rod of iron in that one,' Dad had laughed,

sweeping up the shorn locks into a newspaper, unwilling to scold me. 'She'll go far!'

Mum had me sorted into a different pile though. 'There was a little girl who had a little curl,' she would sing each night, detangling my locks with a sigh, 'right in the middle of her forehead. When she was good, she was very, very good, but when she was bad she was horrid.'

Then, all too soon, I wasn't a little girl anymore. I grew and grew, like Jack's beanstalk. By the age of thirteen I was five foot seven, by seventeen, five foot nine. I was 'statuesque' then, with a cool glare like an icy Norse goddess. In my mind's eye white winds wound round my head and cold fire flew from my eyes. If I gave myself a name it was Freya, goddess of war and battle, death and prophecy, receiver of half the battle-slain dead, like in Dad's other bedtime stories of Norse legends.

People didn't fuss and pet me anymore. They assume if you're tall and straight and don't take too much shit you don't need consideration. Men don't rush to open doors for you or help carry your shopping. There's no primal urge to protect like there is with petite, giggly, pixie women, like Polly, who laugh behind their hands and have doll-sized shoes.

So I made this my virtue. I never slouched, always wore heels, three inches at least, great, tall size eights that clipped on polished floors like jaws snapping. I imagined lightning bolts shooting from my fingers, clearing the way ahead, smiting idiots and smarmy twats with patronising mouths and free hands. When people met me at parties, or for interviews, they would always say, 'You're taller than you look on the telly'. If I knew them, or they were no use to me,

I'd say, 'And you look older' with a Freya frost-whip, electric crackle of a smile.

Of course, being six foot in heels didn't mean I was any sort of match for six foot two inches of man, not at the end. I'd never thought it would. Or perhaps I had. No one had ever laid a hand on me before . . . before that last night. And I can't lie and say I was passive or gentle in life. I took up arms of my own, often enough. I inflicted injuries on others, shot electricity from my eyes and left the slain in my wake. I was never a victim.

Until I was, washed up on a beach, like many before me and all those to come. My body was a sea-softened pulp, existing only to be poked and prodded and tested by lab technicians. How had that possibly happened? To me? In a flash I was no longer a warrior but a missing girl, a dead girl, a victim, a cliché.

That night, in the armchair, I felt sorry for the woman I'd once been. For letting her down, for fleeing the field so easily, the only blood on my hands my own.

After a while I went into Adam's bedroom, looking for solace, and lay next to him. He stirred in the night that was stiff with frost outside and cool inside, so his breath smoked a little. I thought I could see the faint wisp of his life-force sliding in and out and the absence of my own.

'There was a little girl who had a little curl,' I sang, stroking his hair back from his brow. 'Right in the middle of her forehead . . . '

'Mummy?' he muttered, shifting under the covers. But he didn't wake, so I didn't stop singing.

'When she was good she was very, very good,' I crooned. 'But when she was bad . . . '

Chapter Ten

In the weeks to come it became increasingly strange to see myself on the TV. Over and over again I was conjured back into temporary existence by people I'd known and people I hadn't, reborn each night on flickering TV screens, like Doctor Who regenerating into a same yet different version of myself one after the other. Melly Mark II – a collage of sound bites and speculation.

It was always interesting even if it wasn't always accurate, or easy to watch.

Mum, poor Mum – she was always the hardest to see. In my memory she was either smiling and soothing or occasionally faintly disapproving or resigned. She'd never swung to extremes. Indeed, in the weeks before the beach body find she'd made constant TV appeals with Polly on the evening news, looking drawn but dignified. I was probably the only one who could see how her neatly lipsticked mouth and ladylike blouse screamed her mortification at having to be involved in something so terribly tabloid.

Later that veneer began to slip and, as I'd expected, grief didn't suit her. Her face wasn't used to the new shapes it was being forced to accommodate. It warped the lines of her mouth, made her voice harsh when she'd pleaded into the lens: 'Come home, Melly. If anyone knows where Melly is please come and tell us, tell the police. We just want her back. We want our angel back.'

And each time Polly nodded sympathetically.

I believed my mum was telling the truth. She did want me back, her 'angel'. She'd genuinely forgotten, for the time being, that we'd barely spoken in six months, and before that only two or three times a year since Dad died; somehow she'd erased the memory that I'd told her plainly, after the funeral, that Dad had been my favourite, not her – that I'd told her this more than once since, in fits of despair after he collapsed and convulsed his way out of the world when I was just twenty-five, clutching his tired old heart and tired old dreams, dreams I was convinced she'd leached out of him, day by day.

I told her she'd never understood me, was an ambitionless, boring housewife who had never supported my father through his black bouts of depression and great glorious highs of energetic abandon.

Okay, I admit it. I'd been a stroppy, mean-lipped thing to her, teenage and guttural in my rage, even after I passed thirty and should have known better. If I was celestial it was only in my bright, blazing anger, and the glint of my readily drawn sword.

But I did look angelic in the photo she provided for Polly. I think it was the one from my cousin Rhonda's wedding two years ago. A bit of vodka had smoothed the tension of my face, some soft-focus light had worked wonders. I looked handsome in a cool way, like a statue rendered in watercolours. But I also looked kind and honest. Thanks, Mum, for safeguarding my brand.

Later, after my body was found, as people searched for other adjectives to describe me, I was 'delightful' once and 'full of life' many times.

As the 'tributes' and reaction vox pops with neighbours snowballed onwards it seemed everyone had a good word to say about me. My landlady and neighbour was one of the most poignant. Mrs Azzopardi, little old lady, stock model number two; blue rinse hair, pink cardigan, thick glasses, black-and-white cat like Postman Pat.

'She used to knock on my door if there was snow,' she sniffed to Polly, the mic in her face, 'offer to get me milk and bread and bring me a newspaper. Sometimes she'd help me put the recycling out. An absolute angel. A delightful girl.'

Well, I did do that, once or twice. Who wouldn't? You'd have to be an animal not to, surely? There's a universal law about helping little old ladies that even people like me don't flout.

Then there was Mick who served behind the bar in The White Horse, my local pub, who said: 'Miss Black? She was just beautiful, like a princess. Always chatting and full of life.'

I don't ever recall being that chatty at The White Horse. I remember being a bit bolshy at the bar after a few vodkas, on my rare nights off, complaining the TV was too loud. But I did part with many a pound coin for his son's sponsored shenanigans and usually remembered to ask about his sciatica. And no one wants to speak ill of the dead, do they? Or if they want to, they feel they can't.

I suppose Polly, the public face marshalling all these glowing character references, might have been the one with more honest things to say about me, but no one was asking her. How it must have driven her insane during those weeks before and after my body bobbed up, to have to repeat the words 'angel' and 'princess' in conjunction with my name, to be the conduit through which people praised me.

Eager little, itty-bitty, big-titty Polly, desperate to be popular and of use. Always trying to blind us in the newsroom with her megawatt smile early in the mornings, with lukewarm cups of Starbucks coffee, while we were still too 5 a.m.-sleepy to have our defences up; always making a beeline for Eliot with her bee-stung lips. 'Here's your coffee, Eliot, no trouble. Here's your script. Sure, Eliot, no it's no trouble. Just a tad more powder on your forehead, Eliot.'

And then – 'Mel, black Americano for you! No trouble, pay me later. Like the shoes, Mel. Very chic. I picked up your mail from reception, Mel. Here's the library VT you wanted, Mel. I found it for you, no trouble.'

No trouble, Polly Parrot, anything but.

As if I would fall for that. As if I hadn't seen her shaking her feathers at Eliot between pre-records, and down in the editing suite on Sunday afternoons. *Polly want a crack at that?* There are bigger, better winged things here, Pollyanna, I used to think. Things of snow and ice and thunderbolts. And deft fingers.

It's a game, all of it, of course, and we all play it. But if you can't step up then *step off*. That's what Bella should have done. She was in no way equipped from the start. It was too easy.

For months, every time Bella rang the newsroom I'd make some story up ' . . . he's on a job, Bella. He's got the afternoon off. He's gone to buy flowers . . . ', flowers that were imaginary and therefore *she* never received, prompting the question *who did*? It was so easy to trigger that moment's hesitation in her voice, the little hitch of uncertainty, sometimes by pretending to be a tech or work experience girl, disguising my voice when I picked up the phone just a little so she wasn't quite sure who she was speaking to. Telling her he'd been called away for the afternoon when he'd told her he'd be working all day in Cardiff. A seed of suspicion, a suggestion of subterfuge . . .

She'd been easy to manipulate, from the first time she showed up at the office laden with cakes for the Comic Relief fundraiser, a tray of stuff from her own newly opened bakery in Gower. I measured her and sorted her right off. I mean, for fuck's sake, who calls a collection of cinnamon rolls and pecan cupcakes 'signature treats' with no sense of irony? She was wearing fancy dress, too. I mean, not real fancy dress, but a sort of *Arabian Nights* colourful sari and beaded slippers, somehow managing to look cute and winsome in her traditional dress and far less idiotic than she should have.

'Not in fancy dress, Melanie?' she smiled, in that eager-to-please way of hers. 'I guess it's a bit childish but it is for *charity*.'

'But I am in fancy dress, Bella,' I smiled, waving a hand up and down my usual neat dark suit and flicking my hair out of my face, 'I'm ITV News's Julia Somerville, circa 1996.'

When I saw the look in her eye, the one that said she wasn't certain if I was laughing at her because I seemed like such a nice person, I knew she was no competition. Just to make her feel bad for doubting me I put a fiver in her collection box and grabbed two cinnamon rolls. And so it began.

Yes, I suppose Bella would've had something to say about me, too. But no one asked her either. Because I was dead and a saint – a pursuer of truth and justice, a daughter, a girlfriend, an *angel*. If it's on the TV it must be true. See my halo, see my wings, pretty, pretty, shiny things.

Now I come to think of it, sometimes, in Peter's night-time house, when everyone was sleeping, I used to think I could hear wings – outside under the sky, under the ceiling, under the skin of things. I don't think they were mine, certainly not angelic ones, not white and soft like those belonging to Eve's pious figurines. Something else.

The Valkyries were hand-maidens for the goddess Freya, you know, Dad's favourites, despite the Nazi connotations, their wings, black and brittle, soaked in blood. Those wings whooshing and falling in the night outside Rosemary Close, inside my chest . . . were they bringing me my tribute of the slain or . . . Despite my new media status as 'angel' it still came back to that same old question each time:

'Where, oh where will Melly go?'

And the answer? It was always the same, too.

I have to say, I do not know.

Chapter Eleven

After my body was found the weeks pulled haltingly forward while the press waited impatiently for the police to say something definitive about my demise. As usual, the CID, who had perfected the art of stalling some time in the nineteenth century but always felt they needed more practice, said the 'advanced state of decomposition' my body was in was slowing up the test results and formal ID. So, day after day, they said nothing much at all, with many statements that were issued through their press office, technically all the same and equally as empty.

But I knew my colleagues wouldn't be taking this at face value. Behind the cameras they'd be buzzing round like bluebottles asking off-the-record questions like, 'Are you treating this as a murder investigation, Inspector?' and/or, 'Is this a suicide, Sergeant?', even 'Do you have any suspicions of foul play?' hoping someone might let a detail slip, while still pumping any unofficial sources they had for leads.

Even good old-fashioned gossip would have been welcome to fill the news gap, as long as they could stand it up with the usual 'right of reply'. Do you know you can't libel the dead?

They're fair game. That doesn't do much for the grieving relatives though, which always seemed a little unfair to me. But that's the way it is and, since I'd been found on the beach, my background was an open book. Everyone and their media aunt would have been keen to rifle through it, truffling out the juicy titbits with their nosey snouts.

The reporters would be hoping for piles of unpaid debts to emerge, evidence of online gambling addiction or sexy calling cards and unaccounted-for sums of money suggesting I'd been moonlighting as a call girl. During those weeks it was a source of constant relief to me that I'd been so boring but there's always something, isn't there? It was only a matter of time and while it ticked by the winter began to recede with memories of snow, and spring began to raise its face to the sun. I looked out one morning to see great handfuls of flowers and green shoots scattered across the gardens, fields and verges around our house. The world was putting its glad rags back on, getting ready to start another phase of its life while mine was firmly lodged back in a snow pile in February.

Later that sunny afternoon Peter ceremoniously unlocked the garden shed and carried a table and three chairs out on to the paving near the back lawn – he had declared Swansea officially open for the year.

From that day onwards Eve began planting acres of earth-filled pots in the garden while Adam dedicated himself to 'helping', aka ferreting out worms and woodlice, poking sticks and his fingers in the mud. On sunnier afternoons, when Peter was safely at work, Mair started to pop by and Eve made them coffees to drink on the patio. There they sat, wrapped in cardigans, pretending it was already June and therefore not freezing cold. Mair brought her laptop over once and they went online to look at summer-season clothing.

Peter had allocated Eve some money for 'nice classic dresses' for the approaching school-fete and sports-day season. She knew he would want to go with her to the shops, help her pick out 'something suitable', but there was no harm in *just looking* online, she said. Mair gave a knowing smile as she pointed out various items and Eve said, 'maybe' and 'I don't think Peter would like that'.

'You'll want something nice and short-sleeved for the summer though,' said Mair, wearing a strappy neon pink vest atop her tight jeans, oblivious to the chill. 'Can't wear those long shirts of yours when the temperature goes up.'

'Goes up? This is Swansea,' said Eve, attempting a joke, while making a conscious effort not to rub her forearm. She knew the marks where Peter had grabbed her the other evening were hunkered down beneath the wrinkles of the crisp white shirt, sniggering. They still looked purple and obvious. Peter had been unusually stressed at work, of course. Julienne was 'a hard task-master, an unreasonable, ill-qualified, dictatorial woman with no knowledge of finance and even less about managing a budget or a team'. Because of Julienne, Peter was at work more, which was good, but it meant he was also more likely to insist on things being perfect when he was at home, like the other night, demanding homemade pizza and then fussing when Adam got wet sauce-fingers on the sofa. Because Peter never touched Adam in anger.

Then, one wince-bright Saturday morning of birdsong and peeking croci, the radio announced the police forensic collation was complete and my body was being released for burial. Just like that an inquest was officially opened.

Peter, hearing the update on his study radio, said nothing to Eve but decided to attend my funeral. I'm not sure why. Perhaps he felt a sense of obligation. Or maybe it was just grim fascination. His appraisal of the graveside ceremony, from the distant edge of the grass, behind the trunks of the newly leafed spring trees, was cool and speculative rather than compassionate, but I couldn't complain. I was thankful for this whim of his because, since Peter was at my funeral, it meant I could be there, too.

It's not really something you can prepare for, is it? Your own burial? It's not as if I was only pretending to be in the coffin, like in a movie thriller, staring wistfully from behind a mausoleum in Jackie O sunglasses and a headscarf, waiting for my time to re-emerge and right wrongs or reveal terrible treachery.

There was rain that afternoon at the cemetery, drizzly oceans of it, no wind but water, in the air. It kept falling, shifting, slick on the umbrellas, shiny on the coffin lid, slippery on the grass, hovering in the exhalations of the attendees and shimmering on into the evening headlights.

Reporters were there. Polly, naturally, Petra from network paying tribute to one of their own. It was pretty close to the funeral I would have chosen for myself, if I'd had a say in it, and that pleased me for some reason. There wasn't too much fuss, a speech or two, a song by Crowded House called 'She Goes On', which I must once have told Steve I liked in a glib moment.

Thank God it was a closed coffin, though. My mum put a white rose on it and then put her face in her hands. She was weeping and weak-kneed, supported by Steve. She'd always liked Steve. He looked handsome in a broken way, playing staunch and contained in the only suit he owned. I realised Dad was there too, in his way, in the plot next to my mound of earth, under the marble stone I visited on Christmas Days and birthdays. I hoped I wouldn't actually see him though. I wasn't ready for that.

Because I had wondered, as I'd sat next to Peter in the car, waiting at the lights for the turn into the grounds, if I might see more than I bargained for by attending the cemetery that day. I mean, over the weeks I'd spent many a slack and un-edged hour at Peter's house wondering exactly how I had come to be at Rosemary Close; how I'd somehow stayed so long after I should have slid away somewhere else. Surely this couldn't be a cosmic first? I know I have something of an overdeveloped ego but even I stop short of a full-on God complex.

Surely there had to be others somewhere, like me, waiting in the dark, perhaps, asking the same questions? Wouldn't a graveyard be the kind of place where people, things, leftovers like me might congregate?

The thought had run cold around the stone memorials as we pulled up at a safe distance. I glanced around with the memory of a half-held breath, seeking out anyone who looked incongruous – a tall thin man in an old-fashioned suit perhaps, a woman in white, all the clichés and anything in between that might suggest otherworldliness. There was a mixture of fear and excitement pricking my insides – fear I might see something, fear I might not, and under it all, hope that I might not be so very alone after all.

Concentrating on anything unexpected, I thought I saw

something, once or twice, just out of the corner of my eye. It was something about the movement of the light that day, among the mourners. The way it gathered here and there, seeming almost to produce a static shimmer over the shoulder of the vicar, a little blur to the right of the *Evening Post* photographer's long lens discreetly clicking away. But every time I tried to focus on it, to hone in, it evaporated. I told myself it was probably wishful thinking, a little bit of self-induced hallucination. It could easily have been the flowing drizzle, or possibly some water in my eyes.

My dad was definitely *not* there, leaning on his own gravestone in his threadbare woollen 'scripting' cardigan, drinking a mug of Earl Grey tea, which was a peculiar relief. But where he might have been, standing straight as a poker and trying not to step on the tended rectangle of grass was Eliot. Ah, my Eliot, beautifully bereft, suit-smart and shiny of shoe. There he was, even more luminous on the grey day than he was under studio lights.

His curly brown hair, the hair I'd loved to run my hands through, was tufty, as if he had been dragging his fingers through it. I remembered doing that myself, many times, and kissing the slope of his cheek, his mouth. How I'd loved the feel of each fibre of him. How greatly he must have been feeling everything then, his gaze disturbingly blank, his pale blue eyes hazy with bafflement and dislocation.

I wasn't surprised to see two policemen, non-uniformed, standing at a discreet distance, clearly watching everyone – Inspector Murphy and a younger one. Steve glowered at them as he held my mum's arm, both their faces as white as the sky over the bay. But the officers weren't paying attention to them. They were looking at Eliot. Peter, too, was staring long and hard at him, rain pattering on the pulled-up hood of his parka. He obviously recognised him from the TV news but was staying well back so he would not be spotted by the police or anyone else.

As I listened hard to the insides of Peter's head at that moment, it sounded, or felt, something like the words, *that stupid fucking cunt,* which wasn't what I'd expected. I wasn't sure if his curse was directed at Eliot or at my coffin. Peter's was a dark green-black feeling but underneath it there was something twisting itself back and forth and I realised it was fear. It was a bit like the dread I'd felt crowding in on him on my regular visits to his office, but this was more open and uncertain.

Eventually I had to turn away from the mourners, when Peter checked his watch and headed back to the car ahead of the final round of prayers. My last view of the scene was of Eliot's hair shining with beaded rain, some rain in his eyes. I had no choice but to leave as I whispered, 'Forget me, forget me, my love, forget. You will be all right.' And I knew the truth of the words as I formed them. I sent these thoughts across to him as I looked at him for the last time. For one split second the grief was almost crushing, as if I were at his funeral, I had lost him and was standing at his grave, bidding farewell.

In my head I released a sliver of a scream. Peter raised a hand to his ear, a tiny wince breaking across his face. So I put my mouth up close to his ear and screamed a second wordless curse. Then all that was left was the echo of grief, an echo of the life, melting into the mist of evening rain as we drove home.

* * *

The day that my body was laid in the earth just happened to be Eve and Peter's wedding anniversary. Peter had bought her a beautiful posy of roses, delivered by a man in a van, and a delicate silver locket on a chain. She'd cooked dinner and dressed in a blue wrap dress from the approved summer selection they'd picked out together in town.

But I was not in a celebratory mood that night. I hovered around the table remarking to Eve that, new dress or not, her cellulite was fairly disgusting and her taste mumsy, then I sat on the kitchen worktop swinging my legs while she cooked, a sullen and uninvited party crasher. There was a good chance I would be drunken and unpleasant later.

I watched, scowling, as Peter brushed back Eve's hair with his fingers and fastened the clasp of the necklace at the nape of her neck. I fingered my throat where my locket had been – a token of my own love in gold and red stones, lost now, or torn free, perhaps soon to be forgotten.

The bruises had yellowed on Eve's arm. As Peter smoothed her hair from her temple and planted a kiss there, he took her hand and said, 'Happy wedding anniversary, darling – you look beautiful.'

Eve smiled – the necklace was lovely, with a touch of antique Gothic in the carefully wrought scrolls of flowers on the surface. She was genuinely happy. I could hear the clotted pleasure of this tiny silver thing humming between the blue folds of material at her breastbone. And she was relieved that Peter had been pleased with the real leather wallet she'd given him, with his initials hand-sewn on the corner.

By the time they'd eaten their perfectly rare steak Diane, Eve's tension from the detailed preparation of the perfect anniversary had almost ebbed away. She'd had two glasses of wine and I was envious of her, of the imagined feel of the warm red wine glugging down her throat. I could see she was grateful to Peter, for being so kind to her, on that day of all days. For paying those tiny, sweet attentions. For being tender and not a total alpha-male prick for a change.

Surely it was a good sign? It showed he loved her underneath it all, didn't it?

Her gratitude was palpable and sickly in the kitchen, smelling less like Chanel No 5 and more like rotting dreams, like the inside of a coffin, three miles away under a night stiff with rain. She could smell it, too, now and then, the odour of me, of her own pretence, but she squashed it down. She wanted to pretend this was how it always was and was how it could be again, everything smelling of roses.

She loved Peter, she really did, in discrete, small parts she'd stuck together for that night into the image of the man before her, as she hoped he was when they'd met and could still be – handsome, a good provider, a dream catch. What was she without him now? No job, no money of her own. These were the shards of thoughts skipping through the softening core of her being that night. I didn't need to be able to read her mind to know that. By the third glass she was convincing herself that no husband was perfect and perhaps she really should try to be more attentive. He'd been under a lot of pressure. She should try to be more mature, more sensible. Give to receive – offer to have the offer returned – like attracts like. If she could be less clumsy, less slapdash, she might rankle less, irritate less and he would begin to offer to clear the dishes to the sink side now and again, and worry less about what she does when he's out, and tell her she looks wonderful when she chooses her own dress. And return the keys to her wardrobes.

I was sitting on the draining board watching this little kitchen-sink drama. In its candlelit bubble it was a touching and classical marital scene upon which the capricious old domestic gods were smiling. Naturally I was tempted to ruin it – I thought of things to whisper to Peter. I thought of orders to formulate and little doubts to fertilise. But before I could decide on an approach, as the homemade custard tart with real vanilla was produced, Adam appeared in the doorway, trailing Soft Peter and the scent of childish sleep.

I saw him before they did. I saw the look on his face, only half-awake. I saw him smile in the candlelight watching the scene. Somehow a storybook family had appeared in his house. Happy Mummy, happy Daddy. Happy Adam.

'Is it a birthday, Mummy?' he asked eventually, seeing the wrapping paper and the table candles.

Peter turned and smiled. 'No, silly bunny, just a treat for Mummy.'

As he lifted his son on his shoulders Eve stood by the sink in her blue dress like the beneficent Virgin Mary and the illusion was perfect, though something in Eve started to collapse and tear as soon as Peter took Adam back to bed saying, 'Up we go, little man'. The colour of it was troubling, dark and suffocating and it bled out of her into me. She was thinking, *Such a lovely necklace*, but also, *After ten years, how did we get here, to this from where we were? And who we were? I don't know what happened.*

Does anyone? I thought. Does anyone really know how people meet and mate and choose to stick together or not? And how the time ebbs in and out, marked by these little rituals between lovers, between husband and wife? Scenes are set, roles played. I thought about Steve, who, surprisingly, always liked anniversaries and birthdays and the marking of them in restaurants with gifts exchanged and kisses swapped at candlelit tables. I was never that bothered, which was just as well. Eliot and I had to keep our rituals, the few we'd had the chance to demarcate, a secret, because no one in the newsroom had known about us. About our *affair*. You know, because of his wife.

From day one we'd taken great pains to hide it, which must have made my sudden exit extra hard on Eliot who obviously couldn't show any more emotion than for the loss of a colleague. He couldn't reveal his feelings in our daily news conference and certainly not at the graveside. He couldn't show more than would be appropriate for a work friend. He hadn't been able to take his tears home to Bella. He couldn't show anyone how much he'd loved me.

Steve, with his official position as my *actual* boyfriend, I mean the man I'd been dating for four years, had all the weeping and wailing rights if he wanted to use them. He'd managed to hold it together at the funeral so Eliot could hardly have done less. I know I should have mentioned Steve before, in his proper context, it's just that things aren't always as straightforward as they sound, are they? Words are concise while what's behind them isn't. Labels don't always fit snugly where they are pasted. And we had an understanding of sorts.

Steve was my *boyfriend* but he and I had independent lifestyles. He knew I worked weird shifts. He was used to me leaving his place early, getting home to my place late, never being contactable on the phone, going where the news was at any hour of the day or night until the job was done and the edit finished. We were used to our world of snatched afternoons and evenings, scrabbling for the odd Saturday night and the impossibility of forward planning. He chose me. He knew these were the consequences.

He was good-looking and kind, if a bit, well, naïve about the real state of the world and the fact that the socialist revolution really was over for good. He was quiet company – he never asked too much, well not often. He made me laugh. He played the guitar beautifully, though he had an over-fondness for Bob Dylan when maudlin and, of course, Nine Inch Nails when rebellious.

When he asked me to marry him I'd said yes, well, I'd said, 'Maybe soon, not yet though, when I make presenter,' because he'd gone to a lot of trouble to set up 'the proposal' with the ring at the end of the pier where we'd first met. He was sentimental like that.

The day we'd met I'd been filling in for a colleague, reporting on a stranded dolphin that had swum the wrong way into the harbour. Dolphins probably trump dogs in the media stakes. Steve had been taking pictures of the bay doing his freelance photographer thing with long-haired, leather-jacketed aplomb. He asked to take my photo. I refused. He asked if I wanted a drink instead. I agreed.

The stars were out on the night he proposed, two years later. After we left The White Horse he'd said he wanted to walk on the pier to see the moon. It was a pretty night, the sky stirred with stars, but really I was thinking, *It's cold, and I have to be up in seven hours for the breakfast bulletins.* Then he ambushed me with a ring.

I thought if I said no, then and there, I'd have to think of a really good reason why. I didn't think saying, 'Well, sweetie, hopefully I'll be off to London in 12 months and Eliot will be with me,' would be very fair, or very kind, or very in keeping with the moment. And I didn't want to hurt him if I could avoid it. I thought, *there's no rush,* and Steve didn't really want to move anyway. He hated the idea of dirty old, big, anonymous cities.

It's just as well we didn't marry, for his sake, I mean. Who wants that at thirty-four? The stigma, the stone collar, the weight of the word 'widower'. If we had tied the knot the alternative, if I hadn't encountered Peter, of course, would have been a divorce eventually – so that Eliot and I could have married. That's what I wanted by the time the end came round.

'If you want it, grab it, Melly,' Dad used to say, pointing to his little William Blake illustration, the drawing of a tiny man trying to catch a crescent moon on the end of a long stick – the caption simply the words, 'I want, I want'. So if I saw something and wanted it, I reached for it, pulled it to me and shook it until it went limp in my teeth. If people got in my way I cleared the field.

I'd wanted Eliot. What did it matter if he was married, if he wanted me?

I suppose it's true, romantic bullshit though it is, when you meet the right one you know. I knew it with Eliot from the moment he put his hand on mine and said, 'Let me carry that for you, Mel', and weeks later, 'So lock the door, then'. I knew we'd make a great team, in life and side by side at the evening news desk in London, handing seamlessly back and forth to each other before the cameras, shuffling papers at the end for the obligatory credits-up, sound-off chat.

It's hard to explain to someone not in our line of work the coiled and contained pressure of it all, this life – the directed speed, the precision, the rush and roar and then the relief when the nightly news ends and you can draw a breath before you start all over again for the breakfast bulletins.

Eliot got it. He never got annoyed when I checked my iPhone during dinner or before I even got out of bed in the morning, to see what was happening on Sky News or the World Service, because he was doing the same. Steve's world was one of compartmentalisation; work and downtime cleaved down the middle. So I compartmentalised him. I never wore the engagement ring he gave me to work. It'd always felt too complete, too final, as if I'd made a choice and therefore given up all other options. What if my real soulmate caught my eye across a bar one day, then spotted that hard, blue, sapphire eye on my hand, and was deterred and did not offer me that drink? It was not that I wanted to be unfaithful. I didn't want to sleep around. I was just being practical, keeping my options open.

Steve kept the ring. It wasn't buried with me. I was glad of that. I thought maybe as a symbol it might have more certainty for him – a token of a love that would never be allowed to fail, in memory at least, final, uncontested. He could stare at it and pour into it everything he'd hoped I had been and felt for him and it would be faithful where I had not.

Eliot would have divorced Bella in time. I know that.

The dynamics of their marriage had been clear from that night at the Wales media awards. She'd spent three hours looking at her elegant little watch, fiddling with her mobile phone, making a big deal out of the fact she was the designated driver and drinking orange juice.

I've never been a big drinker myself. I don't like the fuzz it creates in my head, not when I'm with colleagues, not when tongues are unshackled and slipped free. I preferred to watch the smiles slide widely and the guards dip down as the shirts come untucked and the shoes are kicked off. It's surprising what you can learn from seeing the soft pink undersides of the professional talkers when they pull off their metaphorical glasses and undo their imaginary buns. That's when they tell you how much they admire you, or hate each other, or loathe their fucking jobs.

Seeing Bella and Eliot that night, I made mental notes, about how proud he was to show her off, so petite and pretty and brown-limbed, in a blue sheath dress. Her raven hair looked like it was combed with sandalwood from a softly scented Eastern story. The more Eliot drank the free Champagne, the more he had fondled her hand. But the more he'd frowned as she'd rung home yet again. 'It's a cold not swine flu,' I heard him whisper to her, slurring a little.

Everyone else was too high on booze on the dance floor to see Bella collecting her silver shawl from the cloakroom, wrapping herself in a shimmering skein of disapproval, fingering her car keys, or to see Eliot returning, angry and a little unsteady to the table, necking down the last bubbly from the bottle.

'I'm going to get a taxi in half an hour,' he said, as I slid into the seat next to him, a wry smile on my face. It said, 'Past your bedtime?'

'Let's celebrate,' said Eliot. 'We deserve to let off steam and stop being *grown-ups* once in a while,' grabbing a bottle from a deserted table and sloshing it into our glasses.

'I don't think Bella would approve,' I said, the proper colleague still.

'We won't tell her then,' he grinned, pulling me on to the dance floor and I agreed, just as I'd agreed, six months later, that it wasn't necessary for Bella to know that what had started that night had become serious between us.

They'd been married for five years and there was no need for immediate melodrama, for a *scene*. Things had to be done carefully. When the time was right we would discreetly go public together and pack up our knapsacks and head for the city streets paved with gold. Ciao, Bella! Then I'd tell Steve.

But they both found out soon enough. Eliot and I just weren't the ones to tell them. Inspector Murphy did that for us. He told them both about where we were the night we were both supposed to have been at the work function in The Gowerton Hotel. He told them about our visit to The Schooner on the night of the Big Snow. And he told them a lot more.

Happy anniversary, all.

Chapter Twelve

Peter was running. Running like something horned and unhappy was on his tail, which perhaps it was. The treadmill incline was set to level three, a slight slope, the speed readout at a lung-shredding twelve, almost flat-out. He was pounding away, arms pumping, little beads of sweat shaking free from his forehead, speckling the read-out panel. I was leaning on the arm of the adjacent running machine, bored and restless.

I'd started accompanying Peter to the gym three weeks before, as part of my ongoing lifestyle research. It was one thing, to watch him at his office each day, to see how he behaved when constrained by his nine-to-five collar and tie, but I wondered what he was like elsewhere, anywhere more unfettered.

It had crossed my mind that his regular trips to the gym could've been a front for something else. Each time he picked up his gym bag and isotonic drink, mixed in his trendy water bottle, pecking Eve on the cheek, it had occurred to me he could be going off to a liaison with another woman. Or perhaps paying visits to one of the Swansea ladies of the night upon whom he could visit any extra-marital urges.

He was always so immaculately dressed when he left the house, so precisely showered, shaved and shirted when he returned. No well-washed hoody and balding tracksuit bottoms for Peter and that alone seemed suspicious. But I was disappointed when I realised it was just what it seemed, part of his veneer of civilisation, his penchant for order and routine, always the councilman, the school governor, never a hair out of place.

Not that there weren't opportunities at the gym. There was no shortage of a certain type of eye candy, the usual gym bunnies, the Marilyns of their environment, younger, tighter, springier, working out in mascara and lip gloss. And it wasn't that Peter didn't notice their attempts to bounce a little more energetically when he was close by, to use the chest-press machines that accentuated their suspiciously round breasts. He just seemed scornful, contempt spraying off him as readily as his sweat. Words that, if they had been spoken aloud, would have sounded like 'brazen' and 'desperate' chafed against his concentration as they fluttered their eyelids and he lowered his.

It was a pretty high-end gym – no council sweat-pit for Peter – peopled by Swansea business owners and highly placed entrepreneurs, their cougar wannabe wives and their 'studying psychology' student daughters. There was also a smattering of professional women a few steps up on the career ladder – spin classes being the female networking equivalent of a round or two of golf. The Retreat charged a couple of hundred quid a month, although you were paying not just for the gym but for the mint-infused steam rooms and lavender rainfall showers, plus a massage suite and various treatments by appointment.

Peter didn't use any of these extras. He didn't network in the minimalist coffee shop either, just got on the treadmill and ran, relentlessly for thirty minutes, losing himself in the rhythm until his joints ached, his muscles screamed and his lungs were popping. Then he strained and grimaced through his weights set, pursing his lips disapprovingly at the MTV stream on TV, the twerking, and jiggling big-butt divas.

His routine had become tedious after the first few times so I occupied myself with the usual taunts, whispering that he was putting on a few pounds, getting soft around the middle, and by watching the other straining members, the chubby older men, pursuing heart attacks.

That night I was distracted by an older woman, who must have had Botox because her face didn't move an inch as her sinewy arms rowed with scary determination. So it took me a minute to recognise Polly, as she came in through the rear door, water bottle in hand, stretching her arms high over her head by way of a warm up. I'd never seen her out of her dolly dresses and heels before. Her hair was pulled back in a high ponytail. She'd taken off her red lippy but left the rest of her make-up on. Whereas I tended to work out in a stretchy pair of black leggings and a running vest, Polly looked impossibly cute in matching Lycra shorts and T-shirt, silver with a pink trim, for God's sake. Her cushiony boobs were only partly reined in by the super-secret support of the bra under her top. I was glad I'd once turned down her offer of the complimentary gym pass she'd been given by some sleazy councilman.

'I can tell you like to work out, Mel,' she'd said, one morning, eying my eight-years-older-than-hers bum as we stood waiting for the kettle to boil. 'They've got great facilities,

Mel. We could do a class, spur each other on, you know. And they do great facials. It'll be fun.'

'Define fun?' I said, before pleading my total over-busyness. I couldn't think of anything worse than jiggling next to Polly breezily shouting 'come on, knees up', or whatever, or having to compare cellulite and conditioner brands in the shower. I'd rather have taken up golf.

While recognition dawned on me, Polly headed for the cross trainer across the room from Peter. She gave the attendant treadmill puffers a quick glance (I do that, too, scope the environment for threats or opportunities), before her gaze fell on Peter. He *was* hard to miss, especially with his impressive physique at full pelt, though Polly pretended not to see him as she fiddled with her iPod on a pink strap on her upper arm, just like she pretended not to notice two blokes wheezing on the stationary bikes eying her up. I don't suppose she minded or she'd have chosen the stretchy running pants option. She can't have been oblivious to the fact that her pert arse was displayed to perfection, bum cheeks flexing and contracting, as she set up a rhythm on the cross trainer's elliptical pads.

It was Peter's turn to glance over next. How could he not? He looked away just as quickly but I knew it would only take him a few seconds to realise that he knew who she was.

'Go on, think,' I prompted, and sure enough he looked up again, this time the look turning into a stare.

Polly had her earbuds in, pretending to focus on the blinking heart-rate display, but she knew he was looking. I saw the self-consciousness shimmer out around her, that instinct that tells you you're being watched, even if your back is turned. We were all prey once, before we dragged ourselves, upright and dripping, out of the seas and into the green jungle – some of that instinct remains if we pay attention. I wish I had.

Peter's stride faltered as he realised Polly wasn't just one of the plasticised entourage always trying to catch his eye. She was something else entirely.

'Ah, hah, yes. A TV star, of a sort, is among us,' I sneered.

Peter slowed the machine to a comfortable jog, trying to look at her without looking as if he was.

'Oh yes, it's Pretty Polly parrot reporter, in the fully ripe flesh. Wouldn't you like to say hello to her, Peter?'

That was the last thing on his mind, of course. I could hear his brain humming, *Could this be a coincidence? Should I be worried she's here, right now just a few days after that bloody funeral?*

He hadn't seen her working out there before, so why now? Though she couldn't know anything about him, could she? There was no link to him and that night, the bloody story she was milking to death? Unless . . .

I was amused by this stream of self-doubt, by the narcissism that naturally made him think everyone else revolved around his small slice of the world.

'What? Are you worried, Peter?' I asked. 'Well there's an easy way to find out if she's on to anything, if she's on your trail. Maybe you should turn on the charm and ask her some questions. I suppose she might know something about the investigation that would be useful to you. Turn the tables, do a little investigative reporting if you think you're up to it. Surely you can talk her round, get some information if you do it carefully? You're good at talking to women, aren't you?'

There was no logical reason for him to approach her but I wanted to see how that little encounter might play out. How would Polly react? Could I point her in Peter's direction with a mental prod? With a little effort, could I make him incriminate himself?

But Peter was resistant, I could feel it. He wanted to jump off the running machine and flee but didn't want to make it too obvious. I wasn't ready to go home so I skipped across the gym to where Polly was getting into her warm-up. It took a bit of effort to separate myself from Peter's side. It felt a bit like wading through chest-high water but I managed it. I thought I saw the air around Polly shimmer a brighter shade of silver as I approached. To my surprise it seemed similar to the light distortion I'd seen at my funeral the week before, only more intense. It lasted just a few seconds before it dissipated.

'Hey, girlfriend, it's *your* Melly here,' I whispered, redirecting my focus, leaning over her shoulder, right at the side of her head. 'Yeah, just when you thought it was safe to go back on the cross trainer. See that guy over there? He's your story, my darling. He's the missing piece you've been trying to sniff out, to pry loose. Yes, you know he's looking at you but it's not for the reason you think, dressed as you are with your tits hiked up and your tight butt. Go on, look back, look at him, at his face. See that beautiful broad chest, those powerful arms. Nice to look at, isn't he? Wouldn't you like to take a closer look?'

Surprisingly, Polly didn't seem impressed. I couldn't detect the usual female appreciation dilating in her pupils. Perhaps she was a woman of some small taste after all, so I tried a slightly different tack.

'Look at his strong jaw. Look at his scar. Have you seen him somewhere before? Something's a bit off about him, isn't it, Polly? Have you seen him somewhere he shouldn't have been? Did you perhaps spot him at my funeral? Careful as he'd been to hide? Think! Go on. What's his story?'

I was mostly talking to myself, not really expecting her to listen, after all we'd never been close. No moment of emotion or proximity would explain why a channel might be open between her and me, like the one between me and Peter. I was mainly up to a bit of mischief. Then, to my surprise she looked at Peter again – right at him. The young, eh? Always eager and impressionable.

As she looked, up into the mirror that reflected him, Peter looked, too. They caught each other's eye and something sparked between them like static. Her curiosity crackled, his alarm flared like a Roman candle. I felt both wince. Peter almost stumbled, mid-stride, but managed to right himself with a soft curse. Polly had the good grace to pretend she hadn't seen this, no doubt assuming it was a reaction to catching him ogling her. She smiled slightly.

'Go on then, go over to him now,' I prompted. 'Seize the magic moment. Don't you want a glass of water? A paper towel? Shouldn't you walk over there, wiggle and shake. Where's your investigative hunger?'

Then Peter lost his nerve. He stepped off the running machine, the belt slowing. He started to towel off and, after a cursory pretend stretch, kept his eyes down and headed for the door.

'No! Where are you going, Peter my boy?' I yelled, realising I'd have to follow him right away. 'That's sooo disappointing. Don't you want to know what Polly knows? Are you really going to turn tail now?'

116

I had to slip through the door behind Peter. I was afraid to linger in case I couldn't get back to him. I didn't want to get stuck in a gym, not even a five-star version, reduced to whispering to overweight chubsters that they really just wanted a plate of cream donuts for my entertainment. I paused for a snatched second to look back at Polly, watching Peter leave, and to beckon her to follow.

'Oh, come on, big boy, you're not running away?' I caught up with Peter, striding at speed towards the lifts. 'You can't think she knows anything? Or can she? Dun, dun, dun!' I made a melodramatic movie soundtrack drumroll on the closed doors of the lift. Then we both heard the door swing open behind us and the sound of tiny trainers approaching.

'Excuse me?' said Polly, speaking to his broad back. Peter became still and solid at the sound of her voice.

'Well, don't be rude, say hello,' I prompted.

His heart was yammering as Polly's feet pattered up right behind us and he stabbed at the lift button with his finger, looking at his heart-rate monitor as if engrossed in his beats per minute.

'Excuse me,' said Polly again, just a foot away, so Peter had to turn around.

Seeing Polly through Peter's eyes I realised how small she was without her heels, almost pocket-sized in her flashy trainers. She barely came up to Peter's shoulders. It would be the easiest thing in the world for Peter to sweep her up in his arms right then, throw her over the chrome balcony, watch her smash on to the tiles of the space-aged lobby two floors below.

The image splashed, dark and vivid over my retinas because it was Peter's own vision, a split-second assessment

117

taking place behind his eyes, as if he could remove this possible irritant with a simple, satisfying burst of precision of strength. It was an automatic reflex, because he had a whiff of fight or flight on him and the flight option looked like it had just failed.

Keep cool, said Peter to himself. He glanced around. There was no one else watching, the reception desk in the foyer below was empty. There was, however, a single-eyed CCTV camera staring unblinkingly at the proceedings. The explosion of thought, barely even acknowledged, left Peter's mind and floated upwards into the ceiling above us. He smiled at Polly, ignoring the bird's eye view he had of her cleavage, but still starting to blush a little.

'Bless! You're busted!' I grinned. 'Polly, meet my nemesis. Peter, meet my, well, whatever the female for nemesis is. You've no idea how much you two have in common. This is the man, Polly, hun. This is the one they're all looking for.'

Polly smiled her usual ingratiating smile. Peter had to speak, for politeness' sake.

'Can I help you?' he asked.

'You forgot this,' said Polly handing him the expensive water bottle he'd left behind by the running machine, in his haste.

'Oh,' said Peter, startled for a moment as the lift doors slid open, offering him an exit a moment too late.

He reached to take the bottle from her. 'Thank you.'

'Hold it,' I said, and Polly actually hesitated. Her grip tightened involuntarily on the bottle so there was a slight tug between them before she let go, laughing a little.

'Thanks,' said Peter. 'My wife bought me this. This would've been the second one I'd lost in two months.'

118

'You're welcome,' she said, but she didn't look like she wanted to leave. 'Look, I'm sorry but do we know each other? It's just, in there, you looked at me like maybe we'd met?'

She gave him her best Pretty Polly smile but I could tell she was uneasy.

'Sorry,' said Peter, 'I didn't mean to stare.' He gave his best charming smile in return. They were quite a pair, performing their roles well. 'You reminded me of someone,' said Peter, after a moment.

'I get that quite a lot,' said Polly with fake modesty, 'especially lately. I'm on the TV quite a bit.'

'Oh,' said Peter, nodding, wondering if he should say it, *Oh, of course, you're on the news*. He didn't want to but was it weirder not to mention it? Or to not ask the most obvious question, as he surely would if he hadn't recognised her?

Really? Are you an actress? What would I have seen you in?

'Oh, right. You're on the news,' he said. 'I've seen you reporting. You must get fed up of people staring at you.'

'Well, it goes with the territory,' said Polly honestly. 'Most people are very polite about it. They want to tell you what they think of some story or other. Of course, there's just one story everyone's talking about now.'

Peter flinched inwardly. 'Yes, of course. Terrible, about that reporter. I suppose you must have worked with her. I'm sorry.'

'I worked with her quite closely, actually,' said Polly, giving her best 'to camera' wistful look. *Round of applause for Polly, once more.* 'But we're all trying to remain professional.'

Peter couldn't resist asking, 'Do you think the police have any idea who did it? You must have your sources.' He smiled that easy Peter smile, full of attention and interest.

Oh Polly, if only you knew your exclusive was standing a foot away smiling like a fool to hide the fear inside him. I could hear it trickling up under Peter's ribs, moving towards his throat.

'Well,' said Polly with a touch of calculated coyness. 'A reporter never gives up her sources.'

'Of course.'

Then Polly's face twitched into more business-like mode.

'Seriously, though. Have I seen you somewhere? I mean, have I interviewed you? Have our paths crossed through work?'

'You probably just saw me here,' said Peter.

'I don't think that's it. I'm sure I'd have remembered you.' She fluttered her lashes a little.

Really, Polly? I snorted, though I realised she must have picked up that line from me.

'Are you in local government?' she persisted.

It was a fair guess. The local authority is usually the largest employer in any area and they get a discount at the gym.

'No, I'm an accountant,' said Peter, too quickly.

Immediately, he regretted it. I felt the rush of anxiety rise as far as his throat and he swallowed hard, covering by taking a sip of water while his inside voice said, *Why did you lie? Why did you say that? That was stupid! What if she sees you at the council meetings now?* But he couldn't take it back without it seeming odd.

'Oh,' said Polly, raising her eyebrows. She was trying to remember something. She was running a mental database search. I felt the words 'leisure cuts' flicker on the back of her tongue.

'Well . . . ' said Peter.

'Oh, come on guys, this is pathetic,' I said, rubbing my hands together. 'Put some effort into it. Where's the sparkling repartee? Peter, at least tell her she has great eyes, or lovely tits or something. Come on, Polly, interrogate this subject a bit further. "What sort of finance are you in, then? Where are you based? What's your name? What do you do? Why do you look so bloody uncomfortable?"'

Thinking of an exit line Peter hadn't realised he was subconsciously fiddling with the scar on his cheek. Polly tried not to stare at the silvery slice of skin as he stroked along its length, over and over.

'Go on, then. Ask him his war story, Polly!'

'Sorry,' said Polly, feigning embarrassment, as Peter realised she was looking at his nervous fingers. 'Now it's my turn to apologise for staring. I can't help the old journalist nose, I'm afraid. Your scar? Does it hide a good old war story?'

She smiled expectantly, adding a bit of fake flirtatiousness to her voice.

'Good girl!' Only journalists have learned to overstep such social boundaries and appear easy with it. I patted her on the back, surprised to see her shimmer a little at my touch.

'Car accident,' said Peter flatly, smiling, though the colour was draining out of his face.

'Do you think that's a lie?' I whispered into Polly's ear. 'I do.' I felt Polly's energy shift into thinking the same.

'Well, thanks again,' said Peter, stepping towards the lift as the doors tried to close. He shoved out the hand with the water bottle and they sprang back long enough for him to step inside and me to follow.

'See you next time, then?' said Polly through the closing doors.

'Sure,' said Peter.

As we slid down and away from Polly, Peter made a vow never to go back to that gym. He'd run the streets instead, somewhere where he'd never bump into that stupid cow again.

'Too late for that, Mr Albright,' I whispered. 'You can run wherever you want, but you can't hide.'

Chapter Thirteen

Dinner was doomed. I knew it and Eve knew it.

For once, I wasn't *directly* to blame. I waited to see what would happen next, as Eve, tense and tight, twisted her new locket at her neck and looked at her watch, standing by the oven.

Adam, at the kitchen table, was concentrating on dressing Soft Peter in some sort of shiny material like a kaftan, with an Aladdin-like turban strip for his head. Peter was in the living room, on the phone, having an increasingly lengthy and loud conversation with Julienne.

Eve kept glancing nervously at the closed oven door, turning the heat controls down, then up, then down again as the minutes ticked by, peering into the depths through the glass. She knew better than to interrupt her husband when he was taking calls from the office, even at the expense of a best shank of lamb. From time to time she could hear the words 'Come on, Julienne' and 'Certainly not, I wouldn't forget that', through the study door.

'Why did it take you so long to answer the phone today?' asked Peter, when he finally sat down at the table half an hour later. He seized his knife and fork. Eve sat down opposite him, picking up a bowl of bread like a shield.

'I was putting petrol in the car, after the park. We popped over after school.'

Peter put out his hand and Eve reached into her trouser pocket, producing the receipt. He checked the time on it.

Adam was playing with a Gruffalo in his lap, the oddly Arabian Soft Peter now sitting by the ketchup bottle. Unsoft Peter gave Eve a hard look.

'What did you do in the park today, Adam Ant?' he asked, not taking his eyes off Eve.

'Played on the swings with Benedict.'

'What is that toy?'

'*Oh no, it's a Gruffalo,*' said Adam with a grin.

'Where did you get it?'

'Benedict's mummy.'

'For the cakes,' said Eve. 'The ones I made for Benedict's birthday party last week, you remember.'

Peter made a 'hmmm' noise and took a mouthful of bread. Then, putting down his knife, he left the table and went out to the Corsa, parked on the drive, checked the mileage gauge, then wrote down the figures in his blue book in the hall. He seemed satisfied with the tally. He sat back down.

I could see Eve was hoping that was the end of it. She turned back to the lamb shank and stabbed the skewer into it, the liquid coming out just a little bloody.

'The lamb is overcooked and clearly not a good cut,' said Peter, trying to carve a slice away from the bone.

'It's the best meat,' insisted Eve.

'Not when it's bloody cremated, is it? Or is it? Help me

out here, Eve.' His voice was loud. Peter rarely raised his voice to his wife, he deemed that undignified.

'It was less well done thirty minutes ago,' said Eve, a slight edge in her voice. Then, 'Do you want some more gravy with it, if it's dry?'

But before she could reach for the gravy boat, the remains of the lamb ended up on the kitchen floor. In just a single movement the ovenproof dish filled with the bone and gristle became airborne before the broad sweep of Peter's arm. It arced over the table, majestically trailing beads of gravy and juice. As Eve jerked back to avoid it, it caught her temple and drew blood, clattering on to the kitchen floor.

The tableau froze.

Adam opened his mouth pre-wail, gripping the Gruffalo.

Eve's eyes became very wide as she raised her hand to her head.

Peter had the grace to look shocked. Then he got up, cool with purpose, took a tea towel from the rack and tried to step forward to hold it up to her head.

'Mummy!' screamed Adam, seeing a red smudge form on Eve's forehead. 'Mummy hurt!' He hurled himself off his chair at her.

Eve pulled away from Peter's touch. 'You bastard,' she said quietly. The words seemed to stun him, as if a bolt gun had been pressed to his forehead and she'd pulled the trigger.

'Mummy!' screamed Adam, trying to climb into her lap.

'Adam, go play in your room, good boy,' said Peter sharply, disentangling him.

'Get your fucking hands off him,' screamed Eve. 'If your friends could see you now, *councilman*, quite the model fucking citizen, aren't you? If Julienne could see her right-hand man now.'

Peter's face became a mask of stillness, his blood beginning to roil beneath. The birds were in flight once more.

'Evelyn,' he said quietly. 'It was an accident. I didn't mean it. There's no need to be vulgar. You're hysterical – you'll upset Adam.'

'*I'll* upset him. Afraid he'll see what his darling Daddy really is? You worthless piece of shit!'

He grabbed her hard then but his voice was steely calm. There was no one behind his eyes at that moment, no one at all. I remembered that look. I remembered it, and the hard hands and the sudden feel of warm blood. I thought of the jagged image of Julienne's breaking back.

'Evelyn, calm down. I do everything for you. After what happened you should be lucky I do it at all. Calm down. It's not bad. Do you want to go back to the hospital? Is that what you want? I can tell them you're sick again. Are you sick, Evelyn?'

I'm not fucking sick! said that razor voice in the room that came from nowhere.

Eve froze at the sound of his words. Her face sealed over, she was battening down. 'I'm not sick,' she said. 'I'm just . . . I lost my temper. You scared me. I'm trying to calm down.'

'Try harder, Eve, or maybe me and Adam will find it better to get along on our own. Look, it's not even bleeding now,' he said, dabbing at her forehead and the greasy brown juice flecking the side of her face and neck. 'That's better. My good girl.'

Eve got up, ran the tap and put the wet corner of a cloth to her head. Peter picked up Adam, crying in the kitchen doorway. Eve washed up the dishes while Peter put his son to bed. I sat on the draining board swinging my legs as she cleared up the lamb from the tiles. I was looking at the cut on her head, hearing the air of momentary anger leaking out of her through the small slit, like a punctured bicycle tyre.

She'd almost made a break for it. She hadn't wound up and in for a change. She'd opened her mouth and words had come out, harsh words, a lash and slash of words – words that might have been my own. But they were already fading. She was sinking back into her familiar role – she was worked into its groove and the groove into her. It wasn't deep but it was sticky. I could tell she couldn't muster herself to pull out of it, even now, at the sight of her own blood.

It was the same old story I'd reported on a hundred times. The same excuses, the same women saying they can't leave. 'He won't let me. I'm afraid, because of the children. Because of the money. Where will I go?' And I couldn't help thinking that, if she couldn't stand up to a man like Peter, maybe she deserved it. Everything she got.

I tried though, that night. I tried to make her see there was another way. I made a full attempt to bring some iron into her spine, to plant a different thought in her head, to make it grow into a root and a green shoot. I tried to make my whispers, hand-cupped to her sleeping ear, a pointer in the right direction, troping towards the light, towards the open front door and the street and away. I tried, I really did. Not for her but because of the look that had been scrawled across Adam's face when he'd cried out 'Mummy hurt!' Because of his small fingers gripped into the Gruffalo's shaggy fur.

Because of these things I spent the night whispering into Eve's restless, half-sleeping head, 'Leave him, leave him. Take your boy. Take your boy while he's still your boy and not his. Before he understands why he's afraid and before he becomes the one who wields that fear.'

I wasn't surprised or even disappointed when she let Peter make love to her the next morning – he whispering apologies, she supplicating with her hands and mouth then showering afterwards until her skin was raw and the sounds of her faked climax were cleaned away.

It was hard to feel pity for someone so weak. For such a victim.

Chapter Fourteen

I never particularly liked this scarf. Odd, isn't it? How the smallest things can have the greatest effect on our lives? The butterfly effect, you know? A butterfly flaps its wings in a rainforest and somewhere in Middle England they get rain at the village fete instead of sun? Yes, it always sounded like bollocks to me too but that was in a different world to this and now I wonder about all the small things. Like this scarlet scarf Steve bought me for Christmas, worn to work with my black coat if I had bright lipstick on.

I was still wearing the red scarf when they found my body. It was the scarf that eventually triggered the dopey landlord's memory.

A few weeks after my body was found the police had held a short reconstruction that played out on the evening and lunchtime news for two days. Well, it was an imagined scenario really. They filmed a tall, blonde woman, whom I assume was a police officer from her stilted performance, walking along the Mumbles streets above the prom. She wasn't really that much like me, too plain, not confident enough as she walked past The Rising Sun pub to where my car had been found, jangling the keys in the lock, getting into the car then getting out again and walking off.

There was no CCTV in that particular street. Despite the door-to-door enquiries no one who lived there had seen this happen. The police were clutching at straws really. They said they'd found some CCTV footage of my car snaking through traffic along Fabian Way, towards the Mumbles end of town, earlier in the evening but couldn't identify the driver because of the quality of the tape and the gloomy night. It was a fairly desperate attempt at bolstering the appeal but they got a result.

Then, weeks later, the landlord of The Schooner called in to say he remembered a tall, foreign-looking blonde in a red scarf, who'd come into his pub that night back in February, the night of the Big Snow. The night Melanie Black went missing, confirmed Polly, nodding for the camera as she interviewed him in front of his well-stocked bar with a back-drop of glasses and shorts bottles.

The Schooner was nowhere near The Gowerton Hotel, where the initial police searches had taken place, where the conference had been. Until then there'd been nothing to physically place me anywhere else on the night I went miss-ing. In the absence of hard evidence the police had probably worked on the assumption that my car had perhaps been stolen, or dumped down in Chapel Street by someone else. But once the landlord came forward it seemed more likely I had driven there myself and walked the five minutes to The Schooner.

'No, she wasn't a regular, I'd have remembered,' said Bill Brady, self-consciously polishing a pint glass. 'Course I watch the news but not very often, every night's spent here, behind the bar. Been away for a few weeks in Tenerife with the wife, got a place out there now for the winter sun, you know. Goes end of March into April each year. Sure I saw the appeals back in February but the news never said she was anywhere near here. The newsreader off the telly – they said she was seen down by The Gowerton Hotel. Didn't think nothing of it, did I? Didn't know her car had been found down this end of town till now. So right away I phoned the police.'

By the time this new information was being delivered on air by Polly the police had no doubt switched their search to the other end of the bay. They'd have been reviewing all the council CCTV for the Mumbles area instead of the town centre, though there were no cameras near where my car had been left, none belonging to the council or the local pubs that showed anything untoward. But, as Bill Brady told Polly, with some pride, he'd informed the nice Inspector chap he should try the pool club down the end of the street. 'It has private CCTV, discreet like, after a few break-ins last year, to tape *youth annoyance* and what-not.'

So, that night, courtesy of the pool club videotape back-ups kept by the club secretary, a probably bleary-eyed police officer had found me. There I was, on screen in black-and-white moving pictures; black coat, red scarf, that would have been bright as blood against the whirls of white and the snow-banked pavements if the images had been in colour.

And I was with Eliot.

When the appeal went out and they showed the footage of me walking, my arm twined closely with that of my slightly blurred companion, asking, 'Do you know this man? Are you this man?' it was obvious it was Eliot.

Okay, maybe the average member of the public wouldn't have known that at first glance. They wouldn't know that Eliot often wore a navy Paddington Bear-type duffel coat, but they must have seen the resemblance in the newsroom right away, as soon as Polly watched the pictures sent by the police press office. The images were a bit grainy but we all know our friends and colleagues when we see them, don't we?

Bella must have seen it too and recognised her husband right away, her husband with another woman. Her husband and me, when she'd had her suspicions about us for so long but never spoken them aloud because Eliot wouldn't do that to her. He was too trustworthy. And I was always so helpful when she called the office, so nice. And I wasn't his type, Bella being all burnished brown and ebony of hair and yummy-mummy and Chanel No 5 sugar and spice – the exact opposite of me.

Yet that February night I'd gone to The Schooner to meet him. I'd chosen it precisely because it was out of the way of our usual haunts. It was long enough after the alcoholic orgy of the Christmas and new year period and usual 'Dry January' for people to want to come out again and blow off some steam, meaning Eliot and I wouldn't attract much attention.

It had snowed half-heartedly for a few hours that morning, but settled by lunchtime into a cold, clear freeze. The gritters had been out and the main roads were passable with care. A Thursday night was busy enough for us to melt into the crowds. Even Eliot, who was on TV every day at breakfast, lunch or dinner, could look ordinary in a woollen hat out of context. And if we were spotted there'd be no need to act suspiciously – we were working on a story, obviously.

I'd sprung a surprise on Eliot that night, a weekend away at the London conference I'd finagled for us in March, but as a teaser, a little trailer, a night in a cosy hotel down in Pembrokeshire together. I'd managed to swap my shifts that weekend. He'd be there for the livestock conference overnight, as part of one of his documentary slots for the *Wild Wales* nature show. The perfect excuse to be away from beloved, boring Bella and her overrated Bakewell tarts.

The streets were slippery so I'd swapped my newsroom patent heels for the black lace-ups I always kept in my car, not fashion-conscious footwear but useful in bad weather or when setting up pieces to camera on muddy verges.

The Schooner was full of light and chatter, sitting and standing groups of people and squeezing room only between the backs and feet and tables. The chill outside was making everyone nest and coddle and Eliot and I joined them, squashing into a tiny, panelled nook by the jukebox. I didn't take off my coat or scarf right away. I wanted to warm up first.

Eliot was quiet during our first drink, while I told him of the plans I'd made. He didn't place his hand on the nape of my neck or my knee as he often did. He went to the bar for another drink too quickly, as if he wanted an excuse not to speak to me. He was gone a long time and when he came back he smelled of cigarettes, as if he'd nipped out the back for a quick smoke, even though he was trying to quit. To hide my annoyance I stood up to put music on the jukebox, to cover the stalled conversation, waiting for him to tell me what was bothering him.

'Do you take requests, love?' asked landlord Bill then, battling through, past the jukebox, to collect glasses. 'You're a tall one,' he said as I drew myself up with my pound coin for the slot.

'What would you like?' I offered. I didn't really care what I listened to.

'Bit of the Rolling Stones, darling?'

'Yeah, all right.' At least he had some taste.

I popped on 'Time is on My Side'.

That turned out to be incorrect.

'Look, Mel, I don't think I can make the thing this weekend,' Eliot said, nursing his second beer. 'Bella's getting suspicious. I've had to change my shifts anyway, go up on the Monday instead, come back the same night. I meant to tell you.'

Bright and breezy Bella, getting suspicious? Surely not?

'Maybe it's time to tell her,' I said. 'Maybe *I* should tell her, spare her the pain. We're only delaying the inevitable now. She has to find out sooner or later, Eliot.'

'No she doesn't,' he said.

What became clear, once Bill the landlord remembered me and my scarf, and the Rolling Stones, was that Eliot had lied to the police about seeing me that night. He'd painted himself out of the picture and that was not good. It's not about how it is; it's about how it looks, or how it can be made to look. Who knows that better than a journalist?

Eliot would have given the police his routine statement when I first went missing, along with the other newsroom staff. It would only have been a few standard details, about when they'd each spoken to me last, when they'd seen me leaving the newsroom in Cardiff that night, etc. Eliot had clearly told them our agreed cover story, said he'd been at the conference in The Gowerton Hotel at the opposite end of town and I can't say I really blame him, for wanting to keep himself out of it at that stage. In those first twenty-four hours, when I hadn't turned up for work, everyone would've thought there was a strong possibility I might still waltz in at any minute, smile flaring, explanations at the ready.

Eliot wouldn't have wanted Bella to know where he'd been if it was not absolutely necessary. So what if no one could remember seeing him at The Gowerton Hotel? It would've been full of people, he one face in the crowd. The police had probably given him the benefit of the doubt – we were just colleagues, as far as they knew, anyway he had an honest face, a trustworthy face. That was his brand.

It was obvious this had happened because, if he'd told the truth, admitted we'd been together in Mumbles that night, the police would've focused their search there at the outset, instead of messing around by The Gowerton Hotel and searching the harbour. My car would have been found within hours.

Once the police changed their search area and found the CCTV from the pool club, thanks to landlord Bill, things looked different. The *we were working on a story* line wouldn't have held water, even if Eliot tried it. More importantly it wouldn't explain why he'd withheld vital information regarding my whereabouts from the police for so long. Unless he had something to hide.

Once Polly had recognised him in the footage she would've told Bron the editor straight away. Watching the grainy appeal on the media room TV I imagined Bron inviting Polly and Eliot into her glass-cube office for 'a chat' that everyone would have been able to witness, sans sound. I imagined her calling in Andy from legal services, tapping her pen on her teeth as she did in morning conference when she was about to rip someone to shreds, saying 'What the fuck were you playing at, Eliot?' then advising him to go to the police to 'revise' his statement while he could still appear to be volunteering to do so.

'The BBC has an image to uphold,' she would have said, 'There are integrity issues here, for God's sake! I'm disappointed in you, Eliot. We have to run the footage – Polly has to make the appeal. You've sent the police on a wild goose chase. You do realise you've hindered their investigation for months by holding this back? Good God! What if evidence has been lost because of the weeks they wasted looking in the wrong place? This is a serious matter, Eliot!'

Bron would have started to distance herself then. She would've been wondering what, if anything, further police investigations, with Eliot as the focus, might reveal. Late-night phone calls on our work numbers? A janitor who might come forward saying he'd seen us rearranging our clothing when stepping out of editing suites after hours? BBC expenses abused for little romantic liaisons on the licence fee? That would be the worst of all.

She couldn't have known then, what I already did, that the police would have checked my bank statements and credit card transactions, found the reservations I'd made for that double room in my name, at The Grange Hotel in Pembrokeshire, for the night after I disappeared. A detective would probably have visited the hotel to see if I'd turned up that weekend, just twenty-four hours after Steve had reported me missing, in case I'd been playing silly buggers following some *domestic,* had a row with my bad-boy leather jacket-wearing boyfriend, you know women!

Steve would've told them we hadn't had a row and that we certainly hadn't been planning a break together because I was supposed to be working. The police might have suspected that the reservations were not for me and Steve at all. I'd pre-ordered a bottle of Champagne, a classic indicator of a dirty weekend liaison if ever there was one.

Steve would've been a suspect, naturally. They always look to the spouse or partner first, especially if there's a mystery hotel booking in the mix, a suggested unknown party, a hint of the possibility of jealousies and rivalries. Oldest motive in the book.

But Steve had an alibi, thank God. He'd been covering that wedding for a friend in Newport until 2 a.m. I hadn't been concerned about anyone getting the wrong idea about Steve. But Eliot? He was in a whole lot of trouble. Because I'd loved him and he hadn't wanted to hurt his wife by telling her he loved me. And with me gone, he had no alibi at all.

It still might not have been much of a problem if the results of my post-mortem had been different, if they hadn't changed the narrative that had no doubt been circulating around Swansea since my body had been found. People would have whispered it. I know I would have. It's a familiar tale. *That poor girl. Probably a terrible accident, fell in the sea. Drunk, most likely. You know young women these days. The state they get themselves in.*

I'd hated the idea of this. Not just because it wasn't true, but because I didn't want something so mediocre to be my final epitaph. *News update – Reporter death was accidental, says coroner.* A few too many, a patch of ice, a watery grave. The banality was an insult. But the post-mortem results changed the game.

The police had clearly been sitting on them for their own good reasons, but as soon as the 'mystery man' CCTV appeal aired the details came leaking out. I expected one of the coroner's assistants was the source. Polly was good at that sort of winkling questioning – she knew lots of young men in places like the coroner's office from her time on *The Post* and had no doubt made a nuisance of herself with wheedling phone calls and smiles until some nugget of information chipped loose. However she got it, she was the one to break the news.

'The BBC has been led to understand that Miss Black had a hairline skull fracture, and a head wound,' said Polly ominously in her piece to camera at 6 p.m.

Investigations had shown there was a small amount of water in my lungs but not enough and not in the right places. I hadn't drowned, I hadn't struck my head or been injured as I fell into the sea, as speculation had suggested. I was already dead when I went into the water. My 'unexplained death' was now certainly a case of 'foul play'.

'Isn't that right, Inspector?' demanded Polly, door-stepping the harassed-looking Inspector Murphy on the steps of the coroner's office, live. She was talking to the side of his head and his back as he fussed his way to his car but the answers weren't the point – they could wait. The questions were what counted.

'What do you have to say about allegations that this investigation has so far been incompetent, Inspector?' she shouted, 'that inexcusable mistakes have been made, such as missing important CCTV footage of Miss Black that could have been gathered months ago? The slow follow-up on reports of her car? Inspector, do you have anything to say about your lack of leadership in this investigation?'

It was as masterful an ambush as I'd ever seen, I have to give her that. How much she'd come on in the past three months. I can't deny I was impressed, the Inspector obviously less so. Even though he was officially stuck with 'no comment', and therefore had no way to defend himself until an official police statement could be made, Murphy's face said it all.

'Well,' said Polly, turning back for her camera sign-off, staring into the lens.

'Amid questions of the veracity of the police investigations it now seems clear that the person responsible for Miss Black's death is still at large. The BBC understands the PM report shows a very telling detail.' She paused beautifully for just a beat. 'There is the evidence of a deep, thin puncture wound in Miss Black's back, below her right kidney.'

In more common parlance, I'd been stabbed.

Chapter Fifteen

When the fresh angle hit the national news it made sense that I hadn't seen Eliot on air for a week or two. I'd thought maybe he'd been taking some 'personal time', you know, to grieve. It was never actually said that he was a suspect – the official line was that a thirty-six-year-old man was 'helping police with their enquiries' – but I knew it was the case. More than that, he was *the* suspect.

I remembered the way the CID officers had stared at Eliot at my funeral weeks before. Perhaps they'd had suspicions that he'd been lying to them all along and were looking for telltale signs of guilt even then. Either way they'd evidently known for a while that mine was not just an 'unexplained' death.

From day one the CID would've been under a great deal of pressure, from senior officers, and the public, to get to the bottom of things. With my being a 'public figure', or at least a known face, the investigation was always going to attract far more than the usual scrutiny. With TV and newspaper allegations of sloppiness and 'blundering' beginning to circulate, they'd have needed to show some progress to save face.

The instant they'd discovered Eliot was the man in the footage, that he'd been with me that night and kept it to himself, they would have 'invited' him to the police station to answer some questions. He would've had to come clean about our affair, all of it, especially when they started checking his comings and goings and communications including his mobile phone. Not that it would've yielded many secrets. I knew there was no string of telling messages or incriminating texts flashing in the memory like a trail of breadcrumbs between us. We'd been too careful for that, sending only messages that could be passed off as work-related. Eliot had been thorough about deleting his call history, too – all reporters are. It's easy to rack up dozens of missed messages a day, fill the memory and overlook that one 'big scoop', that exclusive to end all exclusives, that might be buzzing along the lines from a whistle-blower or source, tangled up in a full voicemail box.

But to a police eye that, in itself, might look suspicious, as if Eliot had been trying to cover something up, a cool act of self-preservation, determined to remove all links to me once the dirty deed, whatever that was, had been done. And there'd certainly have been some calls from his house to my flat landline, and rather a lot of calls from my flat to his house. Those could not easily be explained away as work issues, not at 11 p.m., when Bella must have been at home, sometimes even at midnight, or past it. They spoke of more than just a casual affair, of an involving relationship. Perhaps even an obsession?

Then there was the input of the gaggle of neighbours and acquaintances ready to sidle into view with the slightest wave of a notepad, reporter or police officer-style. People are always just one wink away from pouring out their 'take' on any given subject, handing out their thinly sliced bits of second-hand information, eager to add their unique perspective to the public brew. Why should my case be an exception? All those juicy chunks of gossip had no doubt been fed into a big and troublesome pot that everyone was happy to stir.

Eliot knew this.

If Peter had been oblivious to it he learned how it worked the day after Polly's big reveal, at one of the council meetings. It was 'full monthly', all councillors attending, and I was sitting to the right of Peter after spending the morning with him in his office. General chatter and the clink of cups prevailed, the heads of services absorbed in discussing the improved canteen food under the new contractors and the pleasant possibility of a dry weekend. But it was still impossible not to overhear Marilyn, sitting a few seats down our side of the table, chatting about the still shocking revelation about 'that poor reporter girl being stabbed'.

'Well, technically the police term is still "suffered a puncture wound", of course,' said Marilyn knowledgeably to the fat girl from HR, 'but what the heck does that mean if it doesn't mean stabbed? I mean, dress it up any way you like the poor girl was still *murdered*.'

She was obviously enjoying the whole saga, despite insisting to anyone who would listen that it was very alarming and likely to frighten off some of the summer visitors, and the councillors should be working more closely with the police to reassure people that Swansea was still an area of low crime and a safe place to live and visit.

'Well, my Moira says, you know, the PCSO,' she whispered, loudly, 'that apparently that Eliot Masters guy, that's the reporter they've had in to talk to, is a nasty piece of work, despite looking like butter wouldn't melt in his mouth.'

She paused for effect, letting the words take hold of her listeners. 'Oh yes, that's the man they're talking to about it, you know, "helping with the enquiries", though, of course, that's not official. Well, apparently that Melanie was seen with a black eye once, and a cut on her cheek. She said she'd got hurt in some media scrap, so her landlady says. My Moira did the door-to-door checks with the neighbours, you see, and the old lady told her she hadn't believed that's how the girl got it, a bruise like that – said she might as well have told her she walked into a door!'

'That old chestnut,' said the fat girl, knowingly.

'Exactly!' said Marilyn. 'Well, apparently that Eliot was there, in that Melanie's flat, the night she got the shiner, well, you know what that means. And the old lady told Moira she'd heard raised voices and then crying. She said she often heard crying from the girl's flat after he left there. And he was there quite a bit, if you get my meaning.'

Peter's ears had pricked up by this point, though he continued to stare down at his papers, his lips a thin line, determined not to catch either woman's eye. My mouth, on the other hand, must have been hanging open as I stared at Marilyn, listening to this ridiculous bit of semi-gossip made fact by two women I didn't even know. Crackling with annoyance, my fingers burned to reach out and smack the smug smile off Marilyn's face. 'What a load of old crap!' I shot at her, though I knew she couldn't hear me.

I clearly remembered getting that black eye. It'd been the day of the shale gas fracking protests and I'd been caught up in a charge of crusty, dreadlocked protestors rushing one of the chain fences in the sluicing rain. I'd lost my footing in the slurry of churned earth, fallen forward and knocked my cheek on a concrete fence post. Eliot, packing up from his lunchtime live, had pulled me out of the scrum and taken me home. It hadn't been worth reporting it to the police; these things happen at demos.

Had no one told the police the real explanation for the bruise? I guess Eliot must have, but who'd believe him now? And the raised voices Mrs Azzopardi claimed to have heard in my flat? What the hell was that about? Me on the phone to my mum, possibly? I'd rung her later that same night, after a shower and a whisky, just hoping for a friendly-ish voice after Eliot had gone home, but we'd argued of course. I might have cried later, with frustration or impatience. I don't remember. I hadn't realised the walls were so thin. Mrs Azzopardi had always seemed deaf as a post, or pretended to be.

I thought of all the times I'd helped her out with groceries during the snow. What a cow! I should have shoved those cartons of milk up her little old lady arse!

'Well,' said Marilyn, really warming up, 'Moira says . . . ' but I didn't get the chance to find out what other rumours had originated with Swansea's most indiscreet PCSO because the chief exec arrived and Marilyn had to shut up.

I couldn't stop thinking about it, though. So this was what they were saying about Eliot? About us? Such tawdry clichés, yet they could be considered antecedent to motive on Eliot's part, *a history of violence* – a loaded phrase.

Added to the lies Eliot had told, circumstantially it would look bad. Piece by piece I could see the police assembling a trail of evidence leading to him, now evidently deemed not only a cheating liar but 'a nasty piece of work'.

It was only a matter of time before his name and the gossip leaked out to the wider press (besides Polly). They probably already knew the identity of the *thirty-six-year-old man,* they just didn't have official confirmation to name him. I'd spun stories out of almost as much, or as little, backed up by that wonderful right of reply that Eliot would soon need to consider.

Of all the things I wanted for Eliot, this was not one of them.

Peter and I sat through the rest of the meeting, neither of us paying much attention to what was being said, both thinking about Marilyn's words and about Eliot. I was afraid for him and Peter was afraid for himself. Because, of course, he'd been there too, at The Schooner that night, he just hadn't been caught on any CCTV cameras like Eliot had. So far.

It's the smallest things, right? Coincidence or luck? On Peter's part, it had been where he did or did not park his car. And the decision he'd made to ditch a dull round-table event for a pit stop at the pub, to figure out how to tell the committee, the very men around this table, nodding like fucking dashboard dogs, that they could shove their polite explanations and apologies and their 'it's for the good of the whole council' platitudes up their pathetic collective arses. The butterfly had flapped its wings for Peter that night, so there we were, at 7 p.m. near the pub, Peter and me, where neither of us were supposed to be.

Did we attract each other like dark matter that night, on some level we didn't even sense, something magnetic and clinging? Were we already skin-sharers in some way, without knowing it? We played some of the same games, certainly, him and me. I'm not too blind to see it now. We both used the double-sided edges of our respective weapons in the war of the sexes. He controlled, I manipulated. Was that it? Why we drew each other in? In the days and hours and minutes before the end, did he feel me coming like static in the air, did he sense what we would share when the lightning hit?

Slowly but steadily I came, before and after, scritchy-scratch at the door, down the chimney at night, then on all those nights afterwards when I watched him in his house, a fluttering of whispers and wings. An angel, perhaps? Like the TV tributes said, but surely an avenging one, with a shining sword made from brittle and polished words.

As Peter and I sat side by side, watching the news in his media room that evening, Inspector Murphy finally came out and said it. He had no choice, thanks to Polly – the official words were already redundant by three days.

'I can now confirm that we are treating Miss Black's death as murder,' he said.

When he spoke the words, made finally so by his saying, I placed my hand on the back of Peter's neck and slid my fingers under his skin, across the place I imagined his spine to be. I pulled myself to him, into him. I felt the knobbles of his vertebrae, the wet warm shudder as I flicked my nails on the bone at the base of his skull in a strange embrace. I could feel his alarm, his panic, his doubt fermenting. He was seeing us again, seeing backwards to what happened that night and forwards to what might be to come.

'That's it,' I said. 'You remember,' as I twined around him like a serpent, sinewing around him, making him shiver. For a moment he closed his eyes, so he didn't see Eve, paused at the crack of the media room door, laden with fresh towels, staring at the photo of me on the TV screen. The golden daughter, girlfriend, friend – *the murder victim*. She saw Peter's face, too, cold and glazed, the ice-pick frown between his closed eyes.

Catching sight of her he forced himself to click off the TV screen. 'Fucking reporters,' he said suddenly, with venom that startled us both. 'Women like that are always trouble. Women like that get what they deserve.'

Then an odd thing happened. After his words a scream erupted silently from Eve's mouth, sharp and brittle, splitting my head in half though it had no sound.

And there were words with it – like blades, whirring, cutting.

That stupid fucking cunt! she said to herself.

Then she walked away.

Chapter Sixteen

That was the first time I really heard Eve's voice, the voice of the other woman inside her, I mean. Not her everyday, outward, 'Hello, darling, more tea, sweetheart' voice but something very different. I felt it passing through me, like a shock wave through water and I knew that a barrier I hadn't even known existed had broken between us, something that had been keeping us separate all those weeks.

It might have been the word 'cunt' that burst the membrane. *Stupid fucking cunt!* Women don't generally like that word, do they? I do. Though I rarely said it out loud, I muttered it under my breath daily; a blunt blow directed, for example, at that sleazy Sky reporter Phil Finnegan always poking round my patch, or that weaselly bloke who repeatedly tried to short-change me at the petrol station. Out on the air it has a satisfying thud, doesn't it? It always hits home.

Or maybe it wasn't the word itself that created a hole in Eve's head and allowed me to look in. Maybe I'd just never listened hard enough because what could Eve possibly have to say worth listening to? What could she have had to contribute to the conversation over all those weeks except the likes of *Buy more tea, clean oven, I'm so sorry, darling*.

I realised then I'd heard Eve's other voice before. I'd heard it the morning I'd arrived at the house, in the kitchen. It was the voice that had said, *I only need one!* when Peter had mentioned genies and wishes at the breakfast table. And it'd been in Adam's bedroom when he'd spoken of Peter's mum, Adam's gran, 'gone to be an angel too young'. *Like fuck!* it had said.

Then it had been the voice in the kitchen that exclaimed *Dear God. It can't be true,* when the radio had said my body had been found.

Once I grasped this I realised I could hear her other voice all the time if I chose to. It was as if our different wavelengths had finally coincided and the signal between us was clear. It was something of a revelation, listening in.

After Peter made his usual inspection of the car mileage, to ensure Eve had gone to the supermarket as she'd said she had, and nowhere else – precisely 2.35 miles there and back, I heard her say, *Bastard, bastard, bastard* while she steadily poured his tea into a cup and smiled.

When he handed her the wardrobe keys, and watched her select an outfit for a parents' evening or council event, to which she was expected to accompany him, she said, *Big man, big fucking joke.*

When he gave her a new angel figurine for her collection, as recompense for reddened wrists or sharp words, I heard her say *I hate these bloody simpering things!* while she thanked him with a smile

Okay, so it wasn't a cerebral or literary commentary but it had a nice sound-bite quality. It intrigued me so much that I didn't go to work with Peter for a few days, as I had been for those past few weeks. Instead I stayed at home and listened to Eve's head. It quickly became clear that she'd acquired another pay-as-you-go mobile phone since Peter had smashed the one from the flour bin a few months before. I could see in Eve's head how Mair had dropped it by one afternoon, when I'd been with Peter probably, fresh from the packaging with £15 credit on it.

'I dropped it in the loo,' Eve had told Mair, lying blithely, then hidden it in the vacuum cleaner bag, somewhere Peter would never look. She'd been making calls on it, every few nights when he was out at the gym or running. I realised she'd been calling her mum, who was pretty ill by the sound of it. I'd been right about the unlikelihood of the *fancy man* at least. Eve had been checking in regularly with her and Nora, her carer, who came each day and sorted things out.

I knew right away that Eve liked Nora and trusted her. The texture of her in Eve's thoughts was like cake mixture, rising in an oven, sticky, warm, comforting. I could feel the gratitude deposited from all the months Nora had helped out with Eve's dad, when he'd been so ill, back in the day, because she used to work with him at his electrical shop. Capable Nora, solid Nora, of the grey hair and smoker's teeth. Nora who could get away with saying, 'Come on now, Betty, no slouching when there's Scrabble to play' and 'How many potatoes do you want for supper? And don't say one because one isn't acceptable, my girl,' because it came with a wink and a ready grin. Nora, with her *I'll ask you no questions and you'll tell me no lies about how your little boy is always sick and you can't visit your mam any more, Evie*, attitude.

Eve used the phone to check in with Nora every few days, getting an update on her mum's condition before Betty insisted on being handed the phone. Then Nora would pretend to scold and her mum would laugh. Except when she heard something silent in Eve's greeting, something brittle under the forced lightness.

'Talk to me, Evie,' she would say then. And inevitably later, 'You should let me talk to him about this. It's time he heard a few home truths.'

But Eve was also using the phone for other things. Such as calling her GP to order her blessed prescription of the contraceptive pill. I'd seen her popping it in her mouth each morning, naturally, but I hadn't realised she was doing it in secret. I thought she was keeping it tucked out of sight in her tights' packets because of Peter's distaste for *women's things* – he never could bear to see untidy Tampax wrappers in the bathroom waste bin once a month. It made sense now, that I'd heard him say more than once, 'I think it's time for a little sister for Adam. Big families are happy families. Now you're getting better, Eve, let's just see what happens naturally. It'll be different this time, darling.'

Eve had nodded, and kept getting her prescription through Mair.

The days with Eve took on a slightly different cast once I knew all this. When, in the afternoons, getting ready to make dinner, she switched Peter's radio to South West's Hard Rock Nation, and tapped her foot to the straining larynxes of Def Leppard, Iron Maiden and even Nine Inch Nails, I couldn't help but applaud silently.

When I watched her take scissors to the seams of the trousers Peter bought her so she'd have to buy different ones, or knock the heels of the sensible court shoes loose against the dressing table, as she had been doing all along, I smiled.

I can't tell you how surprised I was at Eve's secret defiance, after being near her for so long and missing everything. Actually, I was embarrassed. My research had been lax to say the least and I'd broken the reporter's first rule: made lazy assumptions that I already knew her and her story.

So, by the end of a blustery June week, beginning to wonder what else there was to learn about Eve, I gave Peter a break from my company for a whole day and went on a school trip with Eve and Adam. I needed a break from the house and the office – and doesn't everyone deserve a day out once in a while? A change of scenery was as good as a rest, even if it meant sitting next to Eve on a stuffy coach, cocooned within a knot of warm little bodies, wool cardigans and plastic rucksacks.

Without Peter at my side I'd been ready to engage my iron spine, to fight the disorientation, the dizziness and nausea I was sure would come at the doorstep. But to my surprise the transition wasn't too bad. I didn't feel sick at all. I'd been growing stronger over the spring and the promise of sand and sea was like a welcome wash of cold water over me. Perhaps it was because Langland Bay had always been a favourite place of mine, where, as a child, Mum would take me to paddle and poke around in the epic rock pools on any day with a trace of sun. It was one of the few places that made Dad perk up for a few hours and shake off the fug of apathy he wallowed in at home every time he came off his pills.

His eyes were alive when he was scanning the breakers, spotting crabs or their claws in the bubbly rock pools, pointing out purple-blob anemones to me. And I, determined as always to pin his gaze on me for as long as possible, had embarked on fearless pranks and adventures for his benefit, climbing high on the foot-ripping rocks, rushing thigh-deep into the waves, just to see him smile and hear him say, 'Fearless, that one.'

How I'd relished Mum's anxious little smile as she called, 'Be careful, Melly!'

Though, to be fair, she was the one left to pick me up and clean the grit out of my scratches and nicks when I overreached that last step, real or figurative.

Years later Eliot and I had gone there together, tripping up the twisting, gorse-spiked cliff path to Caswell, the next bay along, wrapped in coats, scarves and the anonymity of a bitter winter morning. We'd spoken of our future, then, or I had. Staring out at the heaving, sage-coloured sea I'd felt a longing for him and his easy, knowing company that stretched out to the striped horizon and towered like the storm clouds in the offing. I'd told myself I wouldn't bring it up with him again, I wouldn't tarnish the day with it, but I couldn't help myself. I asked him then when he might tell Bella about us.

He hadn't wanted to. It wasn't good timing, he'd said – her birthday was coming up in a few days. I could see his reluctance to hurt and harm, even if the cost was his own happiness.

'You shouldn't really call the house, Mel,' he said, 'she'll start to think it's weird, those hang-ups and late-night queries about scripts.'

'Well, let's not talk about banal Bella, this is our six-month anniversary,' I'd said, pretending I wasn't hurt, grinning. 'What have you got me, then? Give me my present.'

'You can have it later.'

'No, no, patience is not one of my virtues, as you well know!'

I rugby-hugged him then, feeling teenage and silly all of a sudden. I tucked my hands into his coat, up into his jacket beneath, rummaging in the pocket which he hadn't seen me watching him pat a couple of times since we'd left the office. 'I know you've got me a surprise in here. You can't put one over on an investigative reporter.'

'Don't, Mel, knock it off,' he'd said, laughing, trying to twist out of my grip, but I'd already grabbed the little paper packet and was running off up the path towards the headland.

'Mel!' he called after me, picking up his pace to catch me as I'd known he would. I wanted to be caught and folded into him, snared. I pulled open the packet.

'It's lovely,' I said, pouring the little round locket on a gold chain into my hand. 'Is it antique?'

'Yes, Mel I . . . it's from a little shop I found . . . Look, Mel . . . '

'I love it,' I grinned. 'It's the most beautiful thing anyone's ever given me.'

And it was. And I was so happy because that was just like him, to pick the perfect thing. And it was beautiful, old gold, the little red Venetian stones set in it so pretty, so girlish, not like anything anyone had ever bought me before, warm and yellow and pretty, pretty for a pretty girl with small feet and giggles at the ready.

'It's amazing that this is how you see me,' I said, snuggling into his coat for just a moment.

He smiled and kissed me then. 'Mel, I really do care about you, you know that. I don't want to hurt you.'

'Then don't,' I said, holding him like I would never let him go.

His hair was blown by the wind and it was as I was thinking of Eliot's hair, reliving the rush of feeling it triggered inside, that I somehow entered Eve's head. As she sat down on the rocks, surveying the sand, it took me a moment to separate her memories from mine, to realise I'd slipped sideways right into her, on the wave of emotion that had filled her and filled me, for different reasons.

And once inside there was so much to see.

Chapter Seventeen

They were pictures from another life, the ones I shared with Eve in that moment. They came in like a rushing tide of old scrapbook feelings and I drowned in them. It wasn't like sharing Peter's bursts of energy, dark and bird-black, or Adam's primary-colour splats of emotion. It was as if someone had run a cable between us and I could be in her head and under her skin, at one and the same time.

First I saw her father: thin, sallow, patient, confined to bed by heart failure; Eve, handing him the oxygen mask; Eve, in her school uniform-sleeves and slip-on shoes, carefully carrying a teapot, milk in a jug, a cup and saucer, on a tray to him. Stirring in his sugar, smiling.

Then I saw Peter, calm at his desk in the bank, in town, understanding of the pale, pretty art student in paint-splattered black, eyes ringed with kohl and the shadow of sleepless nights, asking for a little help with her overdraft. Her dad's care was so expensive, his electrical repair business all but on its knees now, her cheeks burning pink to say it, her insides cold at the thought of such pleading.

But it was okay. She'd never need to worry about bills and money, he'd said, this smart and handsome man who opened doors for her and pulled out her chair and offered her his handkerchief. He'd take care of it, if she'd let him. In the little Italian restaurant by the harbour he'd said it, over spaghetti Bolognese, over a single candle, a scene absurdly and beautifully like the Disney film *Lady and the Tramp*. Like in the old VHS copy she'd rewound to shreds as a girl, watching it in the living room, while Dad coughed and spluttered upstairs.

Then Dad was dead and gone and Peter helped sell the house and find the tiny place for Mum in Mumbles, his own mum already dead. I saw her clearly for the first time, Peter's mother, Mrs Edith Albright, through Eve's memory of photographs and newspaper clippings; the famous lady councillor, the Iron Lady of Mumbles. Though Eve had never met Edith, she'd died before she'd met Peter, her dad had known of her from his own union days, spoken with grudging respect of 'the old battleaxe'.

Then, in a bright and feverish scene, I saw Peter sitting at the tea table in Eve's mum's new house, a lemon cake glistening on the table before him, while Eve tried to hide her mum's gin bottles under the kitchen sink before he could see them, pushing mints into her mother's mouth and squirting air freshener on her.

Then I was at their wedding day. Eve was staring at herself in the bedroom mirror, in a winter-white two-piece skirt suit Peter had chosen, afraid she might want to wear one of her 'gothic numbers' for the ceremony, at the hotel Peter had chosen, with the guests Peter had invited. He hadn't wanted her to worry about the details, he'd said, while she was still grieving for her father. He'd take care of everything. Just as well, because she'd had no guests to invite, only Mair and Mum, and Peter was less than pleased with Mum because her nose was red-veined and she was wobbly and clearly had miniature vodkas in her handbag for God's sake!

In a flash, as clear as if it was before my own eyes, I saw the torn, pink silk lining of the cheap handbag and the empty vodka bottles within, the saddest thing in the world I've ever seen, and Eve shushing Mum, I mean Eve shushing *her* mum, and taking the bottles and tossing them into the bin with the remains of the buffet.

Then we, *she* was big with Adam in her belly, and I felt him move, in me, as he moved in her. It was no illusion, the hard feet on taut skin, the kick of acknowledgement, *I'm here, pay attention,* and Peter's hand on the fluttering skin, right at the time when the rules had begun. *What to eat for the baby. How to dress appropriately as a married woman.* This did not include goth-metal T-shirts, old jeans and paint-splattered shirts.

Then his tight hand was on my arm, *her* arm, and the tight words and the disappointment in his eyes and the hot fire of tears when he said she'd need to quit art college because of the baby. Then there was Adam, a ball of fuzzy pink skin, unexpected hair and clutching fingers. And the fingernails, the miracle of them, miniature crescent moons, so small yet so wonderful.

Then the black-cloak sky and crow-caw of the afternoons of *the bad time* were on us, like black tar, weighting Eve's arms and legs into the bed and turning her face away from the daylight. Adam was now a weight she couldn't lose but couldn't carry. And Peter's disapproval, that she was tired and crumpled and tearful all the time rather than radiant and maternal and milk-smelling as he'd imagined, that was worst of all.

And then *that* day. The day my Eve was born. The day she lashed out at the squawking baby monitor with one sweep of her arm, smashing it against the bedroom wall because everything inside her had boiled up to one brilliant moment of movement and she had to strike something. The day she took the car keys and left the house in her hideous flowered smock, leaving Adam in his cot because he wouldn't stop driving the nails of his screams into her head . . . and drove to the pub and stayed there for an hour, drinking three glasses of red wine back to back; oh the wound of the look on Mair's face when she'd turned up to get her, after she'd told her on the phone where she was and not to worry but could she check on the baby later – the fear, the disgust, it had been more than Eve could bear.

Then came the lashing eyes of the doctor and nurses, and more rules at home – the car keys given over and the phone put out of reach for the time being, the shoes locked away while she was too tired to argue, too grey and heavy to resist. It was 'for her own good', so she couldn't go anywhere inappropriate again and hurt herself.

Because Peter would help her get better and be a good wife and a good mum as long as she wasn't in touch with that sot of a mother, because this little episode clearly showed Eve would end up just like her, pissed and asking for money, money all the time, and hiding vodka bottles in her handbag and making him ashamed.

His own mother would never have stood for it, if she'd still been alive. *But she isn't,* thought Eve. She'd been in the

159

ground for more than twenty years and what would she know about it?

It wasn't all Mum's fault. She hadn't been able to cope with watching Dad getting thinner and fainter and greyer every day.

'Take him his tea, love,' Betty would say, and even then Eve had known her mum was taking a swig from the whisky bottle in the sideboard to fortify herself to go and help him eat his dinner. Then it had been 'just a few to get me off to sleep, love' and then a few to ease the long evenings and dim the sound of the long raspy breaths from next door – then, when he'd died, what reason was there not to finish the bottle, and the next. It was a slippery slope, wasn't it? Giving a little more each day until you lost your footing? She understood that better than anyone.

She'd defied Peter in the beginning, ignored his hectoring edicts, albeit in secret. *She's my mother for Christ's sake*, she would think. *She needs me and I have every right to see her*. It hadn't seemed to take a great deal of courage, once she was back on her feet, to bundle baby Adam into the car, into his little seat, to drop by the house for just half an hour. It was only once or twice a week, when Peter was safe in the long council meetings he bemoaned for days before and days after. Just the sight of Adam gurgling and laughing through his big brown eyes seemed to do Mum the world of good, put the pink back in her that had been stolen by the cirrhosis yellow.

Peter hadn't been as fanatical about the car mileage then, just checking it every so often rather than noting every fuck-ing mile in his little Domesday Book. Until he'd come home unexpectedly that day, found the drive empty, and she'd had to make an excuse about taking Adam for a check-up at the doctor's and getting the dates mixed up, because she knew he'd ring the surgery to make sure.

After that Mair had helped out once or twice, picking them up and dropping them off but it had become dangerous once Adam had started to talk – God forbid he should fumble out the word 'Betty' or 'Nanna', or 'Nora'! Then she'd had to tell Mum she probably wouldn't be able to come for a while but she'd phone as often as she could, except for that once, when Mum was so poorly and a phone call hadn't reassured her at all, and look where that had got her. And the lies she'd had to tell that night and since . . . because she never said in so many words that Peter, her husband, had forbidden it, because, in the twenty-first century that sounded absurd even to her.

It happens slowly. You make excuses for them. You try to give them the benefit of the doubt – see it from their side. The side that is not the one, for example, that had gone to the pub and left an infant squalling on his own in an empty house, and their side seems almost reasonable in that way.

And soon their cool groove works its way into your head and you hear their voice in it, almost as your own voice, round and round in the notch, explaining to your colleagues why you're giving up your art course, explaining to your mother why it's best she doesn't see her daughter or her only grand-child. You make the excuses because he is, after all, paying the money each month, into Mum's account for the carer, so that's the deal. What could be more reasonable than that?

You allow it, all of it, because they touched something in you once that was calling out to be looked after and taken care of, and he is taking care of things, isn't he? Aren't all women looking for the right someone to surrender to? Someone worthy? And she'd made her choice freely – and these were the consequences, and here she was, wound in marriage sheets as taut around her as hospital restraints.

This was what I was seeing, as Eve stared at the sea, until Adam's voice broke in, splitting us apart in an instant.

'Time for ice-cream ... Mummy, Mummy, Mummy!' he yelled, through our bubble, the membrane breaking, throwing me out of her head as quickly as I had slid in. I tumbled free, dizzy and breathless on to the rocks beside her. Adam, sandy and salt-smelling flew into her arms, and into my arms, and was still inside me for a moment longer before the last thread broke.

Trembling, I watched them jump up and race across the sand to the ice-cream van on the concrete ramp, smiles white and wide as the bay and the sky, hands warm in each other's. As I jogged to catch up, following two sets of bare feet along the hard sand, we inhabited a moment in a perfect world, one without Peter in it. I knew it and Eve knew it and that knowledge made her smile. It lasted two whole minutes before it became hollow and slippery, because that world was only borrowed and had to be returned by the end of the day.

Later, after eggy sandwiches and orange squash in cartons, Charles's mum offered to take the boys paddling so Eve could take a break. As soon as they headed for the waterline Eve pulled out her sketchpad. Sitting next to her, I really looked at what she was drawing for the first time that day, in the big red pad, with the silver pencils never far from her fingers. It was not a book of pictures like the ones at home, cheerful and robust and primary coloured. Besides the bunnies and the Thomas the Tank Engines this pad contained other characters. Not the approved illustrations of Peter's choice but pencil-drawn women, winged-maidens, wielding swords, women soaring on clouds and the backs of horses, proud and stern, with cold fire in their eyes, some with wings like angels, but angels of fire and purpose.

It wasn't Tate Gallery stuff, more like goth-metal art – album illustrations via *Lord of the Rings* – but good nevertheless. The one she was drawing then, with swift, smudgy strokes of her pitch-black charcoal, could have been her, I thought – though not quite. The face on the pad was stronger jawed, sharper nosed, haughty of feature. She looked triumphant, sword aloft on the back of the north wind. I felt all too clearly how Eve's book was a book of wishes; the wishes of warriors gathering their slain, rearing up between its shaded leaves.

Then Eve began to hum the first few bars of 'When You Wish Upon a Star' to herself, quietly at first, but gaining energy with every moment. 'If wishes were fishes . . . ' I whispered.

As the wind bounced back and forth along the circle of cliffs I almost thought I could hear whinnies and wails and blade singing against blade. The light surged in and out, close and back, singing through me, sweeping in like the tide around the children and their gurgling laughter, hovering, humming on my skin with many voices.

At the end of the afternoon, after the application of rough towels to cold little feet, we piled back on the bus, which soon filled with chatter and spilt orange pop. As we swung towards home the driver's radio began to play Queen's 'We Are the Champions', and some of the older kids started to join in, waving their arms back and forth to the chorus. Eve joined in, too, and it was the first time I'd heard her voice, throaty and tuneful. Not even in the quiet of the house, with Rock Nation for company, had she given herself licence to sing. So I joined in, too – our voices rising together along the road, one silent by necessity, one made so by practice.

I almost started to like Eve that day.

Chapter Eighteen

There's nothing new under the sun, right? I know Shakespeare said it but I always hear the words spoken in Eliot's voice. It's a reminder of all those afternoons when the day was ticking by and we finally acknowledged there was no real news to report and it was time to get creative, i.e. call a few rent-a-gob politicians and generate some outrage. It's all the same in the end, what we package up and broadcast. Power, death, jealousy, sex, money, ambition. Variations on a theme recycled through the day in twenty-minute bouts.

The media feeds everyone these same stories over and over, until they believe they are the truth, that's what Dad used to say, resignation in his voice, after he'd had to quit his job at the broadsheet and go into cosy weekend radio because of 'that business' with the libel threat.

'We absorb what we're fed by the evil box in the corner, Melly,' he'd say, 'become fat on it. The fear, the desire, stuck on the same merry-go-round and we can't get off. The difference is that people like you and me, we know it – we can try and think independently.'

'People like you and me,' he said, as if a fourteen-year-old girl was a full person already and might understand the workings of his heart and mind, or her own.

The trouble was I didn't really agree with him. Surely journalists bring order to chaos, don't they? Sift out and arrange the facts, make them clear and clean for the readers and viewers? Pick the matter from the morass, the pearls from under the feet of the swine. I'm not saying we offer gospel truths but is it such a bad thing to have order?

That's what I used to think, watching the news with him on winter nights, the wind of uncertainty outside, its fingers testing the house for weaknesses. And inside me, mesmerised by the visions of the women I wanted to become more than anything else in the world, the women, right there in the corner of our living room, on the screen. The awesome Anna Ford, the marvellous Moira Stuart – the newsreaders – with gravitas enough to make sense of murder and mayhem and far-off wars.

From this side though, I see that Dad was partly right. We fall prey to so many influences in our lives, direct and indirect. How do we really know if the thoughts or the flashes of things we think we believe and feel are our own? Can we be certain they were born deep in our own brains, original as sin, new and shiny in the morning? Or are they put on, second hand, absorbed from what someone told us once, what we heard? Whisper, whisper in the background, a TV or radio in another room, almost inaudible so we didn't know we were listening.

I was always so certain that I knew my own mind, and yet ... shuffle the usual questions, lay them out. Who am I now? What's my story? Who or what made me? Who spoke and made it so? Am I just an echo? A stubborn hanger-on? Something that slipped through from somewhere else when it shouldn't have? A mistake. Am I a new thing or an old one, returned from the darkness, hiding in shadows, recycling myself in words? Am I really alone? Are any of us? Ever?

I kept thinking, about my funeral, about those shimmering tricks of the light around some of the people there. The flaws in the picture, interference in the air, that everyone else seemed unaware of. I had seen something similar, around Polly, that day at the gym, when I had approached her. I'd seen something very like it, once or twice, just in the corner of my consciousness, on my field trips – once in a council meeting near the chairman's right hand. Then there had been that day on the beach, when I was caught up in the singing throat of the surging light, full of voices.

The more I thought about it the more those shimmers, that shifting, looked like whispers. That probably doesn't make much sense, but if you were on this side it would. The line between the senses is different here, between spoken word and thought, between what is seen and what is sensed. I'd begun to suspect that looking and listening could be the same thing and I was learning to do it from a new perspective. I was still new to it, unpractised, but ... What if ... those shimmers were like whispers? Could someone, or something else's lips be moving to make them? Would they speak to me if I could just learn to listen? Would that be good or bad?

I wonder if Peter ever asked himself something similar, when things started to go wrong for him, if someone or something was talking him into a dark place? If he ever suspected the presence of the seed I'd planted in his head, growing branches and thorns, watered with my words. All that whispering I did, every day, my rolling updates and bulletins, the social commentary, the dissection of daily events, telling him how he should think and feel.

'He thinks you're a fool, you know, that tosser from housing. She's laughing at you every time you leave the room, that girl from accounting with the big tits – way out of your league, Mr Floppy. You're a bad boy, you should be punished. Don't cry Poor Peter, little rabbit, whining's such a nasty habit. Two and two is five, add a one and subdivide. Check the balance, hurry along. Are you sure it isn't wrong? Are you sure? Are you sure?'

It must have been hard, to ignore someone telling you constantly that you're a pathetic bastard, even if you think you can't hear it. That you really don't know toss-all about the finances you've been dealing with since school – my words, and the saying making it so. But did Peter at no point suspect the presence of that critical little voice, playing on all his insecurities?

For example, did he think he alone was responsible for that fiasco in the council meeting on the day of the budget?

It was a thing of beauty, that June morning, watching Julienne, tight-lipped, tapping the end of her Parker pen on her pristine pad of paper, a death knell in stationery, noting the glances cast around the table between the grey men and their piles of papers.

Since March an old story had been enacted in the council offices of the Swansea borough – a previously promising man, a responsible man, was reaching a certain difficult age, affected by family pressures perhaps, by disappointment in his expectations, by stress, starting to slip in his work, beginning to behave erratically and inconsistently, making mistakes.

Things certainly didn't look promising for Peter that morning, late *again*, looking preoccupied, fumbling with his files. His face was already hot and flushed when I took my fingers and slid them behind his ear, cupped my hand to that shell with the sound of the night sea inside and told him he was worthless and everyone knew it.

No one was terribly surprised when he stuttered and stammered through the very important papers. No one was mollified when he apologised to the chief exec, only to get all the figures wrong, lost his place, apologised again. But the best thing was saved for last. The final page of his report, with copies before each member at the table, was missing. When the group got to the end and turned the final page, the expected summary flow-chart had been replaced by a magnificent doodle of a giant cock and balls.

It was a wonderfully bulbous and winking penis, stray hairs popping out of the scrotum, like the ones you see scrawled in marker pen on the backs of toilet doors and graffiti-magnet shop walls. Okay, it was a particularly childish prank. And I didn't *make* him draw it exactly, or force him to put it under the pile for photocopying. It was the end result, a bonus, you might say, of what I'd been saying all day and all week before the very important meeting.

'Peter, you're a massive cock! Yes, you are. You're a joke! A tool, a positive fool. You'll never keep your cool.' And variations on a theme.

'Is this a joke?' asked Julienne, recovering first, flushing scarlet through suppressed fury rather than outraged delicacy. A table's worth of grey heads shot up to meet her gaze then plunged back down at their papers, trying to melt themselves out of the scene through the backs of their chairs.

Peter looked aghast. The chief exec looked aghast at Peter. Peter swallowed, trying to find something, anything, to say.

'That's not mine, I don't know how that got there,' he spluttered, as silence clattered around the room and back, ball-bearing hard. 'Really, it's a mistake. It's someone's idea of a joke.'

'Do you see anyone laughing?' asked Julienne, her voice sharp enough to slice marble. 'Good God, I've had enough of this. This is the last straw!'

My face split into a grin as she gathered up her papers and swept out of the room without another word. I was still stretching when the chairman Brian Barnstable found his voice and suggested a ten-minute tea break.

'Er, Peter, could I have a word?' he asked, as the chief exec strode after Julienne and the others followed.

That morning was a definite triumph for me. At last, a tangible outcome I could take credit for. Over the weeks I'd tried doggedly to replicate the success of the 'phone in the flour bin' incident from April. On many occasions I'd concentrated hard and told Peter to put his hand on the hissing gas burner when Eve was cooking, or to stick a fork in an electric socket. But something had always interfered with my ability to make him obedient. Self-preservation, perhaps? Or maybe I just hadn't been able to replicate the precise force of an order without a suitable emotion to act as a trigger, like the rage that had made the flour bin pierce Peter's conscious mind and turn into action. That morning in full council, I could see I was really starting to gain control over the chaos in Peter's head.

'Never mind, poor little Peter,' I crowed, that afternoon, while he sat at his desk, head in his hands, long after everyone had left the building and the sounds of council bureaucracy had dimmed and disappeared. 'You're not the first man to have a nervous breakdown. A midlife crisis. You won't be the last. They know the story. They know how it goes. Originality is overrated; the old ones are often the best. Perfect Peter, wants to cry. Perfect Peter doesn't know why.

'But you will,' I whispered. 'You will.'

Chapter Nineteen

The next afternoon Peter left the office early and drove out to Adam's primary school. It wasn't his collection day so, instead of greeting Adam as the children poured out, he parked a little way away from the gates, carefully avoiding Eve. He sat very still until they drove away then turned and watched as Kyle got into Bella's car across the street. Did I mention that Kyle was Eliot and Bella's boy? He visited the house, just that once, on a play date with Adam.

I can't tell you how pleased I was when I realised we were following Kyle and Bella out of the village because I knew I had made Peter do it. I'd somehow achieved this feat by thinking all the previous night and most of the day that I really, very badly, wanted to see Eliot again. I communicated this to Peter by feeling it deep in my bones and heart and blood and making it surge loudly while Peter tried to sleep and eat and work – *I want, I want, I want*, I whispered. So, evidently, Peter wanted it too.

I smiled in anticipation as we tailed Bella along the winding road above the beach, through the field-flanked lanes and up the hill into the small hamlet where they lived. She parked outside the garden of the stone cottage, as I had known she would.

I knew the house, of course. I'd sat outside it enough times in the past few weeks of my life, when I'd never seemed to be able to get hold of Eliot on the phone. When I just wanted to see what he was up to, to feel him near me, even if I couldn't touch him. Or talk to him, when he hadn't been answering his landline or his mobile.

It was one of those restored stone character cottages, not flashy, with a small and tasteful extension at the back that extended the kitchen with sympathetic wood and glass. From outside it'd always been easy to see Eliot inside without being seen, especially in the dark evenings when the Christmas lights had been on. I'd watched Bella padding around the kitchen, aproned and smiling while Kyle coloured pictures at the table and Eliot, working on his laptop, offered advice and encouragement.

He'd never really looked at home there, to me. There was something in the way he kept glancing wistfully towards the phone when I rang it, as if he really wanted to answer but was letting the machine get it for form's sake, with Bella right there.

As I always had, Peter parked his car well back on the green patch of grass in front of the bus stop, where it couldn't be seen from inside the house, even if someone were to look out. *Go on then*, I thought, *now that we're here get out of the car, that's a good boy*, itching to make the most of my field trip. After only a few moments of hesitation Peter got out and sidled around the garden wall at the back until he came to my old spot by the pear tree, well hidden. From there we had a clear view of Eliot, looking tired and pale, coming into the kitchen to greet his wife and son – well, he was still grieving – but he looked beautiful to me, as he always had, real and solid and safe.

Bella, chocolate-skinned and petite and pettable had to play up to him, of course, giving him one of her theatrical hugs, running her hand down his stubbly cheek in a way that made my stomach knife with jealousy. Unsuspecting, bright and breezy, Bella, the world's friend, the 'Hi, how are you? Come over for drinks sometime, I'll cook some lovely nibbles' woman. She hadn't been a very worthy opponent, to tell you the truth. When you describe your *talent* as making a mean coconut cake or Victoria sponge it takes the edge off the suggestion of an equal battle of minds. But battle is battle and all's fair in it.

During those long old days in the newsroom it had taken nothing, just a moment, for me to delete Bella's messages from Eliot's work phone. I'd seen him put in his pin number often enough and he always left it in his jacket pocket. It'd been the work of a moment to smudge my lipstick onto the edge of his jacket or shirt collar, where he couldn't see but I knew she would. I'd been sure she'd put two and two together sooner or later and come up with three's a crowd (and she was number three). Such clichés yes, yet so effective.

She'd been slow about catching on, certainly, but she would've left him, I'm sure, if she'd known how he really felt about me. If she'd seen how he fucked me, the urgency, as if he was trying to drown in me and swallow me up at the same time. Though it was perhaps only half a dozen times in total I could tell it was forever. Yet it seemed, from outside looking in that, despite the news of our affair, she must by then have been aware that she was 'standing by him'.

We watched them, Peter and I, Eliot sitting at the kitchen table, Bella setting out the mugs, then sitting opposite each other, hands linked across the tablecloth, drinking tea. We watched as they sipped and smiled and spoke in a way that looked soft, even through the window glass. I watched as Eliot started to clear away, pulling on some rubber gloves and running the water for the washing-up.

I wondered how it was that the sight of something so simple, so domestic, could make me hum with violence. The memory and longing for the feel of his fingers made mine itch, made me want to reach out across the garden, burst through the glass plates, grab Bella's head and slam her face against the table. At the same time I was thinking, *I love you, Eliot. I miss you.* And there were other words, a stream unleashed, pouring out of me unbidden, *beloved* and *happiness* and *bitch* and *why* and *I'm sorry,* and *I hate you* and *I'm still here,* clutching my hands together as if I could clutch his heart between them and draw it to me.

I noticed Peter was rubbing his hands together, too, his head also full of words, but not my words, as I might have expected. He was thinking something odd. He was thinking just three words – *fucking bastard* and *gloves.* He was seeing a pair of gloves in his mind's eye, black leather, expensive, hand-stitched. It took me a minute to realise why, and why he then started to think about his mackintosh – the one he'd worn the night we'd met and hadn't seen since.

We only stayed a few moments after that. Despite my exhortations to stay, Peter was suddenly very anxious to get home. I couldn't override the swift stride of his legs to the car, cutting our visit short, or the heaviness of his foot on the accelerator as we headed home.

'Where's my mackintosh, Eve?' he asked, still standing at the front door before he even put his briefcase down or hung up his keys. 'My black one. You did get it from the cleaner's, didn't you? I asked you ages ago and I haven't seen it since.'

'Oh, yes, I must have forgotten to tell you,' said Eve, appearing as always to help him out of his coat and hang it up. 'They couldn't find it at the cleaner's, darling. When I went to collect it – they didn't have it.'

'What do you mean, they didn't have it?' said Peter, freezing with one arm still in his jacket.

'Well, when I went to collect it they didn't have the bag corresponding to the ticket or something. Some sort of mix up, they said.'

'What?'

'I know. They searched everywhere. It's very annoying, darling. It was such a nice coat. But they were very apologetic. They offered me free cleaning in compensation, up to the value, so that should last us a while, cut down cleaning bills.'

'Compensation?' shouted Peter, throwing his jacket to the floor, making Eve take a step back 'What use is that, woman? I don't want compensation, I want my bloody coat!'

Then he grabbed the glass of wine she'd been about to hand him and tossed it on the floor. The glass didn't break on contact with the thick pile but the red liquid spread wetly on the cream carpet at the foot of the stairs. For a moment Peter stared at it then put his hand up to his face, to the silver scar on his cheek. He opened his mouth as if to speak but simply swallowed, dropped his hand and walked into the kitchen to pour himself another drink.

Eve let out the breath she'd been holding and opened the cupboard under the stairs, fishing in her huge cleaning basket for the Stain Devils and a sponge.

Chapter Twenty

I was more careful from that day onwards. Since Eliot was no longer reading the daily news bulletins I found myself missing his face more and more but I was also nervous of thinking about him too much, in case it sent Peter back to his house. That was the last thing I wanted right then because I sensed I'd made a mistake, making Peter go there, putting Eliot in the forefront of Peter's mind. Peter's thoughts about Eliot were not of a shade I liked.

There was no escaping Polly on the TV though. She was heading the TV interviews about my case exclusively by then, sporting an expensive-looking haircut and a new trademark blue coat. I'd become *her* story and it seemed she had dibs on all the developments. It was unsurprising then, that she was the first on-air with Inspector Murphy and the fresh appeal in early July. Murphy, somehow still clinging to his post as senior investigating officer despite the criticisms of his team, had obviously chosen Polly to impart the information first, probably thinking if you can't beat 'em, use 'em.

He was standing outside the grey cement foyer of Swansea

Central Police Station and looked gravely into the camera when he said, 'I need the public's help once more.'

He was suited-up and smooth-shaven, but looked dusty with tiredness, a look we all recognised on CID officers heading long-running, slow-moving cases, let alone 'blundering' ones. He was focused, though, as he revealed that some new information had come to his attention and he wanted to make another appeal, for a man who'd allegedly been seen with Melanie Black the night she vanished. The man had been seen leaving the pub, The Schooner in Mumbles, with Miss Black at about 8 p.m., or perhaps walking into it, he said. He wanted very much to talk to the man as he might have vital information about the sequence of events that night. He also wanted to hear from anyone who might have seen Miss Black with the man. The incident room phone lines were manned and ready, he said, with another serious stare at the camera.

Then, prompted by Polly, he gave a typical description of a white male, about six feet two inches tall or thereabouts, with dark hair and a black trench coat.

'There is a suggestion that this man might also have been seen walking along the Mumbles seafront sometime after Miss Black left the pub,' he emphasised. 'It's possible they left together.'

Polly, standing beside him, just in shot, nodded sagely at appropriate intervals as the incident room phone number scrolled across the bottom of the screen. She seemed oblivious to the fact that the DI had managed to make the whole thing sound both thorough and vague at the same time, as if, in an ironic twist he himself was *not* oblivious to, he was wasting police time by indulging in this latest bit of speculation.

And I could see why. The description of another man at or near the pub, must have come from Eliot, because no one else had been around or recalled seeing me so far. I remembered then, how I'd seen Eliot circling back along the seafront that night, the night of the Big Snow, in his car, a few minutes after we'd left The Schooner together, a few minutes after we'd argued again, after I'd threatened once more to tell Bella about us. And much more.

It made me wince to remember how I'd stalked off to my car in a high-energy huff only to find my grand exit delayed by a flat car battery, drained by the cold as the snow started to pick up and the road turn a slow, creeping white. Eliot had looped past in his car a minute or so later, peering out of the driver's window, on the lookout for me. At the time I'd been glad, glad that he was feeling guilty about his own storm-off, had had second thoughts and had come back for me. But I hadn't shown him that I'd seen him. I'd just made sure he'd clocked me walking along the street with Peter. Knowing he was watching I'd hugged in closer to Peter's arm because I'd wanted him to be jealous for a change, to see me with this tall, handsome man and know he wasn't the only one who could play games and keep secrets.

Eliot must have given the police that description of the 'other man'. It was a good way to deflect attention from himself but I can only imagine how they must have received that 'new lead'. *It wasn't me, guv! It was the other guy!* The cynicism about this so-called second man had been written all over Inspector Murphy's face. There's always one, isn't there? A lurking male, intent on no good, collar up, eyes down, hands twitching, the stranger full of danger!

'Was there anything else about this man, Inspector?' asked Polly gravely, obviously prompting him to continue the appeal. 'Any *distinguishing marks*, perhaps?' a pure police and journalist phrase if ever there was one. Clearly the little exchange was prearranged.

'Oh, yes,' said the DI, looking openly embarrassed. He cleared his throat and said, 'Possibly, Polly. It's possible the man had a scar on his face. On the right hand side,' then he raised his finger and drew a line from his cheekbone down to his mid-neck. Peter, sitting at his study desk, elbow-deep in work papers but listening intently, froze. I smiled as his hand went automatically to the side of his neck, to the silvery streak there, mirroring the Inspector's downward motion.

'Oh dear,' I smiled. 'That's not good is it, Peter dear? Newsflash! They're on your trail now. They're sniffing you out. They're coming to get you. Poor old Pitiful Peter, the net's closing, *Mystery Man*. Tick-tock, look at the clock. Time's a flying, we must be good-bye-ing.'

Peter knew he was the second man, naturally, and at that moment he knew for sure what he'd long suspected: Eliot had seen him with me and remembered him. His recollection shivered between us in the evening light, like a stone dropping into water, rippling outwards in larger and larger circles around us. I could feel Peter reliving the moment he'd watched me and Eliot arguing in the street that night, while he'd stood in the doorway of one of the other pubs, trying to get a cell phone signal, to call home. I felt the images replay, first *That's definitely that bloke from the TV*, and then, *What a prick!*

I shared the echo of the smug burst of pleasure Peter had experienced a few minutes later, when he'd seen Eliot cruising past us, but it was quickly replaced by another flash, from earlier in the evening, an exchange near the side door of The Schooner, by the delivery entrance, the smokers' corner. Peter had been finishing a cigarette, puffing a couple of times and stubbing it out, wondering whether or not to get a drink or go home, then Eliot's voice had asked, 'Got a light, mate?'

In the flare of the lighter, and the bulb of the alley security light, I saw Eliot's face cupping the lighter and heard him say, 'I'm supposed to be quitting.'

'Me, too,' Peter had said, annoyed at having to share his quiet corner with some prick wearing a Paddington Bear coat, as if he was a twenty-something student not a man in his late thirties, a man he half-recognised from somewhere, but couldn't quite place.

'Tough day?' Eliot asked then, out of politeness.

'Oh yes.'

'Me, too. A woman problem, I'll bet?'

'You could say that.'

'Me, too.'

As soon as I saw this, Peter's hostility towards Eliot made more sense. Peter had been worried about him all along, since that night, wondering if he remembered that cigarette break in the alley, agonising over how well he'd actually seen him in the gloom. And what that could mean.

He'd been hoping Eliot hadn't seen his full face, maybe just his profile, his coat and height and hair and other general characteristics, in the dark alley with the security light behind him and maybe in Eliot's eyes. He'd been wondering if he'd recognised him as the man walking along the street with me later. But at that moment, watching the appeal, Peter knew for certain he'd been seen closely enough for

Eliot to glimpse the silvery scar on his cheek . . . Peter's most distinguishing feature.

Until that moment Peter had been confident, cocky even, that he'd been the invisible man that night, on my last night as my old self. That he'd slipped into and out of the evening without record, forever lost in the night streets, free from blame, out of trouble. But for the first time panic was knifing through his head, the rustling birds in his blood throwing up more and more questions.

What if, now that the police were looking for someone specific, he had been caught on one of the other CCTV cameras in other nearby streets, placing him in the surrounding area? What if there were witnesses, who might remember a detail like his scar, if their memories were properly jogged? Kick-started by the claims of the good-looking, nice man from the TV who said there'd been a stranger there.

And he knew that, although it had taken the landlord of The Schooner three months, he *had* eventually remembered me at the jukebox in my red scarf. What other someones might there be now, waiting to appear, to remember one crucial detail? Sticking their hands in the air and saying, *Excuse me, officer, I'm not certain but* . . . ? He knew people tended to notice the scar. Some asked about it. Women especially, and then he spun them his story about a foiled mugger with a flick knife and a grateful old lady and watched them melt before him.

And that Polly girl, that evening at the gym . . . Oh God, she'd remarked on his scar. They'd spoken about the investigation. He hadn't told her who he was and it was nothing on its own, but were she and that Eliot prick friends? Might they be talking about him right now? If a finger was

183

pointed, even in his general direction, was he safe? Couldn't those CSI men find all sorts of things on clothes, even months after an event? The TV programmes suggested they could never really be cleaned off, things like blood, right? And he thought again of his mackintosh, missing from the dry-cleaner's, the coat he'd worn home . . . after . . . Did that mean his car seats might have traces on them, or something on the steering wheel, fibres, smudges? It was not good. Not good at all.

As soon as the news appeal finished Peter flicked off the TV and slugged the last few inches of his nightly brandy down in one. He had an uncontrollable urge to sneak off to the yard for a cigarette while Eve was in bed and Adam was snoring. He needed it to calm him down, clear his head, help him think things through.

Peter had smoked until he was twenty-five but given up until he'd sneaked his first one in years with Eliot that night. After that, with a little encouragement from me, his cravings had increased and, following the cock-drawing incident he'd finally bought a pack from a garage.

As he lit the Regal on the patio and took his first sharp inhalation, a picture was already forming in his head. It was made from surges of fear and something rare for Peter, for Perfect Peter – uncertainty. In the very middle of it all was Eliot's face. Standing down by the garden shed, taking throatful after throatful of cigarette smoke into his lungs, it was a knife in his stomach and in his eye.

He kept glancing up at the bedroom window where Eve was sleeping. He didn't want to have to explain what he was doing out there at gone 11 p.m., his head exploding. But all he could think was that Eliot was a reporter. What if Eliot himself recognised Peter after all these months, finally put a name to his face, because he realised he'd been at a council meeting one time, or an election vote count that Peter had attended? He could've seen him at one of those parties he was forced to attend on behalf of the authority, like the one at The Gowerton Hotel, with all-round handshakes and smacking of lips on arses. He'd been there the year before. Had Eliot?

In theory Eliot could put a name to the memory of his face at any minute, spot him in a tax and finance story from an archive or in the local paper. And Eliot's son went to Adam's school. Had Eliot ever been to a parents' evening and seen him with the PTA? Might he do so in the future?

I'd seen how, when Kyle had come to the house that once, not long after I first arrived, Peter had told Eve, in no uncertain terms, to break off the friendship. 'They're just not our sort of people,' he'd said, because the last thing he'd wanted was Eliot picking the kid up from a play date. He'd been playing it safe.

But in the months since, with no sign of any problem, he'd started to think he was in the clear. That's where I'd made my mistake because, over the past weeks, I'd inadvertently put Eliot right back in the front of Peter's mind. I'd encouraged him to seek him out for me. I was afraid because, though the July air was soft, the night scented, what roiled off Peter was black and bitter – alarm and anger, and envy, too. Envy of Eliot's job, his flash car parked outside his character cottage and his biddable wife who, presumably, never called him a bastard or left her baby wailing in his cot while she went to the pub to get drunk.

He sat down on the edge of the patio and drew in a long

breath. It was the closest he'd come in a long time to thinking about me – about what had happened between us. *It was just a drink,* I heard him think. *It wasn't my fault. None of this is my fault.* It was exactly the same excuse he always came up with, the familiar vindication he felt, when he twisted or gripped some part of Eve, every time he hurt her. *She* made me do it. *It was her fault.* The pity followed close behind, self-pity, that he hadn't found himself any woman who was worthy of his time, who saw what he was – able to bestow their undivided attention, their undying devotion.

A great and spectacular moon surged over the trees and down upon us then, washing over him and through me. In all those weeks, turned to months, I'd never got used to the fact I had no shadow. Watching the moonlight sift and skein through my skin and bone made me shiver and Peter shivered, too, holding the cigarette in his lips to rub his hands together.

Before I could stop myself I was thinking of Eliot, huddled round the back of the pub in Pengelly with me, in a cupped-hands-excuse to be together, outside, away from the eyes of others, his face lit in the match flare as we huddled in the chill under a great moon haloed by a ring of light.

I want, I want, I'd thought, trying not to look at his lips, trying not to cough as the unfamiliar nicotine hit the inside of my forehead.

'You don't smoke, do you?' Eliot had laughed.

Such small things are we made of, the words between cigarette puffs, 'God, you're really something, Melly. So smart, so tough – I wish I was more like you.' Such minute moments we overlook, with time smirking nearby, ready with the coats and hats, opening the door to kick us out.

'Tick-tock, tick-tock,' I said to Peter, under my breath,

under the garden moon, and Peter muttered it too – 'Tick-tock, tick-tock.' The same words slid between us as both of us were seeing Eliot's face.

The moon slipped in then and, for some reason we both looked up at the same time to see the glow of the nightlight from Adam's bedroom. Adam was standing in his window, pudgy fingers splayed against the glass – his mouth making the shape of the word 'Daddy'. So Peter stubbed out the cigarette.

'Hey, little man, you should be asleep,' he said, ushering him back under the Thomas the Tank Engine quilt cover a few moments later.

'Sorry, Daddy. Your nose is cold. Who were you talking to in the garden?'

'No one, Adam Ant. Daddy loves you,' he said, kissing the top of his head with a mouth much softer than when he had kissed me.

'Kiss for Soft Peter,' said Adam.

Then Peter lay down and closed his eyes. Almost at once, on the bed next to his son, he started to doze. Eliot drifted from his thoughts like curls of his son's breath from his open mouth. His fear and uncertainty began to distil into pictures in his head, around a series of images, grainy and faded – pictures of a small boy, lying in a bed not unlike Adam's, in a room not unlike his, long ago.

'Story, Mummy,' says the boy, in Peter's head, as he snores.

'Not tonight, Mummy has to work. You're too old for that rabbit.'

The boy hugs the flop-eared bunny to his chest as Mummy pins on her red party rosette and says she'll see him tomorrow.

'Margie will bring you a sandwich,' she says, already looking at her watch, smoothing her perfectly coiffured hair, leaving again. She's always leaving.

Then Mummy is home again and, though laughing softly at first, she is very cross to see the boy standing at the foot of the stairs in his pyjamas instead of in bed, because Mr Bettle is with her again, red-faced, beer-smelling, helping her off with her coat. But the boy won't go to bed as he's told because he wants to know where Daddy is and Mummy says how many times does she have to tell him that Daddy is not coming home and Mr Bettle will be coming around now.

When the boy starts to cry, fat round tears plunging down his already wet cheeks, Mummy's hand comes up and strikes him like a whip.

'Tears are for little bloody girls,' she shouts, as the boy, stunned and stumbling, loses his balance and falls back on to the stairs and slithers down to his knees.

'Easy, Edith love,' says Mr Bettle. But it's too late, the boy's already fallen on the glass he was holding because he came down to the kitchen for a drink, because Margie had gone home ages ago, and Mummy was not there again and he'd been so very thirsty. Now the boy's hands are full of bits of glass and somehow his face is covered in blood, warm blood that splashes in great blobs at the bottom of the stairs on the nice, clean carpet and Mummy is crosser than ever.

'You're about as much use as your bloody father,' she says and, as the boy cries through the night, both Peter and I know there is nothing new under the sun, or under the stars.

Chapter Twenty-One

The next morning Peter was not happy. He convinced himself it was because his eggs were not right again. They were too firm. There was no dippy yolk. And he *really* wanted another cigarette. He still wanted to quit, well, to quit starting back up – but how was he supposed to do that when Evelyn couldn't even boil fucking eggs properly?

He ignored Eve's questioning frown as he left the table and lit up a cigarette from his pocket, standing by the open back door, blowing smoke into the yard. He was waiting for her to say something as she had last week, when she'd smelled it on his clothes and he'd insisted it was just one at work to ease the stress. He almost wanted her to ask him then, if he wanted a pack of those patches or one of those e-cig things, then he thought he might have something to say in return that would tell her to mind her own business, but she was silent. He watched her pouring tea from the china pot, his face like a brewing storm.

'I'll make you another egg, darling,' said Eve, with her ray of sunshine voice. (*Pedantic, pathetic excuse for a man that you are*, said her other voice.)

'There's no time,' he snapped, taking in a long breath of smoke and spitting it out towards her.

'Don't have it then!' she snapped back, intent on not burning Adam's porridge. 'Have a cereal bar in the car.'

'A cereal bar?'

Eve put the pan down, reached for a cereal bowl but it was too late. Peter, stepping towards her, said he'd like to remind her that cereal bars were not for bloody grown men doing a full day's work. Reaching out he grabbed her hand and stubbed his cigarette on the pale, smooth flesh of her inner arm, just below the elbow crease. Eve cried out, but only a little. She wasn't that surprised, really. Most of the cry went inside along with the pain. She sucked them both down as she heard Adam's elephant feet above, hitting the top stair.

There were words inside her certainly, at the moment the circle on her arm sang bright and dark, her other words, the other woman's words, short, sharp, bludgeoning, queuing up to burst out – but also the usual ones that said, *If I leave him he'll take Adam. He'll tell the doctor the depression is back. They'll believe him, they always believe him.* And they were the words that won.

Silence surged from her mouth. It carved through my brain like a chainsaw screaming.

Peter released her wrist, calling sharply for Adam who came bounding into the kitchen, full of smiles.

'Come on, kiddo, can't be late for school,' said Peter, flicking the cigarette out of the back door. 'Have a bit of Daddy's toast on the way. Coat?'

Then they were gone. It was surprising how, after a moment, no sense of what had occurred lingered to taint the rising light of a summer school day, except the faint wisps of cigarette smoke over the table. Eve walked to the sink and ran her arm under the cold tap for several minutes. No expression crossed her face as the water streamed and splashed. *I'll need to wear those long-sleeved shirts for a while,* she thought. She left the pan on the stove and the dishes on the table, wandered into the living room, sat down, put her head in her hands.

She wanted to call her mum. The urge was an ache in her chest, an iron fist twisting her lungs. She wanted to pull on her shoes and run coatless the two miles to the Mumbles, to the yellow-blanket warmth of her mother's arms, not caring if people on the quiet avenue stared, if the commuters in their cars glanced in concern or teenagers with school bags sniggered. Once there she would pound on the door of number twelve and fling herself into her mother's bony embrace like Adam often hurled himself into hers, in simple, uncomplicated need.

Instead, in one explosive motion, she swept the neatly symmetrical magazines from the coffee table before her and Adam's Transformers sprayed on to the floor. The action came before the idea, like a whip-crack. There was no thought in it, just instinct, as she swung round and pounded the back of the sofa with her fists, panting through the grille of her clenched teeth. The barrage lasted thirty seconds before her fists smarted and she forced herself to breathe.

This is not sensible, she told herself, and she was determined to be sensible about such things because, if she was not, she might lose her slight grip on the world completely and fall off it into oblivion, again. And she knew she couldn't really leave the house because Peter would call soon, checking up on her – she knew he would. He'd hear the different background noise if she was not at home and ask her to check something, to test her, like he had before. He'd ask for the date on a bill in the rack on the mantelpiece or the serial number on the TV he always seemed to have a note of, pretending he needed it for insurance or to pay a bill, but really just to make sure she was where she said she was.

Just phoning Mum wouldn't be enough, in fact it could be the last unsensible swipe at her self-control because Mum would certainly hear that catch in her voice, in the way that mothers alone can, where everything unsaid is stuck like a bone under the larynx.

Then Mum would say: 'Get out of there, love. Bring the little 'un. You have a place to go. You'll always have a place to go,' as she had the time Nora had wheeled Mum into the hospital room to visit her, after the red wine incident, when she'd been 'getting her head right'.

But how could she run to Mumbles when Peter would know exactly where she had gone? They couldn't hide for the rest of their lives behind the wooden door of the house, with Nora on guard like a fairy-tale ogre to ward off the wolf at the door – the soft-speaking, doctor – convincing, plausibly – suited Mr Wolf who would never allow himself to be separated from his son.

'Dear, God, dear God, dear God,' she chanted aloud, and it was the first time I'd heard her say anything like a prayer. 'Help me, help me, send me the strength, send me a way.' And I knew why this plea had come now, because it had been getting worse for her those past few weeks, since the trouble at work, since Peter's description had gone out on the news appeals. I'd started to feel just the teensiest bit bad about it, to be honest, its effect on her. The cigarette was just the latest development and it was directly down to me. After all, I was the one who'd told Peter he really needed that cigarette, 'Have a cigarette, just one, just one won't hurt, will it, darling Peter? One puff, Peter, puffing Billy. Peter, Peter, fag-end eater.'

And I'd been whispering to Peter all night, every night – 'They know it's you, they know it's you. The police will break down your door and haul you away! It's already too late. You might as well turn yourself in now. While it seems noble and you can pretend to be full of remorse.'

Part of me knew Eve would be on the end of Peter's reprisals but, before the smell of singed flesh, and the all too graphic sight of the tiny hole burned in her skin, I hadn't realised I'd started to care, that something had been changing in me since the day we'd spent together at the beach. Since I'd been inside her head. Since the fluttering feeling of Adam inside her had been inside me, in the drum of my belly, kicking off from the starting blocks of his life. It had been a complete surprise to me, that visceral and clinging sensation, because I'd never wanted children. I'd been sure of it. And it wasn't just because I wanted to be a *career girl*. I simply never thought I had it in me – the capacity for unconditional love. It scared me, to tell you the truth, the thought of the late-night crying, the high temperatures and rashes, the falls and scrapes, the needing, the feeding, the reassurance. The uncertainty. The chaos.

And if I couldn't embrace it fully what business did I have bringing a life into the world? I didn't want to be one of those mums who treat their kids like accessories, dumping them in childcare or with frazzled grandparents. Or, frankly, those annoying ones who can't understand why it isn't a given that they absolutely must have the first choice of leave every half-term and bank holiday because of their 'childcare issues', leaving the unencumbered ones to pick up the work because our desire to spend three days in the pub with our other halves or the weekend sleeping is less important.

But Adam had unscrewed something inside me, like a tap. He was leaking himself through drop by drop, filling the fearful spaces within me with eggy fingers and constant humming. Some nights, when Eve was lying on the bed next to him, reading, I'd lie next to them both. Seeing how completely their two halves made a comfortable whole I'd realised how alone I was, and had often been. How, even in company, I'd often felt walled off, in a little glass box at the front of my brain, watching the world go by, while the light and thought pooled and rose around me, suffocating and deep. Echoing like an empty well under iron winter skies it was filled with the relentless tick-tock of my thoughts, a slip-and-slide monologue impossible to silence. And when it had seemed as if I might finally crumble under the weight of it all there was my father's voice urging me into battle with his, 'Iron spine, girl,' so I couldn't lie down for a minute, even if I'd wanted to.

Then I had met Peter and found myself there, every night, with Adam and Eve in their temporary bedroom Eden. In that corner of the blighted garden where Peter was God, making the rules and meting out the punishments, somehow I felt less alone than I had for a long time, and it began to cross my mind that I had a duty, as part of this new family. It was a duty to the child, who was not mine but was as close as any had ever been, because if Eve stayed with Peter, how much of a monster would he make of Adam by the time he was a young man? How long would it be before Adam began to transform from the clean and white-winged angel he was into the dark image of his father?

Could I really stand by and allow the years ahead to shape him into something so cruel? Something that would ring with brittle contempt for all women, even his mother in the end, schooled in forms of violence, subtle and explicit? Children are so fragile, so malleable, so unformed, and yet they, least of all, can choose their guardians. Could I really let Peter pipe the tune for Adam to follow? Eventually it could lead to only one place, years from now even, a lifetime away but still there – the end destination.

Adam still had his clean white wings. He was still unsullied whereas Peter was destined for somewhere sooty and hot with gnashing of teeth and no leaf tea and no soft-boiled eggs.

I stared at Adam for a lifetime that night, into the small hours and onwards through the years. Just before daybreak I thought of Eve's small prayer, 'help me, send me strength' and I knew I had to act, that I could be strong for Adam even if Eve could not. I left his side then and lay next to Eve instead. I thought she might finally be ready, for me to show her the truth. I half-hoped that, if she knew it, saw Peter's real darkness, what had happened that night, she might find her own iron spine after all. The small round burn on her arm would be my way inside her head, its throb backing my story with the ring of truth. She could be my weapon, my sword.

'Go to the police,' I whispered. 'I will tell you what to say. They will know how to look for, and make truth from the pieces I'll give you. Through your saying it will become so.

Through evidence and facts they will do the rest. All you have to do is tell them who to look at and where.

'Remember Peter's mackintosh, the stain on the sleeve? I can show you how he got it, right now, tonight. And the other things he did. This is the man you serve – the one you excuse and placate. This is what he has done. What else will he do while you gather up your courage?'

I whispered these things, trying to show her in my head by remembering and running it along the frequency of her mind, like that day at the beach – to show her the last time I'd been with her husband. I wanted her to feel his hands on me, to feel my surprise and then fear, to see the sky wheeling above white and low with snow and hearing the approach of the waves.

But there was something sticking in her head, no matter how hard I tried, something keeping me at bay, tangling my truths at the edge of her dreaming like a wall of twisted thorns as she slept inside. Her denial was too strong. No matter how hard I whispered and tried to make my blood like hers, my heartbeat remember, there was a circle I couldn't break, around the part where my words might pierce and burn in pictures, and I didn't know why. Self-preservation is, after all, one of the strongest barriers to overcome and some truths we simply have to ring-fence and hide even from ourselves, like Peter had. Because, if we admit them, what then?

Just before the 7.30 a.m. alarm sounded, when I'd spent the night trying to plant seeds in Eve's head, willing them to grow, she finally turned her back on me. Still in her sleep she pushed me out of her head, back into the sunlit room. She murmured aloud, 'No. You're not here. You're just a dream,' and breathed me out.

For one moment before she expelled me, I saw the colour and texture of the visions under her eyelids. I saw my own face, the snow on my hair. But she pushed the imagined nightmare back to the edges of sleep, burrowing under the blankets.

'I'm sorry, so sorry, but you're not here,' she said again, sharply, firmly, as her eyes opened on the empty room.

'Who are you talking to, Eve?' Peter asked, turning over beside her, a flicker of annoyance in his half-awake voice.

'No one,' she said staring at the ceiling, 'no one at all.'

Chapter Twenty-Two

The TV and newspapers went wild when Eliot was arrested. It had been bound to happen, I was only surprised it had taken so long. Out of habit I'd already scripted the story in my head, sorted it into intro and clips, how it would be played out on the screen. It looked bad. It always had.

As soon as Eliot had been formally interviewed he would have been forced to admit meeting me in his car, the night I disappeared. He would've told the CID that we'd sat inside his BMW for a few minutes, the windows puffed white with our breath. The CCTV would have supported this and the rest of his story part of the way, of us walking together towards The Schooner just off camera, of us returning to his car later, me storming off, then him returning to his car alone.

The police would have pieced together how it could have gone from there, from those flickering black-and-white images patched together with statements. They couldn't be sure *exactly* what had happened, not with the camera blind spots, but there was more than enough to apply for an arrest warrant. They couldn't charge Eliot right away but the arrest would justify and activate those crucial forensic searches they needed to make, give them leeway to dig and push and press and hope something would shake loose from his story and inside his house and his car.

Because, by then I knew there was all sorts of 'circumstantial evidence' gravitating around Eliot, like asteroids in orbit. They wouldn't look good under the forensic light of day, underlined in officer notebooks, bullet-pointed in briefings and highlighted in statements given beneath unforgiving lights into interview-room microphones.

The police finally had a solid suspect, in the right place at the right time, with no alibi for part of the night, plenty of excuses and a history of suspected violence, black eyes, shouting and tears. Men like that, well, *you know what they're like.*

Once the searches were conducted, Inspector Murphy and his gang could have found plenty of things to cement the appearance of Eliot's guilt, enough for senior officers and the Crown Prosecution Service, enough to offer the public a tentative suggestion that they were *on to their man*, redeeming themselves for earlier oversights.

I'd thought it through and realised there might very well have been traces of my blood in Eliot's car, just a smudge or two, dry and dark, nothing extreme or conclusive but still damning in detectives' eyes. There could easily have been stray fibres, too, from my black winter coat, on examination, fingertip and thorough, some of my long, blonde hairs, found in his car boot.

Eliot would've tried to explain these away, his face approx-imating that of his honest and trustworthy TV brand, but it had expired. The men and women interviewing him, in the presence of his lawyer, were sure he was an adulterous, lying, scumbag who'd cheated on his wife and lied about his dalliance with a lovely, delightful, angelic girl who had come to harm in his vicinity.

In spite of this, Eliot would've tried to explain, calmly at first, how I'd cut my face in that media fracking scrum, *bled like a bastard*, my words, into tissues in his car, after I'd refused to go to hospital. But that was *his* story and my landlady, that lovely old dear with no reason to lie, knew otherwise.

'Of course she was never in my car boot!' Eliot would have said, outraged, and astonished. 'Why the hell would she be? What exactly are you suggesting?' Self-righteous, furious, his legal representation telling him to calm down and answer the questions because he had nothing to hide. Then Eliot would've explained how my coat had been stored there many times during shared outside broadcasts, folded in the back, how easily a couple of my hairs could have been on the collar, transferred to the boot carpet and his car blanket.

'What a convenient explanation, Mr Masters. But I'm here to inform you that you are under arrest . . . '

Pretty Polly was practically overcome in all her reports that week. Eliot had once been the best thing that had ever happened to me, now we'd both become the best thing to happen to her career. Polly was becoming a serious player, the focus of at least three live links for network TV regarding Eliot's arrest. When London comes calling, you answer! I imagined she wouldn't be too long in Cardiff once she'd taken my story to one conclusion or another. Ah well, it looked like she was finally learning to own the game and play with the grown-ups. I could hardly blame her for that. Poor Eliot, though. From reading the news to being the news – never an easy or welcome transition.

At least I was physically out of the picture. No one was harassing me outside the Swansea nick or scrummaging me to my car in a tangle of flashbulbs and tripod legs. How I hated seeing Eliot's gaunt face in the pap snaps. I wished I could say something to him, anything would have been better than our last conversation at The Schooner and afterwards. It broke me in half to recall how our last words to each other hadn't been sweet nothings, paired with soft caresses, tender, to be treasured, but exchanges filled with accusation and spite. Insults had been aimed and thrown, announcements made that had changed the shape of the world and my heart.

We'd been walking away from The Schooner, towards his BMW when he'd said it, 'Bella's pregnant again.' Just like that, in the frosty evening silence, out of the wide blue yonder, with no attempt at building up to it, easing the blade in.

I stopped still, in mid-stride. I think I laughed, out of astonishment, out of terror, out of the disbelief that he of all people could throw in such a tired cliché, for God's sake! But he didn't laugh. He didn't smile. He hadn't smiled all night.

'It wasn't planned, Mel,' he said quickly. 'But we want the baby. I'm sorry. I can't do this anymore, me and you. It's not fair now.'

'Fair to whom?' I asked automatically, wondering, with sharp rage whom it had ever been fair to and whether he'd believed equitability was a relevant factor when he'd been thrusting inside me, moaning into my ear how breathtaking I was.

'To everyone, to Bella, to you,' he said, doing up his top coat button, putting on his gloves, 'to Kyle.' He sighed then, took both my hands in his. 'It's been a mistake,' he said.

A mistake? Like Bella getting a bun in the oven? I'd pretty much assumed that, since Eliot and I had been having our affair, he hadn't been sleeping with Bella at all, that things were cold and fraternal between them, their interactions merely habitual pecks and chaste end-of-day cuddles. But unless hers had been an immaculate conception it seemed I'd been badly deluded. He'd been doubling up on the goodies all along, working up a sweat with her when we weren't together. But which one of us had been the warm-up, which the main event?

Fingers of icy fire started to work their way up into my throat. Either way, he'd cheated on *me*! I was supposed to be the one he loved. I felt sick and sweaty as I tried to digest the words he'd spoken, their implications, trying not to retch at the whiff of Bella's Chanel No 5 escaping from the collar of Eliot's coat, as if she were still clinging to his neck even then, kissing him *goodbye, darling* . . . sliding her hand into his trousers, he unbuttoning her blouse.

Eliot and I had been a mistake, apparently, a 'wonderful, exciting moment of madness', but nothing more. These were the words he used, while his lips kept moving at me. He 'cared' for me, he was so 'grateful' to me, for the way I'd made him feel, alive, vibrant. But he loved Bella. He was so very sorry but he had to end it.

Grateful? Dear God! That was the worst word of all. It exploded like a pipe bomb between us with maximum carnage. Disbelief and contempt sprayed off me in all directions, twisting and tearing. Eliot saw my face break apart and dropped my hands, taking a step back. The icy fire poured out of my mouth because I didn't believe him. Not for a second. It was inconceivable that he really meant what he said, and I told him so, right there on the street, with the prickle of snow in the air and the tang of frying chips on the breeze. *He wouldn't leave me. He couldn't leave me. I wasn't going anywhere. I was staying right there.*

Because I knew it was all for show, his little performance. It had to be. He simply wanted me to talk him out of it. He didn't want the baby at all. He was just panicking and reverting to his default setting of *doing the right thing.* And I knew, I knew if I told Bella about us she would see it was doomed, their marriage, the charade of this new child, a fake life, an illusion that they could be happy, an honourable but empty gesture he was making to stand by her, nothing more.

I said this to him. I tried to take his hand again as we stood by his car. I tried to talk softly and calmly, but he shook me off. He sighed. He used an approximation of his reporting voice, calm, steady, trustworthy, to say that we'd been a wonderful moment in his life but that moment was over. It was just sex, really. He could see that. He'd been flattered, flattered that I was interested in him, someone like me, so independent, so beautiful, that I could want him. But he loved Bella. He wanted her, their life together. He'd been confused. He knew he'd been a fool but he needed to be with his family.

It was a good performance, sincere, on brand. He was trying to make me hate him, to make it easier for him to be a martyr, but I was willing to fight for both of us if he wasn't. My sword was drawn, my hand raised. I could deliver the blow if necessary. Wasn't that what he always said he loved about me? My uncompromising nature, my fearlessness? I stalked away from him towards my car.

Would I have told her, I wonder? Would I have told Bella everything, like I threatened to then? Standing by my car, grabbing the front of his coat, then jumping in when he pushed me away, locking the doors and turning the key – saying, 'It's time to grow up, Eliot. It's time to be honest!'

Probably, I would have. I think he believed I would, that I'd drive to his house, hammer on the door, shoot thunderbolts of truth at his divine wife, set fire to his family fantasy.

He banged on the window, panicking, 'Mel, for God's sake, be reasonable.'

'I'm going there right now,' I said. 'It's time the three of us had this out. You should come, too. It'd be better together, coming from both of us.'

For the first time he looked genuinely alarmed, confused, as if the story was not playing out as he'd planned. It had started with the promise of being one thing and then become something else. Eliot did not like surprises and last-minute rewrites.

'Mel, come on. You knew what this was. You of all people! You're too realistic. You knew this wasn't some dumb romance novel. You're not one of *those* girls. I respect you too much to think you ever thought that. It was a last flush of youth, a midlife crisis thing. A fling. We needed that. *Both* of us.'

'Well, let's see if Bella believes that,' I said, through the couple of inches of car window between us. 'I'll put it a bit more subtly of course. I won't tell her you said I was the world you turned on when you saw me in the studio each morning. Well, I might.'

'Don't you fucking do that, Melly,' he shouted, finally losing his cool.

I don't think I'd ever heard him raise his voice before. It didn't suit him – he wasn't the righteous hero type really and he wanted me to do it, that was obvious. He wanted me to make it easy for him. That way he could still be the good guy and that was fine with me. I had no problem being the villain. The bitch. The other woman. The home wrecker. If that's what it took. It was just words – received words and wisdom, an old tale. For his sake I'd don horns, paint my face red and play the devil himself if I had to.

But the car wouldn't start. One flat battery altered the course of the evening.

Should he have left me there, then? In temper, in the snow, with a car that, as I turned the key, rewarded me with only a splutter and wheeze. My dramatic departure was one thing but I didn't want *him* to leave. He didn't get to turn his back on me and walk away. No one does. So I wound the window down further and tried to take his arm.

'Let's go there now, Eliot, and tell her,' I said. 'I love you. You love me. She can't spoil that.' I touched his cheek.

'What is wrong with you?' He pulled away. 'You're a big girl, get a fucking grip. Stay away from me and stay away from my wife. Go home to your fiancé! Remember him? Remember Steve, that poor, stupid bastard!'

Then he walked away, away from my sprouting tears, freezing as they hit the frigid night air.

At that moment I was pure white rage in a black winter coat in a blue metal box. I wanted to summon the electricity from my eyes, send it to my fingers, smite him, burn a hole in the back of his childish fucking Paddington Bear coat, a lightning bolt through his heart. Honest Eliot. Admirable Eliot. Slain for fleeing the field.

But instead I just sat there shivering, shaking with adrenaline, slumped over the wheel.

If Eliot had taken me home Peter wouldn't have had the chance to offer to help me. He wouldn't have appeared in the car window with his disarming smile, poked for show under the raised car bonnet then offered me a consolatory drink.

Why did I go with him? With a man I'd only seen once, across a room at a council function, weeks before. *Well, at least he isn't a stranger,* I thought, and he was handsome and warm and easy. I wanted to fill the void that the thought of Eliot leaving me for his own pregnant wife was suddenly forcing open inside me.

'You can't wait for a taxi in this,' Peter said, as I waved my phone around, out of the car window, trying to get a reception. 'The snow's starting up again. Have a drink with me and I'll call you one, or I'll take you right home. I promise to behave.'

'What makes you think *I* will,' I said, giving up on the car, getting out and pulling myself up to my full height. It was an effort, to gather my cold northern calm, to tuck my great Norse wings under my coat, to pocket my weapons and take Peter's offered arm, but I did. It seemed like a gesture of protection and I needed that, right then.

Peter was decisive. As he steered me back to The Schooner I was almost flattered. I felt like a doll girl for once, pinned on to his arm, one who needed taking care of. Perhaps I could lay my head on his shoulder, just for a minute, just to catch my breath, just to think. But I didn't think enough.

An hour later it cost me my life.

Chapter Twenty-Three

As I'd expected, Eliot was released on bail forty-eight hours after his arrest, 'pending further enquiries'. I watched his hurried exit from the police station on the TV in the council canteen, with Peter. It was lunchtime and, while Peter poked at the half-eaten chicken curry before him, I watched the press clustering outside the doors as Eliot emerged.

Polly was in pole-position at the front of the scrum. She'd probably had a tip-off to arrive before the others. *The Post* were taking photos, too, their cameraman Aled and his beer belly jostling and shoving with some Press Association freelancers I half-recognised from other, similar scrums I'd fought for footing in, in days past. Peter watched wearily as the BBC Wales management team issued a statement, read soberly by Polly, saying Eliot Masters had been permanently withdrawn from broadcasts until 'the matter could be cleared up', and that the BBC was co-operating fully with the police investigation.

Peter's eyes were ringed with the soot of another sleepless night. He sighed, rubbing the crease between his eyes. By that time he was always awake long before the sun rose, relentless and bullying in his bedroom window each morning. He rarely slept before 1 or 2 a.m. any more so he was spending his days in a sleep-deprived, cotton wool-covered fug, sucking down coffee and chasing it with pills to soothe the fiery headaches that flared up in the afternoons.

After the 'cock' debacle, Mr Barnstable had had a word with him about maybe talking to HR, hinting at the effects of stress, of a 'midlife crisis', had suggested some time off. Peter had insisted he was fine, pretending he was not becoming more and more visibly sloppy at work and sometimes even 'borderline incompetent' (Julienne's words). He'd taken to spending more time than could easily go unnoticed in the council canteen, chain-drinking Americanos while gazing balefully at the sheaves of papers before him.

Marilyn, who generally spent a lot of time hovering around the canteen looking for comrades in gossip, had noted this and so 'just happened' to be getting a cappuccino when the footage of Eliot pushing out of the police station came on the TV.

'Not good, is it?' she said, materialising at the end of our table, cup of froth in hand. 'For the area, I mean. When young women aren't safe to walk the streets of our town? Don't you agree, Peter?'

I was still pissed off with her for the 'nasty piece of work' gossip at full council but she did have a point. I'd seen how that sort of thing could have a ripple effect of alarm on communities, making people ask, why her? Why there? And, could it just as easily have been me, or my wife, or my daughter? Since Eliot was now being touted as the likely guilty party it meant there was probably no random maniac on the loose after all, but I was curious to see what Marilyn would come up with next. Thanks to her PCSO daughter with the big mouth she'd continued to be a stream of rumour-mongering over the weeks, enjoying her role of 'woman-in-the-know'.

She stood her ground, her face shining pinkly as Peter clutched his papers in front of him as if they possessed the repelling powers of a crucifix. His face was fixed intently on the flat screen but Marilyn was not deterred.

'It's just a tactic, you know,' she said, cocking her head to the TV, determined to make him look at her with those blue eyes of his, 'letting him go on bail. My Moira said so. They'll probably make a charge soon.'

She leaned in closer than was necessary, lowered her voice. 'I shouldn't really be saying this but they've been doing searches of his car and so on, found some interesting *forensic* stuff. They're looking for something in his house, too.' She dropped her voice even further to a theatrical whisper, 'Something that ties him to the scene.'

Peter's gaze swivelled slowly to meet hers.

'You know, Moira, my daughter,' she said, taking Peter's silence as permission to continue. 'She shouldn't be telling me, but I'm her mum, it's not like I'm going to go blabbing to all and sundry, only you, but they're looking for blood, and a glove. You see, they found one on the dead girl's hand, a black leather glove, not her own glove apparently.'

She leaned in so closely that I felt Peter wince at the smudge of chocolate powder on her lipstick. She was enjoying herself.

'They keep that sort of stuff back you know, from the press, one or two little things, because it's the sort of thing that only a killer would know about, right? A *significant detail.* Boyfriend said it wasn't hers, the glove. He'd never seen it before. It was a man's glove, like a driving glove. They think it's the reporter's – they've been looking for the other one. That Eliot fella says it's not his glove either, but then he would say that, wouldn't he! Moira thinks there might be fingerprints inside maybe, something like that, who knows, DNA and so on. She wouldn't say any more but apparently they're some posh, special gloves, handmade and they're looking for the place that made them.'

And then I heard Eve's voice in Peter's head, clear as a bell tolling only for him, 'Happy Birthday, darling. Do you like them? They're driving gloves, for the winter. Look, Pete, they have a special label stitched in, only a few hundred pairs made. Very exclusive.'

And then his own voice, on the day I arrived at their house, when I was still dizzy and blank and vomiting as they left for the parents' evening, 'Evelyn, where are my black gloves?'

Peter didn't have his gloves. I'd been wearing them that night. He'd forgotten that he'd given them to me when we walked along the prom, because my fingers were freezing. Such a gentlemanly gesture.

My first thought was that Marilyn was talking through her arse again. Journalists know that while the public think CSI is akin to modern magic, it really isn't anything like as slick as it seems on the TV. Fingerprints wouldn't be viable from inside a glove, left for weeks in salt water. If Peter had never been fingerprinted, which was likely, it wouldn't matter anyway. There'd be nothing on the system to match them to. It was a stab in the dark at best. But Peter's head was already running ahead, full-tilt, before the glow of Marilyn's stained insider smile. He was genuinely scared. I could feel it rattling inside him, around him. He was wondering what might happen if Eliot finally remembered him, put him at the scene, and if the *very exclusive* glove-makers had a list of clients and orders that showed a Swansea address . . .

I would've bet any money that the barmaid, if not the landlord of The Schooner who'd remembered me, would recognise handsome Peter Perfect if confronted with an actual photograph from council files showing his little silver scar. Peter was thinking the exact same thing. I could hear him crashing it all out in his head, drowning out Marilyn.

'My Moira said that that Polly woman, the other BBC reporter, has been in to the station more than once, full of theories, kicking up a fuss,' gabbled Marilyn, well into her stride. 'First she had this idea that someone had followed Melanie Black from the big do at The Gowerton Hotel she never seems to have turned up to. Which is pretty scary because that would mean it could have been one of us, someone *here*.'

She looked around under her dropped lashes for dramatic effect, as Peter's mind started to fog with the memory of that day at the gym, of Polly asking him what he did for a living, of his lie.

'Lots of our people go to that every year as you know,' continued Marilyn. 'As if anyone here could be a *killer*.

'Then when it came out about the Eliot Masters chap that Polly was all over it, saying that Masters was apparently a bit of a *player*, was a shifty bugger and had "tried it on" with her more than once, but that she wasn't interested. Moira thinks she *bats for the other team, know what I mean*.' She gave a lewd, exaggerated wink. 'Moira reckons this Polly had a mega-crush on Melanie Black and is gunning for

211

Eliot because he'd bad-mouthed her, telling this Polly she shouldn't trust Melanie, she wasn't the angel she thought she was. She had a right set-to in the nick about it, with the DI, when Moira was in the next room, saying this Eliot character was no Mr Perfect and what the hell were they going to do to pull their fingers out of their arses and get to the bottom of it?'

Finally she drew breath, before adding with evident enjoyment, 'Quite dramatic isn't it? Like a soap opera, all those jealous rivalries. *The plot thickens.*'

She leaned back, sated at last, but almost sloshed the rest of her cappuccino down her blouse when Peter got abruptly to his feet.

'You stupid cow,' he snapped, his hands forming into fists, trembling. 'You shouldn't be talking rubbish like that to me or anyone else. Your stupid daughter should know better. This is a police investigation, for God's sake, woman. You could get in a lot of trouble. If I hear you talking about this again I'll put you on an official warning. Get the fuck out of my way.'

It was almost comical the way Marilyn's smile slid off as Peter gathered his files, glaring and crackling. Heads turned and Marilyn's mouth fell open wide enough for me to see a tiny piece of lettuce or something stuck in her bottom teeth. I got the strong impression she was about to burst into spectacular sobs as Peter moved to push past her. But at that moment Julienne, standing unnoticed a little way behind him at the vending machine, said, 'Peter, can I have a word with you, please?' in a loud, calm voice.

'Excuse me,' said Marilyn, her eyes swimming. 'I'd better get back to the office.'

Julienne raised a perfectly arched eyebrow but said simply, 'Peter, will you come to my office, please, *now*.' It wasn't a request.

'I didn't mean to upset her,' said Peter, realising that other people were now looking over. 'She's just . . . she's a silly woman, gossiping, spreading rumours. It's inappropriate.'

Julienne gave him a look that signalled he of all people wasn't in any position to comment on what was or was not appropriate.

'I'm not interested in your tiffs with staff,' she said, turning on her patent high heels, expecting him to follow hotly on them. Once in her office, after Peter had been led through the corridors like a child following the headmaster to his study, she finished her sentence.

'What I am interested in is your explanation of this.' She didn't sit down but handed him a report in an open blue folder.

'What's this?' said Peter, blindsided for a moment.

'You know perfectly *well* what it is.'

She tapped a French manicured nail against a box showing the figure £1,420, then used the nail to tease a kink of hair out of her eyes. 'See anything incongruous?'

'No,' said Peter, reflexively. Then he flicked the pages back and forth with the cover sheet. 'Wait, yes, there's a mistake here. This should read £14,200.'

'Yes, it should, as you should well know, since it's your report. This is the money set aside for the social housing budget from the contractors – luckily they spotted the mistake before we were tied in.'

Peter looked at her blankly. I could tell from the silence in the front of his head that he didn't actually remember filling

213

in the tally sheets. Probably because I'd done it with him, whispering and chattering over his shoulder the whole time, treating him to some hard rock choruses of my choosing.

'This is a serious error, Peter. It's a little difficult to explain how £13,000 almost vanished from the budget.'

'It's just a mistake, Julienne. I'm sorry.'

'Yes, or perhaps you had other plans for the money once the transaction went through?'

At once, Peter was alert, the clarity of his outrage cutting through his irritation. He saw what Julienne was building towards a few seconds after I did and responded defensively, 'How dare you? Why would I? Are you suggesting I would deliberately . . . for that? That's not even half a year's salary for me! It's pennies. That's outrageous.'

'It's *council* pennies. We all know you've been distracted lately, Peter. Your work has been regularly below standard since I took over this department. I *hope* this is a mistake. I hope that's all it is. After that disastrous presentation to council your work has been slipping. There'll have to be an investigation to get to the bottom of this.'

'It's a mistake, Julienne. I'm very sorry.'

It cost Peter a great deal to say this, to her of all people, to apologise, but he did. The sound of the blood-birds battering their wings against the inside of his chest was almost deafening but he managed to keep the chill out of his voice.

'Is that necessary? An investigation?'

'Perhaps in other circumstances it could have been overlooked but it's not the first time you've made a mistake, is it? Important emails have gone missing or were not replied to, copies of documents were not saved to the secure files. I've heard the chatter, around the building, and I've had an unofficial complaint from someone in accounts. I think it's time we evaluated your capabilities.'

'You're enjoying this, aren't you, you arrogant bloody harpy?' he spat, a mouth full of fury and feathers.

'Really, Peter, I'm not Marilyn. I don't get tearful at being called a few names. I'm a professional – you should try it some time.'

Peter's fists clenched as he took a step towards her.

'I've been here fifteen years, Julienne. My record is unblemished so far. That should count for something.'

She didn't flinch. She didn't modulate her voice up or down, just kept it flat and cool. 'Perhaps it's time to see exactly what that is.'

'I won't stand for this. This is a vendetta against me. It's your dislike of me, it's bullying. It's slander. I'll go to the chief exec about this.'

'He's the one who asked me to speak to you,' she said quietly.

I think it was the pale sound of the pity in her voice that punched the air out of him. He stood staring at her and I waited for the burst of hands to finally come, for him to take that final step and show her who and what he really was. I imagined how it would look when her blood spilled on his hands and on to her pale-green carpet.

He wanted to. Oh, how he wanted to. *I want, I want, I want*. He wanted to grab her by the throat and choke the self-satisfaction out of the arrogant little bitch, land a punch on her tight jaw, her blushed cheekbone and feel them crumple, watch the tell-tale red stain her teeth.

I wanted it, too. I wanted to watch him finish himself, to see it happen – to stand on the heaped bones of his career and reputation and laugh without restraint into the skies. I'd certainly earned it, my front-row seat to the final act, the result of my hard work and influence. A little collateral damage is always expected in these things. Julienne was a grown-up girl. She could take one for the greater good of the team.

An urge as sharp as my own expectation was firing through Peter's every gym-honed sinew. In that second I knew it'd take only the tiniest push from me, a little lubrication to make him slip off his restraint once and for all. What a thing of beauty it would be, Peter's ultimate humiliation. Peter Perfect reduced to violence – to attacking a woman – brought so low, made primitive and muddy before the grey-shell people he despised. Nothing could hurt him more than that. It would be a fitting revenge.

So I leaned right up to his ear and said: 'Go on, Peter, she asked for it.'

As soon as I said the words, his fists, already clenched at his sides, twitched. They say revenge is a dish best served cold but I learned right then how the heat of the moment has its uses. That was where Peter lived after all, in the hottest part of a split second, molten and liquid, when his leashed temper snapped free.

Something in Julienne's face spasmed, closed in on itself as she saw for the first time what I did, the man before her, stripped bare of the niceties of office civilities and modern manners, pared away from the illusions of equality in the manner that eventually counts most, in feet and inches and pounds per square inch.

At that second I wondered if the same look had appeared on my face, that night of Big Snow, just a moment too late.

I wish I could say for sure that it hadn't, that I'd been ready and armed and proud and unafraid. But if wishes were fishes . . .

I wish we hadn't been interrupted then. I wish there hadn't been that knock on the door, the face in silhouette through the frosted glass that brought everything up short. Things might have turned out differently if Julienne's secretary hadn't stuck her head in and said, 'Sorry to interrupt, Ms Henry, but Mr Connelly is here to see you now.'

'Just a moment, Jane,' said Julienne to the door, but not before she had taken two steps back behind her desk, putting it between herself and Peter.

The moment was defused – the detonation never occurred.

Each waited for the other to speak. Julienne recovered first.

'Continue your duties for now, Peter,' she said after a moment. 'We'll schedule a review immediately and an opportunity for you to offer your explanations.

'That'll be all.' She gestured to the door. 'Send Jane in, please.'

I had to hand it to her, it was an iron-spined recovery. She managed to sound steady and dismissive and I was simultaneously pleased and disappointed that Peter hadn't wiped the ghost of a smile off her face with his fists.

What could Peter do then but leave, walk back to his office and sit down in silence.

What could I do but comfort him. 'Poor old Peter, pitiful Pete,' I said quietly, stroking the side of his sweating face with the back of my hand. 'Peter Albright, what a sight.'

I could hear him thinking to himself, *I mustn't panic. That bitch can't do this. It was a mistake. I can clear this up.* But he wasn't sure of that. He wasn't sure of anything much any more. After a moment or two, slicing up from underneath the rising tidal fear that he was losing control of everything, were two far more simple thoughts.

My gloves, and *That fucking nancy-boy Eliot Masters.*

Chapter Twenty-Four

It was Peter's turn to pick up Adam from school that afternoon, so naturally I accompanied him, but my thoughts were elsewhere, stuck back on the jagged, bloody edges of what had almost happened in Julienne's office. They were also snagged on what Marilyn had said about Polly and Eliot in the canteen and I was struggling to make sense of it. Could Eliot really have been trying to get together with Polly, like Moira had suggested? Could he have made a pass at her? More than one? Surely not? Eliot didn't do casual flings. He'd always said Polly was a simpering schoolgirl with the brains of a Barbie doll.

And why would he have said such a thing to her, about me? That I couldn't be trusted? We'd talked about Polly of course, about all of our colleagues, shredding them to pieces, laughed about it in the sweating bed sheets, downing cold beer from a bottle, eating takeaway. He'd taken part just as eagerly, laughing.

'Remind me never to get on your wrong side, Melly,' he'd spluttered.

And Polly? Could she really have had a crush on me?

That's what Marilyn had suggested with a snigger. Of course it was just gossip – nasty, salacious gossip. But then . . . all those coffees she used to bring me on earlies, those breezy compliments offered with a half-drop of her Bambi eyes, the hanging around the editing suites always trying to be useful. Had that been for my benefit?

'I think I can learn so much from you, Mel,' she'd said once, at my elbow, watching me edit a breaking-news piece, right down to the on-air deadline, cutting footage and laying down a voice track with two minutes to spare to the Live light, while the directors jittered and panicked. 'What do you think, Mel? Will we make it? Is it a good story? Is he telling the truth? Will it stand up with the lawyers?' What if all that breathless admiration in her girlish voice hadn't been put on because she just wanted part of the glory? Had she admired me, and maybe more? Even in the twenty-first century we still forget that suitors come in all shapes and sizes.

She certainly seemed to have got the bit between her teeth on my behalf. Had she heard me that time at the gym? Had I sunk my suspicions into her and they'd caught and held tightly because she actually *cared*? All that time had she really just been trying to impress me, to become a seeker of truth and bestower of justice, just like me? Or how she imagined me to be. If so I was seriously starting to question my ability to read people. Everyone seemed to be becoming someone else, changing their clothes and their faces. Myself included.

With my thoughts flying away at all angles, it took me a minute to realise that Peter was parking his car outside the school and brightly coloured scraps of red-uniformed children were already flinging out of the gates towards us.

An Adam-shaped flash of scarlet jumper and grey trousers detached itself from a teacher's hand and was pulling at the car door. Peter smiled at the sight of him and, for the briefest moment, the raging fists that had been buffeting his insides all the way from the office softened. But it only lasted until he saw Kyle, bounding towards his mum's Corsa across the road, until he realised Bella wasn't in the driving seat this time.

Eliot didn't get out of the car and I can't say I blamed him. I don't think it was because it was obvious he hadn't shaved and his hair needed a good wash. Who wants to face the worst inquisition of all? The school-run whispers and nudges of the yummy mummies and their nannies in their Boden and Barbour and bright self-awareness:

'That's him, the TV chap. The one, you know . . . the one who was arrested over that bad business with the reporter girl.'

Peter watched Eliot buckling Kyle into his junior seat as he buckled Adam into his own restraint, then started up the car.

'Where are we going, Daddy?' asked Adam, yawning. 'I'm tired. We had lots of running games today and a treasure hunt. Want to go home now.'

'Soon, Adam Ant, sleep with Peter bunny for a bit,' said Peter, turning out of the school gates, following Eliot's car out of the village.

As we drove, everything inside Peter started buzzing like a barbed-wire tornado. On the outstretched arm of the coast road, bubbling between the green verges and grey-green sea, I could hear the fragments of Peter's brain talking to each other and I didn't like what I heard. *Bitch*, and *I'll make it all right*, and *fucking reporter*, and *I've worked too hard, too long*, and *I can fix it, must fix it. Fucking bitch, all bitches. Little shit. Little preening TV shit.*

In the long lanes the Corsa sailed on, oblivious to Peter's big, black people carrier behind, predatory and slick, and the thought that stuck out of Peter's head suddenly as sharp as a spear. *Drive him off the road*, it said, glinting and lethal. *He'll go over the cliff easily. Do it now, before he can identify you, before he leads the police to you. Without him it's all nothing. They won't know who you are if you get rid of him. If he dies they'll think it was a suicide, because he was guilty. Because he knew what was coming. He knew they were coming for him. End of story.*

In that moment, horrified as I was, this actually made a sort of sense, because it made sense to Peter. It was an alternative explanation to my end, one that wrote out the mysterious scarred man and pointed to Eliot's assured guilt. Loose ends would simply unravel without Eliot there to hold them. No eye-witness – no firm ID. There might not be any customer records for the men's gloves. That little piece of actual physical evidence, seemingly so crucial, could easily come to nothing. Eve might have picked them up off a display case, paid cash. *Anyway*, Peter was thinking, cleanly and clearly, *I could tell them I left them somewhere at any time, in a council meeting, or a pub one night, even the pub the girl had been in.*

Without Eliot to pick him out, put him at the scene of the crime, make that first, vital link, the chain failed. But that wasn't the only reason that Peter wanted to lash out at that moment. Peter wanted to hurt Eliot right then because he couldn't hurt anyone else. He couldn't hurt me anymore. He hadn't been able to hurt Julienne in her office when he'd

222

wanted to. The rage generated and swallowed down had to go somewhere or split him open. The thought came out of the open door of the hot place inside him and said:

Drive him off the road . . .

It wasn't a weak or idle thought. It was sickeningly fleet of foot, keeping pace with Eliot's car as he picked up speed. Even as Peter began to lower his foot on the accelerator it had a target lock and soon the noise in the car was deafening, roaring, full of fists and bones and striking feet.

Dear God, no! I thought, shaken into panic. *He's really going to do it. But he can't. Not to Eliot, not my Eliot.* Then, almost as an afterthought, at the bob of a small dark head in the rear seat of the car in front, I realised – *Dear God, the kid's in the car, too. Kyle is there, too.*

Peter accelerated harder, closing the distance between us and the Corsa bit by bit.

'No, dear God, no!' I shouted, over and over again. I'd never wanted to touch something, anything, so badly, to batter my fists against Peter, grab the wheel and twist it away, stop what was coming. Instead all I could do was cup my hand to his ear and yell, 'Stop it, Peter. Pull back, go back!'

But it was harder then, harder than it had ever seemed before, to make him hear me, to break through the black stinging rage clogging the lines into his head – so clear was his intention. I knew, somehow, that it was precisely because I was so afraid that Peter was not. I was giving him power. He was feeding off me this time – the current running the other way. My fear was making him stronger rather than making him stop, like all men of his kind.

In desperation I started to sing. I sang as loudly as I could, to stop myself thinking, to stop myself feeling – to staunch the terror and helplessness that the thought of Eliot's body, dislocated and drowned at the foot of the spray-soaked cliff, made stream from me – to break the link.

I sang the lines from 'When You Wish Upon a Star' over and over again, with rising cold fire, my voice raucous. The car radio went up and down and in and out in time with the waves of my voice, like waves of static were hitting the car. But, although Peter stuck his hand to his brow as if the ice-pick had been inserted there, he gripped the wheel even harder.

Just do it at the bend, swerve into his wing, it'll take him over. Right over and down, into the sea, out of your life. Problem solved.

His words filled the world and I knew, as we came to the bend, that the road support fell away there and the cliff edge was close and crumbling, the blue-white booming sea far below punching at the pebble bank of beach. And there was nothing I could do. Nothing at all.

'Eliot my love,' I said. 'I'm sorry. I'm so sorry.'

Chapter Twenty-Five

When the school bus came towards us, around the corner from the opposite direction, Peter hit the brakes out of reflex. Eliot, in front had done the same and we almost careered into the back of the Corsa, tyres losing traction, slipping forward. But we stopped short of their bumper by about two feet. The wheels of the Corsa skidded on the gravel but slid past the missing metal guardrail by just an inch and somehow clung to the road.

A cloud of herring gulls, disturbed from the cliffs below, exploded into the sky. Eliot hit his horn and I could see the silhouette of an angry wave directed at the bus driver who hadn't slowed down at all. As the coach swung by I could see the kids inside, unconcerned, waving and sucky-sticking their mouths up to the window like suckerfish.

'Fuck!' yelled Peter, slamming his hands against the wheel.

'Daddy?' shouted Adam, jolting from his doze in the back seat, 'why are you shouting at the school bus?'

Adam, said the inside of Peter's head, as if he'd just remembered his son was in the back of the people carrier he'd wanted to make into a remorseless weapon of impact.

Something inside him ignited and the blackness receded. Both cars were caught in the freeze-frame before the world stuttered and restarted. Peter watched as Eliot's Corsa pulled off in front.

'Nothing, Adam Ant, nothing to be frightened of,' Peter said after a moment. 'We're going home now.'

He leaned back to ruffle his son's hair. 'Tell me what you did in school today, little man.'

I slumped back in the seat as Peter started the car and pulled a U-turn at the next junction. He was chatting to Adam about running races and making sand shapes, but I could tell that the thought about what had almost happened had started to crystallise into an intention. It hadn't slid away with the moment; it was out and circling around us, fuelled up and full of purpose. If not that day, then another, when Adam was not with Peter and no eyes were around him, somehow, he could and would remove the last obstacle.

I wasn't oblivious to the irony of it, of what I had helped put in motion. By thinking about Eliot I'd kept him in Peter's head. By worming my way into Peter's thoughts I'd cracked his arrogant, confident, irreproachable Perfect Peter shell, made it buckle with uncertainty. Then I'd served him up to Julienne and what would come next, with a thought that had to find its way out into the world somehow, somewhere.

And Eliot would end up paying for it, or Kyle or Adam, or all of them at once. That wasn't supposed to be the end of my story, especially when I realised, not much later, that I hadn't really been the one to give birth to that terrible thought. It had been there inside him all along, long before we met that night, deep inside Peter, a thought to destroy, buried in the hot place. All I'd done was pry open a very old door.

* * *

'You're a bit late,' said Eve, 'where have you been?' as Adam tumbled into the hall and Peter shuffled in behind him, carrying his rucksack and coat. Adam already seemed to have forgotten the excitement of the near miss, pulling his school bag out of his father's hands with excitement.

'Look, Mummy,' he said, about to burst. 'I made you.'

'Made me what, sweetie?' smiled Eve.

Adam huffed with happy frustration, 'Nooo, I made *you*. Look!' and he pulled a large wooden peg with black wool hair and a pink marker-pen smile from the flap pocket of his bag. The peg was wearing a blue dress. He held it out to Eve, a vast grin on his face.

'Oh, how beautiful,' said Eve, 'my clever little man.' Then she dropped into a crouch and mother and son folded snugly into a single hug.

For a moment Peter looked crestfallen, his face filled with jagged longing.

'Boys make dolls at school now?' he said, quietly.

'What, no present for Daddy?' asked Eve, glancing up.

'Mrs Lewis said Daddy's hair is still drying,' said Adam. 'We're making families for Family Day.'

'Let's go and put Mummy in the kitchen then, where she can help me get dinner ready. Sausages for you tonight.'

'Yay!' shouted Adam, barrelling away from her into the kitchen.

'I'll be in in a minute,' said Peter, his face now closed, heading for the stairs.

'Everything all right, darling?' asked Eve. *In for one of your moods, are we?* said the other Eve.

'I'm fine, just going to change.'

Once upstairs, and into jeans and a sweater, Peter sat down on the bed. At first I thought he was staring at nothing, sulking about the present Adam had given Eve, but I soon realised he was gazing off into a distant memory, one existing just beyond the surface of the photograph of his father leaning on the top of the dresser.

Staring at it alongside Peter I could see some small resemblance between the eyes of the man leaning on the Allegro and the son sitting next to me on the bed.

'What? Does little Petey miss his daddy?' I asked. 'Come on, tell the nice lady what's making you so glum.'

I asked more out of habit, my ingrained desire to goad him, but I got what I asked for. I didn't even have to prod about in his head. A whirlwind of serrated images poured out of a place inside him I hadn't known existed, a place he'd kept chained away in the dark, even from himself. The events of the day, of the weeks, of the months must have made the lock brittle because the images and emotions exploded outwards like shattered glass.

I could see what Peter was seeing: a sixteen-year-old boy. Beneath the boy's gangling limbs the contours of a man were starting to show but his face still carried the softness of a child. The boy was standing at his bedroom door smarting under the red wheals left by his mother's tongue but he was the one shouting, almost crying, 'You didn't even tell me he was ill. I never got the chance to say goodbye.'

I felt the edge of the words split my skin and looked down, expecting to see red slices appear on my arms, but the images were changing as fast as I could grasp them and the boy was weeping.

'Dear Christ, boy, are you still crying like a girl?' said

228

the mother. 'You've never been any use to me, just like him. Couldn't even die with some guts – lots of people get cancer and don't blub and whine about it. If he'd had the guts he'd have ended it himself, six months ago – that's what I'd do.'

And then there was a collage of shouting and pleading and longing, scraps of that moment mixed with a sequence of bite-size pieces of the boy at all ages with wet eyes and an empty stomach.

Peter was watching this from outside, as if viewing each moment all at once. He was watching the almost-man's hands, stronger than he even realised, clenching tight.

Then he was feeling it all.

He was feeling how slight the woman was up close, her mouth open in shock.

How could someone so empty ever have had anything to give me, thinks the boy, the hot fire inside him far stronger than she was or ever could be.

His hands were on her shoulders then, and it was the work of a moment to half-carry her backwards from the doorway of his room to the top of the tall stairs, like a bag of old washing. When he shoved her backwards she fell like a bundle of twigs, cracking on each tread, rolling to a stop at the bottom. When she opened her eyes she started to cry. But the boy was finally done with crying. He headed down towards her, tread by tread, stepping over the hump of the weeping, green two-piece suit, ignoring the pale white face above its collar.

He sat quietly in the kitchen and ate the sandwich he made for himself, the usual dinner he'd prepared most nights a week since he was old enough to hold a knife and butter bread. To cover the stringy cries for help from the hall he turned on the

229

radio to Swansea Sound. The cries were hoarser and fainter by the time he'd eaten his slice of Battenberg cake and made himself tea with yesterday's used bag.

'Please,' said the voice from far below him, as he stepped towards the coat hook in the hall and reached for his anorak. He was late for football practice. 'Please,' it said again as he opened the door. Then the voice stopped.

Later, as the boy's key slid into the front door lock, he listened for any sound on the other side, though he knew there'd be none. He'd brought Rory back for a can of lager. He'd told him it'd be okay since Mum would be at her Labour meeting until at least ten. He stayed at the front door so Rory could be the first inside, to see what was at the bottom of the stairs. It was Rory who phoned for the ambulance, though it was clear to him Mrs Albright was dead. 'There's been an accident,' he told the 999 operator.

Peter was quiet at dinner later. He made a show of admiring the peg Eve on the table and complimented the real one on the nice bit of hake on his plate, but said little else.

All night afterwards his thoughts roiled and churned back and forth through that swinging door inside him until it was hard even for me to tell where the black of his head ended and the black of the night began.

Chapter Twenty-Six

Eve knew something was wrong, when Peter returned from work early the next day, or when she thought he had. He'd actually pretended to go to the office and called Julienne's secretary to say he'd come down with a bug. Then he'd driven out to Eliot's house, sat in the car for a few minutes then stood in the garden for a very long time.

Eve didn't say anything, just made him some tea, passed him his newspaper and a slice of lemon cake, and went quietly to the kitchen to check on dinner. She almost got away with it, diffusing him by radiating her practised calm, her domestic composure. The house was immaculate, her voice soft and coaxing. The beef, slow-cooked and pink-hearted, was rare and right. And Eve was happy not to make too much small talk. She had things of her own to worry about that evening.

She was thinking about her mum, still insisting, as ever, that she was fine, but . . . on the phone earlier Nora had said her chest cold had worsened overnight – she was watching for signs of infection. The last thing her mum's fragile health could weather was a relapse of last winter's pneumonia.

Eve had thought . . . she couldn't bear to think what she'd thought when she got that call from Nora back in February, saying Mum was getting weaker. She'd been so afraid. That night, when Nora called out the GP . . . what had happened, what could have happened . . .

But no, she mustn't think about that and she mustn't panic. Nora had assured her there was nothing to suggest anything more than a bad cold, that Mum had eaten some scrambled egg and some custard creams and taken all her pills. Mum *had* sounded quite chipper for once. She'd spoken about Dad without crying, about some old film she'd been watching on the telly that they'd seen in The Palace Cinema together on their second date, with a bag of chips afterwards and a walk along the prom in the hot summer of 1976.

'I thought your father was so dapper and smart, Evie,' she'd say, 'smoking those roll-up cigarettes and with his hair slicked back.' Then she'd heard Eve crying, though she'd tried not to because she'd been happy to hear Mum being happy.

'Don't cry, love. What's he done now?' she'd asked. 'Is he getting worse? They mostly do, love. They never get better, just worse. It's the way of things. Don't forget, you have a place to go . . . you'll always have a place to go . . . '

For one minute Eve had been overwhelmed by the recollection, of the smell of beans on toast, her mum's sweet whisky breath, nights on the settee with Dad in the big chair, and her heart had broken into her throat like a wave of red memory. It had seemed possible, for that moment only, to break open the bedroom wardrobe with a screwdriver, liberate her shoes and clothes and run with Adam under her arm all the way to Mumbles.

232

But Mum didn't understand. She had to paint on a happy face for a little while longer. She had to think hard and bide her time. Do exactly the right thing.

So her act was perfect and meek and grateful as she cleared the dinner dishes and Peter rewarded her by leaving her alone. It was Adam who ruined it, at bedtime.

'What did you do in school today, Adam Ant?' asked Peter, dropping a dirty shirt in the bathroom laundry basket.

'Kyle and me had lunch together today and he gave me chocolate worms.' He brushed his teeth with a foamy grin. 'Wiggly, wriggly worms.'

'Kyle?' said Peter to Eve, putting some folded sheets into the airing cupboard. The air in the steamy bathroom crackled and the back of Eve's neck stood to attention. She knew what was coming next, we both did.

'I thought I told you I didn't want Adam mixing with that kid?' said Peter. 'I did say that, didn't I? Or maybe my memory isn't what it used to be? Help me out here, Eve.'

'It was Kyle's mum's turn to get the treasure hunt started. She brought the treats for everyone. You know she runs her own bakery. She did the cakes,' said Eve, not turning to face him, opening the cupboard door. 'What was I supposed to do? Say Adam was the only one who couldn't share the treat?'

Peter knew this answer was reasonable but that didn't mean he liked it, today of all days. He glared at Eve as Adam launched an explosion of white spit from his mouth, into the sink.

Adam started singing about a worm at the bottom of the garden, then he looked at his mummy, then at his daddy and stopped. Somewhere in his little-boy brain he knew the grown-ups were about to start shouting again.

'There was a little girl, who had a little curl,' he sang instead, low at first, more insistently when Peter asked,

'Don't you care who has influence over our son, Evelyn?'

'Of course I do, darling,' she said, with her best reassuring smile. *Believe me, I fucking do,* said her head-voice. *And I am in no fucking mood for this tonight.* She was thinking that she really had to see Mum soon, somehow, in case things took a turn for the worse, wondering how she might manage it. Maybe Mair . . .

'Won't you be late for the gym, darling?' she said to Peter. *Go on, sod off out, for God's sake.*

'Right in the middle of her forehead,' sang Adam, in a monotone, drying his mouth in a towel.

'Be quiet, Adam, go play in your room,' said Peter.

'Don't yell at him. It's not his fault,' said Eve, a note of impatience creeping into her voice.

'I never said it was, did I?' said Peter coolly. 'And I'm not going to the bloody gym tonight.'

'Okay. Oh, by the way, Julienne rang while you were in the shower,' said Eve, trying deftly to change the subject. 'She didn't sound happy. She asked if you were here and if you were feeling better. I'm not sure what she meant by that. Then she said to tell you that if you're well enough they want to see you at 11 a.m. tomorrow, in the chief exec's office. She asked if you have any paperwork at home and if so to bring it all with you.'

'What did you say to her?' said Peter, taking a step towards Eve.

Almost gracefully, as if such retreat was effortless and artless, Eve stepped out of the bathroom and on to the landing with the sheets still in her arms. 'I said you were perfectly fine.'

'Really, and what did you say about the files?'

'I said you sometimes work at home so I'd ask you to check.'

'Why did you say that? You know I'm not supposed to bring files home.'

'I . . . because it's true. I didn't know that. Is it really a problem, darling? Is there a problem at work?'

'The problem isn't at work, for fuck's sake. You're the bloody problem, Eve, as usual. Why can't I trust you to say or do anything right? You're supposed to back me up. I don't ask for much and yet you can't get the slightest thing right.'

Eve's performance was the exact opposite of Julienne's, placatory and deferential, but it had the same effect on Peter. And perhaps because she was preoccupied with thoughts of her mum, Eve wasn't quite on her game.

'I'm too tired to argue tonight. I have a headache,' she said. 'We're not all perfect, Peter.'

I wasn't that surprised when he shoved the sheets from her hands.

'Stop doing that when I'm talking to you.'

'Oh for God's sake, not now,' she hushed, picking up the bundle and nodding her head to Adam's room. 'It's bedtime. Let's not have a fuss. I have to get him down.'

'When she was good, she was very, very good,' sang Adam from behind his bedroom door.

'I'll bloody say when this conversation is over,' Peter said, following her out of the bathroom.

I saw Julienne in his head then, where she'd been lodged since yesterday afternoon, since the moment of almost violence. Not his wife, not Eve. It was Julienne dismissing him, saying, 'Send Jane in' all over again. His fists had not unfurled since that moment, they'd been thwarted with Eliot, now Eve was close at hand.

'Fine. But it's late and Julienne said to remind you to be ready at eleven sharp!' said Eve.

Peter grabbed her then, pushed her backwards.

'She doesn't order me around and neither do you.'

Eve was startled. 'You bastard!' she hissed, struggling. 'Get your hands off me!'

His hand was on her throat, at Julienne's throat, at the head of the stairs, the tall, steep, hardwood stairs. Eve had no desk to step behind – there'd be no knock at the door to interrupt this scene. By the time she realised it, shocked and suddenly short of breath, her pink-slippered feet were already in danger of slipping on the top step.

We both caught our breath. We both knew the fall was high and long, on to the hard-tiled floor across the hardwood treads. At the very least bones would crunch and crack, bruises would bloom, were already forming under his fingers.

The slightest pressure would force things forward. There it was, the flowering of the poisoned tree I had helped take root. If Peter did this, the police would come for him – he couldn't hide it this time, not if Eve was in the hospital, under the eyes of nurses and doctors, or worse. And Eve would give evidence against him for sure, either with words and images of fractured X-rays and stitches or by her untimely and ultimate silence. Peter would pay – for her, for me, for the day of his mother's *accident*. The day my Peter had been born.

Eliot would be safe then, and Kyle, and even Bella and the baby, and that would mean Eliot could be happy, happy without me after all. Because even after he'd tried to make me believe he didn't love me, and even if it was true about Polly, I still thought I loved him. That was the only thing left that I knew was real and unchanged since the last night of my life. That had to have been real.

In that moment the voice in me was something darker than I'd ever known, darker even than those nights spent twisting myself into the shape of thought and fear. It scared me, I can't lie. It scared me that I could say again, as I had in Julienne's office, 'Go on, do it. She asked for it.' The words were already there, from long ago, from the first time Peter had stood in a place like this and lashed out. He was ripe and ready, full of the intention he'd suppressed since that night his mother had laughed at his tears. The birds were beating their wings in his veins. Now that *I* was calm and unafraid, the thoughts would slide into him like hot spikes, clean and slick. He would feel them like his own and they would be just that, they had been all along.

Then, if Eve lived, she would be free of him. He would go to prison. Adam would be safe. If she died at the foot of the stairs, and stayed true to my example, she could join me in the little Peter harem of the night. Who's to say an eternity here would be so bad with some company – a friend, a comrade, a colleague, an apprentice?

In that split second I thought of the things I could teach her, the places I could guide her. We could have a lovely time entertaining Peter in prison, with me showing her the whispering ropes. Think of the songs we could sing together while he was sealed in those blue overalls and slip-on shoes in a bare cell. Best friends forever, Eve and I, and she could still keep an eye on her little boy, speak words into his ears every day and night to make him come out big and strong and kind and brave and watch over him as I have.

The feeling was so strong it already seemed real but, through this domestic vision, through the bedroom door, I could hear Adam singing, brash and tuneless and angry. I couldn't see him but I could feel his pudgy hot hands over his ears, his eyes screwed shut, leaking watery fury, repeating the same refrain, *'When she was good, she was very, very good!'*

'I wish you were dead,' said Eve aloud, into Peter's face, as he tightened his hand on her throat.

'Careful,' he said. 'Don't you know that accidents happen in the home.'

Then the singing broke off and Adam burst out of his room, right into the middle of us, a ball of hot white light, breaking into the scene.

'I wish Daddy would stop being horrid,' he sobbed, stamping his feet before putting his hands back up to his wet eyes.

I made my decision then. It had been made for me really, long before that moment. It was the only one I could make.

'Let her go,' I said, cold and quiet and certain. I put my hand on the back of Peter's neck and the electricity of the thought flew out of my fingers as the words went into his ear. Adam's eyes grew saucer-like, his total silence more than Peter could stand. He let her go then, his wife, Julienne, his mother, me, all the women in the world who had wronged him, all those bitches – they slipped away at the sight of his son's tears and the feel of my fingers, for the time being.

'It's okay, little man, no more yelling,' said Peter with an effort. He attempted a smile. He stepped away from Eve and, without a word, picked up Adam and carried him back to bed. A bubble of snot emerged from Adam's nose, his cheeks still slippery with tears as Peter tucked the covers under his chin.

'It's all right, little man,' I soothed. 'It's all right.' I couldn't stop myself stroking Adam's head, even as Peter reached out to dry his son's eyes.

'Time for sleep, bunny,' said Peter, managing a smile. 'You're a tired boy.'

When Adam finally quieted Peter clicked on the toadstool lamp and turned out the bedroom light. Under the covers Adam started singing to himself again, low and soothing and I joined in the rhyme I had sung to him on long nights before.

'There was a little girl who had a little curl, right in the middle of her forehead . . . when she was good, she was very, very good . . . '

Adam cuddled Soft Peter even tighter. Eve came in then, a little shaken but smiling like nothing was wrong.

'It's okay, Adam,' she soothed. 'Mummy's fine. Mummy loves you very, very much.'

'When she was good, she was very, very good . . . ' he crooned.

A frown crossed Eve's face when she heard him.

'That's a funny song, little man. I've heard you singing that before. Who taught you that song, Adam?' she said.

'No one,' he replied, already half asleep.

Later that night, there on the sofa, the three of us made an odd little family. Peter was upstairs, feverishly sifting through his papers for the morning meeting, sorting things into bundles with elastic bands, scribbling notes on Post-its. Eve and Adam were curled up at one end of the sofa, he in her lap, legs stretched along the length; sock footed, pyjama-ed, warm, smiling. Adam had woken in the middle of a nightmare and been allowed to come down and have hot milk and a biscuit for just ten minutes that had become twenty, then thirty while Daddy was preoccupied upstairs with the door shut.

The light from the table lamp pooled across the gloom and over the floor, creeping its glow on to Adam's shampoo-shiny head. Eve's fingers ran through his hair and their joint breathing slowed together into a soft pulse. Her voice droned to the words of the book in her lap.

They were drifting and dreaming.

I was cross-legged at the other end, just a finger width from Adam's feet and for a few hours the shadows were pushed back beyond our bodies. Eve snuffled into Adam's neck, blowing tickly raspberries, raising a sleepy squirm and giggle.

On impulse I stretched out a crooked finger, tracing it lightly across Adam's foot and he laughed unexpectedly at this imaginary ticklishness. Eve delighted to hear him, snuffled some more. Taken by the rare sound of her chuckle I repeated the foot tickle and Adam dissolved into giggles. 'Stop, stop,' he wriggled.

I laughed out loud, then. We all laughed together. 'You love your mummy, don't you, you love your mummy,' I said, tickling once more.

'I love you, Mummy,' said Adam.

Later, after Eve had carried Adam back to bed and was

attempting sleep herself, the laughter hung in the lamplight. When Peter came downstairs, to crack open a beer and eat his now cold supper, he looked around puzzled, unsure why the room felt the way it did, unable to see me or my smile from the blackest corner of the sofa.

Thunder was stalking the high hills and low valleys of the bay. Out across the ocean, lightning flared. I felt it in my remembered bones and imagined my fingers crackling with static, bolts leaping from my palms to join it. An answer of white light flashed against the curtains. Peter shuddered. We both bristled and crackled. The hour was approaching.

This particular party was ending, that was obvious to us both. Everyone was getting ready to leave. The lights were going up, revealing the broken glasses and food trampled into the carpet, that one mean drunk still hanging around who just won't quit and go home or pass out. These types of parties never end well. They get out of control in ways you don't expect, with tears and blood and sirens. Someone has to be the adult and call time, be the voice of reason. It was clear it had to be me.

I'd said a great deal to Peter over the past nine months, in the quiet times and day times and bright times and night times. I'd been waiting for the ultimate way to take my revenge, to mete out justice, call it whatever you want. Perhaps most of all I'd just wanted him to suffer, slowly, and feel powerless, like I had before my last breath. But all good things must come to an end; every game finally has a winner and loser. I was tired of playing with him. I knew I had to make my point, cut to the chase, voice the conclusion and then sign off.

I had to say one last thing. And the saying would now make it so. As Peter's eyes closed, heavy with sleep, I leaned in and began to speak.

Chapter Twenty-Seven

On the last night of whispering Peter was dreaming. He was dreaming of us, me and him, on the night of the Big Snow.

The images spooled through his sleep in loops and twists, our versions not identical but overlapping in the places that mattered. And however it was edited together, from whose point of view, I knew the substance and the outcome was the same because there we were, in the night.

Once again he was watching me and Eliot, arguing in the greyed-out street, from the pub doorway, breath flaring. He was watching me waving my mobile phone out of the car window trying to get reception, through the first stray flakes of snow in the air. Then he was walking towards me.

I'd seen him right away, sauntering towards my car after Eliot's departure. I'd been cautious. Well, you never know who's hanging around on a cold, dark winter night. There are some real oddballs out there.

'Engine trouble?' he asked, walking up to the window, blue eyes sharp, cheeks pinked by the bay breeze. I remember turning the key in the ignition so he could hear the limp wheeze.

'Thought as much,' he smiled, 'it's the battery, by the sounds of it.' It wasn't a warm smile exactly, but it was bright and beckoning and I realised I'd seen it before.

I was embarrassed by the thought he'd obviously witnessed the noisy byplay with Eliot a minute before and my cheeks threatened to turn a different colour to the ice cool I was hoping for – but then I thought, why should I care what he thinks?

'One of those nights?' he offered.

'You could say that.'

I was heavy with tiredness, afraid I would become tearful again. I imagined Eliot haring home to Bella, powering along the coast, checking his mirror for the lights of the taxi I could still have hailed to pursue him to his doorstep, to the final confrontation. But my appetite for battle had waned in the gap between the thought and the delayed action. I was cold, queasy, hungry and empty, and I wanted a drink, a large one.

'Use my phone,' said, Peter. 'I've got two bars of signal. Well I did, on that side of the road. But only if you come and have a drink with me while you wait. It's been one of those days for me, too.'

Newsflash, darling, I thought. *I really couldn't give a shit.*

But then I thought of what I was going home to, with Steve away photographing that wedding – the chill inside of an empty flat, the inside of my own head and, no doubt, the ring of Eliot's evermore unanswered phone. Something slipped inside me, something weakened and bent just a degree or two from the perpendicular towards him, softened by fatigue years in the making. There was nothing iron-spined or even iron-filing coloured about me in that moment. I was pink and malleable to the core, aching like the pulp of an exposed tooth. *Fuck it*, I thought. *Why not?*

'Please?' he said.

And I think it was partly the word and the fact that, when I looked into his face, he looked a bit broken, too, a little bit cracked, as if he was trying too hard to sound nonchalant, to keep that megawatt smile glowing, that I relented. What I didn't know then was that he'd been overlooked in the interview for the job of head of finance a month before, that six hours previously he'd had to shake hands with the new boss, *that bitch Julienne Henry, from Bristol, for fuck's sake, like that meant cosmopolitan and brimming with fucking charm and foresight and go-getting attitude for the twenty-first century, like the line of shit the board had tried to sell him when he'd demanded to know what was so bloody special about her, just because she had international exchange experience and fancy fucking ideas of European restructuring. Give me a fucking break!*

It was only later, of course, in his reruns of that night, that I heard these actual words inside him and understood. How he'd had to stand at her side as she accepted the welcome of the *ball-less fucking house-cats of the board. Fucking neutered old cunts!* From the scraps gathered from inside Peter's head I could see how, at that point of the night, he'd just wanted to exert some of the dregs of power left to him, the power of his smooth face and handsome jaw, his charm and will, over a woman. Almost any woman would have done, I think. Even if it was just for a drink, for an hour as suggested, a bit of play-acting, another way to delay going straight home.

He'd wanted to know he could still be in control. Perhaps,

in part, he really thought he was coming to my rescue. I'd seen shards of this in his head and darker splinters since. But that night I just got out of the car, buttoned up my coat, pulled myself erect, shoulders back, iron spine clicking back into place.

'I recognise you, don't I?' he said. 'From the TV news. You're taller in person, and you're younger close up.'

'I've seen you, too, at some of the council meetings?'

'Really, you stayed awake long enough to remember me?'

'You? Well, you stand out.'

I knew what I was doing by using these words. I knew what he was seeing – an upright Amazon, acknowledging his out-of-the-ordinariness. I saw the swell of pride in him, looking more like gratitude than I'd anticipated and that soothed me.

'Come, on, one drink. Let's warm up. I could always drive you home.' He didn't offer his phone then, and I didn't ask.

So we went to The Schooner, to the bar and to the booth where I'd been with Eliot fifteen minutes before (not before Eliot had circled back through the street in his car and glimpsed us together, his face white in the passing windscreen).

So I sipped my glass of Rioja and turned on each of the switches that enabled me to be interesting and interested, charming and charmed, and it was easy with Peter, easier than I wish it had been.

We chatted, we laughed, we drank. I drank more, he just two glasses of wine, probably over the driving limit, but he seemed sober enough to maintain his offer of the lift. But we didn't hurry. I asked him about the scar on his face. He told me he'd got it intervening in a nasty mugging, helping an old lady. I told him I was impressed. He said it was nothing. I told him my newsroom stories and criminal adventures. He claimed to admire my tenacity and unflappable drive.

I'd been flattered by his attention and part of me had wished we weren't sitting in the poky booth again where no one could really see us. Because I wanted the other women in the pub to see the man I'd caught, even if it was just for an hour, even if the one I really wanted had tossed me away.

Naturally I'd spotted Peter's wedding ring right away but I hadn't let it bother me. I didn't ask him if he was married or if he had children. I had no intention of doing anything a wife would disapprove of, well, not too much, and surely a grown man and a woman could have a drink together in a crowded pub? He saw me dismiss the ring, caught my eye as I caught its glow and then rubbed at it with his thumb, but he didn't say anything either.

'Your boyfriend?' he said, with a tip of his head to the street. 'A bit of a tiff, was it? I couldn't help seeing you didn't part on pleasant terms.'

'He's not my boyfriend,' I said. 'He's just . . . We had *a thing*. He's married. It was . . . it's nothing.'

I don't know why I lied. I don't know why I said *it's nothing* in that offhand way, as if I might have been juggling countless, no-strings-attached affairs with married men. I think I just wanted to promote the illusion that we were two people and anything was possible, for it to last a bit longer, until I was drunk and could face going home. Talk of reality, of our other halves and broken hearts, would only have spoiled it.

I probably should've realised he'd taken more meaning from what I'd said, or hadn't said. He'd assessed what kind of girl I was, based on the way he thought *career girls* must be, and he, too, wanted to believe anything was possible. Why else was I drinking wine with him, right? Not asking for his phone to call a cab just yet, and ignoring his wedding ring?

He talked just enough, listened a lot and he really did have the most disturbingly blue eyes. When he put his hand on mine as I reached for the bottle of wine I didn't pull away. When I finally smiled and said it was time for that taxi, he said:

'Reception will be better outside.'

He got up, pulling his coat on and handing me mine. He picked up my scarf and dropped it round my neck, pulling me towards him while he knotted it loosely in the front. He held the knot just a little too long so I had to lean into him for a few seconds before he released me with a grin.

'Come on, reporter extraordinaire, you look like you could do with some air.'

He was right. Once on my feet I felt wobbly. I realised I hadn't eaten anything since lunch and the wine was turning cartwheels in my head and stomach. It was threatening to snow again, out on the street. The sky was light and feathery, the tide on the turn, the loose breakers half a mile out from shore churning the line of black sand and orange-white sky, picking up the lights of the city. Somewhere in the back streets the screeching sound of a snowball fight gleefully split the night.

'Let's walk for a minute,' he said, nodding at my sensible brown lace-up shoes. 'You're dressed for it. Let's go down on the beach for a few minutes. I like the beach when it's dark and quiet. It's peaceful, soothing almost, just the sound of the sea.'

I knew what he meant. Often, when I'd come off a late shift and been unable to sleep, I would leave my flat in town and walk down to the deserted harbour to stare out at the black waves. Occasionally I'd been tempted by the idea of shuffling out into the wide waters, to just keep walking until my feet lost the pull of the soft ground and I floated away. It would have been so peaceful.

That night, with Peter, I had the briefest flash of how bad Eliot would feel if I did it right then, if I just walked into the bay and never came back, stopped fighting and surrendered. He'd know it was all his fault. But of the many things I was, I was not a martyr, nothing so benign.

So I smiled as Peter led me down the deep, snow-capped steps in the sea wall, on to the shingly beach, out of sight of the prom, his hand on my arm, guiding me. I was a bit surprised not to see anyone else huddled furtively down there in the darkness. That end of the beach was a fairly well-known spot for teenage smokers or amorous pairings after chucking-out time. But it was too early for the post-pub fumblers and we had the stretch to ourselves.

The crunch under my feet was nice. The cold air floated up into my head and lungs with the faint memory of fish and chips from footsteps walking above. The town to the east was backlit and orangey. The lights of the iron-boned pier to the west glittered out into the waves. All at once I wished Steve was there, smelling of his leather jacket and Joop aftershave. Steve would put his arm around me, tease me, call me his ice queen and mean it kindly, offering to melt me when we got home. I rubbed my hands together, my teeth stuttering.

'You're cold,' said Peter. He pulled off his leather gloves, gave them to me, and I smiled again because I was being taken care of. I was twelve years old again and my dad, on an 'up' day, was zipping up my coat, pulling up my hood and walking me out on to Langland beach with a crabbing bucket in one hand and a net in the other.

Peter and I walked for a minute or so, down the beach towards one of the old, barnacled wooden groynes dotting the bay. There was no one on the long-railinged prom above but I could hear music spilling from somewhere nearby. I wasn't startled when Peter cupped my face in his hand and said, 'Has anyone ever told you have beautiful eyes – like pieces of arctic ice. So blue.'

'They have, actually,' I grinned.

Then he dipped forward and kissed me. His mouth was warm and I wanted to be warm inside. As he pulled me in to the curve of his body I half-imagined it was Eliot's mouth on mine. I slid my arms around his broad back. His breathing was ragged. Then his hands were unbuttoning and pushing under my coat and he was saying, 'Oh God, I need this,' into my ear.

That's when I realised I didn't.

Chapter Twenty-Eight

'Come on,' he said, pulling at the buttons on my blouse. It was happening faster than I could process, as if I was watching it happening to someone else on a video screen. He slid his hand up my thigh, under my skirt, between my legs, pushing me back hard against the brittle wood of the sloping old groyne. My head reeled, but not so much that I couldn't tell him to get the hell off me as my instinct and outrage suddenly returned.

'What the fuck?' I demanded. To make the point clearer I shoved him back with all my force.

I was expecting him to apologise then, to say he'd got the wrong end of things, or at least shout back and defend himself. I wasn't expecting him to grab me before I'd even caught my breath.

'Come on, no need to play hard to get, sweetheart. I want you,' he said, his hands suddenly manacling my upper arms. 'You've been waiting for this all night.'

And I knew things were veering off script way too fast, and not just because of what he'd said. Hearing what was in his voice and under it, only at that moment was I afraid.

'Peter! Get off me, I said no!'

He twisted me around then, grabbing the back of my neck, hard, without saying anything at all. He was trying to bend me over the groyne. I couldn't break his grip. I always thought I'd kick out and fight if anyone ever tried to lay a hand on me but there didn't seem to have been time for that. I couldn't lash out. I could barely stay on my feet. And I could hear him fumbling with his belt.

Oh God, this is actually happening, I thought, the smell of salt water and seaweed filling my lungs. 'No, don't,' I wheezed, the two least inspired words of my articulate life.

I think it was this more than anything that brought my iron up, cooled my panic and led me to drive my now clenched right fist back, hard, blind, by chance, into the soft sack of his testicles.

'Fuck off!' I yelled, glad to hear the muscle in my voice and an 'oof' of air escaping him.

Somehow the lucky hit made him loosen his grip enough for me to squirm free and twist round. But I was off balance, suddenly staggering forward, twisting my ankle and grazing my knee as it knocked on the pebbles. 'Fucking, motherfucker,' I gasped, taking refuge in pure instinctive profanity, staggering to get back on my feet

'You stupid, filthy bitch,' said Peter as he recovered his balance and his wind. Then, with a blur, his fist connected with my jaw. At least I assumed that's what happened because I saw an explosion of sparks and white swirling snow as my head snapped to the side and I fell backward, twisting, my head hitting the groyne. There was a sharp sliding pain at the base of my back as if I'd been punched in the kidney.

A burst of noise wrapped around us from the prom, somewhere near, yet away, close and above, skipping trip-ping footsteps on the tarmac, laugher, a breaking bottle. I thought I should cry out but I had no breath, just two lung-fuls of red heat and red water as I staggered forward. I put my hand to the back of my head. There was no blood there, but when I put my hand to the back of my coat it came away slick and oily.

I'm ashamed to say it, but for some reason I held out my hand to him then, slick with black. I grabbed at the sleeve of his black mackintosh. He was the last person in the world I wanted to touch, or have touch me, but I didn't want him to leave me on that beach, my head filling with greyness, my legs weak.

'Please,' I said. I think I did, even then hating myself for the word that bore the stink of begging. 'I think, I – something's – I can't . . . '

He slapped my reaching hand away. 'Get off me, you stupid bitch,' he said. Then, he shoved me hard and short in the chest that knocked me backwards off my feet, legs crumpling beneath me once more. For a second he stood over me, looking down from a triumphant height at me, at his feet. Despite my wavering vision the urge to cower passed as I looked up at him. From somewhere within me the ghost of a smile, tainted with scorn, escaped from my clenched teeth

'You spineless bastard,' I said, with as much ire as I could muster, as a fresh burst of hilarity exploded, some-where up on the promenade, what sounded like a drunken cheer. Hearing my words and the faceless laughter around us, Peter's face became a mask of blackness. I wasn't that surprised when he stepped towards me, drew back his arm and punched me again, smack on the side of the face. That one was for Julienne, of course. Both for Julienne and for Eve and his mother and for every woman because they were all the fucking same!

I wonder sometimes what he would have done next, if he would've hit me again, or worse. I've felt it in the moments since, the split second urge that was inside him, to bend down and grab my throat, to squeeze any more words I might speak out of me with the memory of my smile. But suddenly, from above us, came the sound of smashing glass and shouting. It splintered Peter's focus, broke into what I now know to be the hot moments when the door opens and the real Peter strides out. Equally quickly the door snapped shut. He gathered himself, realising how it, how *he*, must look, pulling his coat back into place, smoothing his tie as if he'd just concluded a finance meeting and was ready to leave for the day.

He looked at me then, coat askew, gritted knees, bleeding lip, with something like contempt.

'You're all the fucking same,' he said. Then he turned away and walked off.

And that's where Peter's remembering ended. But not mine.

Time became elastic after he left, unreliable. I think I sat on the sand for a minute or so, my knees refusing to unbuckle enough for me to stand. A half-eaten bag of chips on the pebbles near me released their lingering whiff of oil and vinegar. A plastic bottle without a lid was rocking slightly with each gust of wind. *It's not very clean here,* I thought. *That's a shame.*

It was getting colder, the snow that had begun to fall in the previous few minutes or so, or my eyes, was making everything whiter and dimmer. I kept putting my hand to my back and staring at the black blood sliding across the black gloves. I still had wits enough to be curious about that. *Breaking news – a woman has been seriously assaulted on a Swansea beach!*

Iron-spine girl, I said, over and over, hoping the saying would make it so. At some point I managed to swivel my head and saw above me, about waist height, a four-inch piece of rusted metal sticking out of the old, wooden groyne, a bracket that might once have held part of a jetty or mooring plank. It was slick with blood.

My arms and legs felt slack. After a minute I started looking around for my shoulder bag with my phone in. I spotted it, dropped between the groyne and the barnacled rocks and managed to snag it and pull it towards me. But the phone showed no signal and I dropped it and the bag to the ground. Somehow I got to my feet, started to walk.

Later, I think, I realised, without much interest that the tide was inching in. I croaked for help a few times but time was stretching in and out like an elastic band, my eyes snapping open and dropping shut. I tried to walk back towards the steps but the black on my coat was spreading on to the sand and pebbles behind me in fat splashes. The surf line was getting closer, closer, creeping and whispering. Snow gritted my eyelashes. Then I was sitting again, sand between my fingers.

I held up a hand to keep the snow from my face. I was aware that my nails were in a dreadful state, the neat, home-manicure grimed with sand and blood, the edges raggedy and chipped. Mum would not approve, I thought, and the words *Pretty Princess* bubbled up from the past along with my mother holding my fingers, mini brush poised.

I held my hand up, spread my fingers open against the sky, spanned galaxies with and between them. For a moment the moon winked through the snow clouds and then winked out. The North Star appeared briefly through the flying cloud. I fixed my gaze upon it and the crescent moon curling in and out of view.

I want this not to be happening, I thought. *I want to start over. I want, I want . . .*

And then with a last silent howl at the moon I thought, *I'm not going anywhere, you bastards. I'm staying right here.*

Be careful what you wish for.

High tide was 11.32 p.m.

Peter could never have been sure of what had happened to me that night, after he left me, bruised, bleeding. Though later he must have at least guessed how the end had come. Borne on the back of his dreams on the sofa I heard him asking himself one final time, how it had all happened and why it had happened to him. Why he'd had the bad luck to run into me that night. Not if he'd behaved well or badly, you understand, or if he should feel guilt or remorse about what he'd done. He didn't ask himself that. He didn't ask himself about me, about my pain or confusion, alone and cold, just why and how he'd been in the wrong place at the wrong time for a trouble-making little slut like me to cross his path.

Never in all the fragments I'd gathered out of his mind over the months, when I'd been as close to him as his own bones, had I ever heard a thought that sounded like *I'm sorry*, or even one that bore the abstract weight and colour of regret. All he wanted was to put me away from him and, with it, the worry of what might happen if anyone found out.

But it was far too late by then, to think he could ever be free of it or me. He made his choices, consequences came. Through them I'd found my way into his life and the seashell labyrinths of his ears. I alone, so near the end, could be the one to tell him how to atone.

'It doesn't matter now,' I soothed. 'The waiting is over.'

I'd sworn that night on the beach that I wasn't going anywhere, and I'd meant it. But that didn't mean that Peter wasn't.

'Won't be long, till you're gone, won't be long, till you're gone,' I whispered, sing-songy in the dark, over and over.

I knew it would be better for everyone that way, for me, for Eve. We'd both suffered for loving the wrong men and then for hating them. To the world that watched and watches, women like her, women like me, have polished veneers of perfection. No one sees all the scars and fractures, especially not the men we love. I carried mine inside until I met Eliot, until he told me he'd chosen Bella while Eve had worn hers on her skin. But we weren't so different.

And Adam? Eve was thinking about him as she tossed in her bed above us, while Peter and I were tucked side by side on the sofa like lovers. Her thoughts drifted down to me like snowflakes through the ceiling. *How much of me is in my son and how much of his father? And when will that balance shift and break me in half?*

It won't come to that, I reassured her. *You asked for help and I will give it. I have strength for both of us.*

257

I sent my thoughts up into her head, cold and sharp like the air finally settling in over the house and the world, outside. Deep in the Swansea night the clouds had finally slid away, the transitional thunder quieted and the sky opened into a cold, black drum of November stars.

Lying next to Peter I inhaled him for the last time. I had his scent and mine was all over him. He sniffed in his sleep as if it lingered in his lungs, as I whispered, blade-quiet and precise, into his ear, soft as skin, invisible black smudges where my fingers caressed his cheek. I was silence and scentlessness, I was shadow only, floating through the corners of his vision as I had day after day, in mirrors when his back was turned though he could never turn quickly enough to see me. There was nothing to see after all. No trace of blood and bruises.

But the other forms of violence hung upon us and around us – fingerless, fistless. He and I had perpetrated them all on softer forms than ourselves. I'd used words like shotgun cartridges, primed to explode, released slights so sharp and stinging they pierced the hearts of people like Pretty Polly and Boring Bella. And with 'perhaps' and 'maybe' I'd stuck needles and pins in the reaching hopes of Steve and made him wait. Then, finally I'd slashed at the skin and balled-up restraint of a man, still a boy, but a man who did not reach gently, a man like Peter. Why not use my last words for some good? I'd shuffled us both into our proper places, at last, ready to play my final hand.

It was a long night but when it was over everything was in order. Peter hopped on the train to work, like I told him to, because of the sudden cold snap, the heavy frost, the radio and TV warning of black ice and hazardous driving conditions, renewed snow. Luckily the railway station was only ten minutes' walk from the house and it was fifteen minutes from the end of the line to the council offices. I knew he'd be out of trouble that way, unable to chase around after Eliot for one more day at least, and I needed darkness for what I was about to do. He had to face Julienne and the board that morning but it didn't matter. Either way, whatever the outcome of that meeting, he wouldn't be showing up for work on Monday.

Chapter Twenty-Nine

It was an uneventful day at Rosemary Close after Peter left for work. The schools shut at lunchtime because of the thickening snow flurries so Eve walked the mile and collected Adam at 1 p.m. We all slipped and slid home together, along the frosted pavements, over glassy, frozen puddles, Adam and Eve in their sensible outdoor boots. Once home they had hot chocolate for a treat and played Transformer battles for a bit under the dining room table.

At 5 p.m. Eve was not worried about where Peter was. She'd been glad to see him leave that morning, more than glad to hear him say he might be late and he'd let her know later about dinner. She was grateful for the few hours of extra peace, grateful that he'd rung her at 4 p.m. to say not to wait but to eat without him, if a little surprised to hear him say goodbye so solemnly and softly, it felt like an almost forgotten kiss.

To Eve's surprise, though he'd obviously been preoccupied with the meeting with Julienne, Peter hadn't taken all his keys to work with him as usual. The little bunch was left on the bedroom dresser by the photo of his father. It included the one for the TV cabinet so Eve and I spent a pleasant few hours together watching afternoon game shows while Adam played in his room with Thomas the Tank Engine.

Fortunately Eve's mum was feeling a bit better that afternoon. She'd put down the phone after speaking to Nora, relieved and pleased that her cold seemed to be breaking, promising to find a way to pop by soon.

By the time it was dark she and Adam had eaten some beans on toast and ice-cream and we'd settled in to watch an old black-and-white melodrama together, *The Wicked Lady* in which the fabulous Margaret Lockwood plays a buxom and scheming highwaywoman. I'd watched it once, with my dad, both of us marvelling at Margaret's dastardly plotting. Eve sketched as we watched, versions of Margaret, black-hearted and beautiful, astride her horse, masked, hair flying, pistol in hand.

For a while it felt as if Eve and I were girlfriends, watching a chick flick, eating biscuits (well, she was), giggling about *men, the bastards,* with a laugh. I had a glimpse of how our future might unfold and, you know, it actually didn't seem so bad.

'I'm going to do something great for you, now,' I said, when the time was exactly right. When the hour had come. 'That's what friends do, isn't it? I won't tell you what it is. Wait and see. It's a surprise. I think you'll like it.'

Then I slipped out for just twenty minutes.

I was pleased with myself when I returned, doubly pleased to find Eve still sitting on the settee, oblivious to where I'd been and why. A surge of satisfaction warmed me as I settled back down on the sofa, smiling to myself, glad to be in out of the wind-whipped night to the place I was beginning to think of as home. I was glad that everything was settled at last. I was finished with it all.

Cue exit credits. Lights up.

But everything was finished with me, it seemed. There was one last surprise waiting when Eve put down her drawing pad and switched on the news at six. My face appeared on screen again, smiling and happy. Then there was Polly and Inspector Murphy. At first it seemed they were just recapping the stuff about the 'scarred man', repeating the police appeal, with Polly reiterating that Eliot Masters had been arrested but released on police bail.

Then Polly asked, 'So, Inspector, are there any new developments you can share with us in the Black case?'

That's when Murphy came out with a small revelation, a thumbnail sized one, or perhaps not even that, but still a great bit of breaking news:

'Yes, Polly,' said the Inspector. 'We can now confirm that Miss Black was pregnant at the time she was killed.'

Polly nodded sorrowfully, though not surprised. It had obviously been a set-up and she'd known what he was going to say. Eve's mouth fell open though, mine did, too. *How odd*, I thought. *Why on earth would he say something like that?*

We both gaped at the screen.

'Pregnant?' Eve said.

'Pregnant?' I echoed. 'Really? Are you sure?' as Polly continued to nod, gravely.

As if reading my thoughts, the DI said, 'Yes, Polly, Miss Black seems to have been only a few weeks into her pregnancy. Indeed, she may not have been aware of the fact herself, but it makes this case doubly tragic. That's why we are once more urging anyone with any information to come forward, so we can do our jobs and bring the killer of Miss Black and her unborn child to justice.'

I have to say I was impressed by the Inspector's dignified plea to camera. The use of the phrase 'unborn child' was suitably emotive, despite the fact he was referring to something that had been no more than a cluster of cells. It was definitely a strategic decision on the part of the police, choosing to release the news so far down the line. Even Polly and her unknown sources must have missed it earlier. Unless she'd been promised an exclusive if she'd kept it under wraps for a while. Either way it was the final bit of tear-jerking information the police had left, to try and lever out more witnesses, to prick people's consciences.

The CID must have been sure that someone, somewhere knew something, but they were obviously reaching the end of their viable investigations, time to really make their case with this final calculated tug on the heartstrings, to elicit any guilty secrets and confessions from a silent party, perhaps, someone protecting a friend, a relative, a lover. There's no better conscience-kicking headline than a *dead baby* – a would-have-been, almost-was, will-never-be, dead baby. Kids and babies – best news hooks in the world. Better even than dogs and dolphins. Applause, once more, for Polly.

I looked down and ran my hand across the flat, empty drum of my belly, beneath my skirt band. I tried to imagine a knot of cells in there, clumped together in the dark, once carrying their own spark of life, no more than a pinprick of light, for perhaps four or five weeks at most. It couldn't have been much more than that or I would certainly have known, the date ringed in my diary would have alerted me. It couldn't be true ... even hearing the words and saying them surely couldn't make it so this time. Yet ...

I knew it must have been Eliot's baby. Me and Steve hadn't, *you know*, for about six weeks at least. At least I didn't think we had, it's not as if I'd been counting, but it'd only been now and again, when time permitted. It had been more often with Eliot and I'd been careful, but not careful enough, apparently. Maybe it had been the time in my flat, while Steve had been in Aberystwyth and I'd been taking my pill at weird times because of the double shifts on the tyre fire disaster. That had been the last time we'd really been alone, as it had turned out.

It was a strange sensation, knowing I had incubated a life, even for a short time and knowing that I probably wouldn't have kept it, *the baby*, if things had not happened the way they did. Well, you can't have it all, can you? Despite what the women's magazines preach you can't raise a baby in London and work in a twenty-four-hour newsroom, not until you've made a name for yourself, not while you're still pulling yourself upwards clinging with fingers and toes in every horizontal crack.

But still, it would've been nice to have had the choice. And it would've been a strange dilemma for me and for Eliot to face together. Who knows what he would have said, under the circumstances? He hadn't planned for one more child, then suddenly there might have been two – not so easy to *do the right thing* then.

I realised at that moment that nine months had passed since that night. The imagined baby could've been a real live and inescapable one, if I'd only gone straight home from The

Schooner. For just that moment I felt its absence as a silent scream.

But there was nothing to do except sit there, staring at the TV with Eve, as the DI continued his appeal. He was holding up a sketch of what looked like my necklace, drawn in black and white pen, pretty much the exact shape and design, give or take the odd swirl – my round locket, the one Eliot had given me, the filigree workings on the edge, the four small stones. Distinctive.

'This was Miss Black's locket, Polly,' the Inspector was saying. 'We have reason to believe she was wearing it the night she disappeared. From our extensive enquiries the locket was not found on her body, at her apartment or anywhere else. Of course, we do not yet know for certain where Miss Black died. If anyone found such a locket in a particular location, or thinks they have seen such a locket being worn by someone we would *really* like to hear from them.'

While I was staring at the screen, down at my stomach, then back at the picture of my locket in the Inspector's hand, I'd stopped looking at Eve, but when the report ended I could see that something complex had formed on her face. It was a look I was unused to. At some point over the past few minutes she'd opened her sketchpad to the drawing of the woman she'd sketched the day of Adam's school trip, back in June. She'd finished it sometime since, drawn in blade-straight hair with charcoal sweeps, completed the aquiline nose. It was now clearly a drawing of me, wearing my locket.

That's when it happened, when I saw into the last closed kernel of Eve's head. It was the final barrier, the one I hadn't been able to crack open that night in her bed, when I'd tried to whisper the truth to her, the truth she'd been keeping separate from herself. Staring at what she'd drawn on the page the final tile of the mosaic fell into place. She got up and went to her sewing box in the bottom of the living room sideboard, the one that contained things for making dress-up costumes, full of discarded Aladdin-outfit scraps and bits of thread. She brought the box back to the sofa and opened the lid. Fishing into the bottom she pulled out a little fold of Soft Peter's turban fabric, opening it to reveal something golden inside.

It was my locket. It was impossible that it was anything else. It was one of a kind, vintage, old gold, Victorian looking, four small red stones. A pretty gift for a pretty girl, with small feet, full of ready giggles. Out of habit I reached up and felt for it under my scarlet scarf, expecting to feel the chain wound at my neck as ever, but even as I did so I knew it wasn't there anymore. Only the memory of it still nestled in the notch at my throat, because I knew what had happened that night on the beach.

I knew what had happened when Eve had walked towards me.

Chapter Thirty

'What were you doing?' she'd demanded, as I tried to walk along the beach, clutching my hand to my back. Despite the state I was in, I'd been surprised at her tone of voice, at the anger in it. I was almost amused to hear such a demand coming from this slummy mummy, barrelling along the beach towards me, wearing a stupid green woolly hat and the collar of her coat up as if she was in disguise.

Her car keys were in her hand, as if she'd just pulled up on the prom, jumped straight out and down the steps to ask me this very impertinent question. It was only a minute or so after Peter strode away from me, at least I think it was. I can't be sure because of the wooziness and the bleeding. I hadn't known who she was or why she thought it was perfectly acceptable to march up and interrogate me.

She didn't seem interested in my dishevelled state, standing as best I could, canted against one of the big rocks for support. Her breath was high in her chest, pumping in and out like a piston.

'What were you doing down here, with him?' she repeated.

She raked me up and down with her eyes, my suit, my

coat, but didn't seem to register my reddened jaw, only my ruffled blouse with the button missing, my laboured breath, my flushed cheeks. She'd already drawn her own conclusions about our late-night activity on the darkened strip of beach.

'That man, who just left? How do you know him? What were you doing with him? With Peter Albright.'

She was shaking.

Part of me, the part detached from the dizziness and pain, bridled and crackled. Part of me wanted to say *mind your own business you silly bitch and call me an ambulance because I think I need one*. But her voice sounded far away and somehow it all seemed like too much effort.

'Who knows?' I said, after a long pause. 'What does it matter?'

Everything was tumbling round in my head, the back of my skull pounding. Pain shot through my kidneys and I feared I might vomit. My words came out in the wrong order, edited badly, mixed clips and sound bites from a story that was longer and more complicated than anyone could imagine, one that had started maybe weeks or months ago, before the words 'Bella's pregnant' were spoken, and long, long before that.

'They're all the same, aren't they?' I said. 'Men. Bastards. A quick fumble or two, a bit of fun, then they dump you . . . because even though you're *marvellous* and *majestic* and *beautiful* they love their boring old wives, really. Because it's a mistake, it's just a fuck in the end and their wives are such great homemakers and the mothers of their beloved sons.'

The words, not really meant for her, slid into her as smoothly as the iron paling spike had gone into my flesh not long before. They became part of her understanding of herself and she didn't like the revelation. Then something else dawned in her eyes. 'Wait, I know you. I know you. Don't I know you?' she muttered.

'Maybe. I'm on the telly,' I said. 'Melanie, from the news.'

'And you're having an affair?' asked Eve. 'You're his ... mistress.'

The accusation sounded ridiculous, antiquated, as if I'd entertained Eliot at a London townhouse, serving Martinis while wearing a pink negligee. I chuckled, I think, or maybe it was a gasp.

'Sure, if you like, that's as good a word as any, sweetie. It was love though. It had to be. As if that bland and boring homemaker could really have her hooks in him, with her Chanel No 5 and her fucking *baking*.' I sneered at the memory of Bella's *signature treats*, 'as if he could love that stupid, fucking cunt.'

Eve's face became solid then, well the two floating halves of it I could see did, because the snow seemed thicker than ever, almost a whiteout.

'Don't you say that! Don't say that, you bloody whore,' she screeched.

'Yeah, that's me, evidently.' I was holding the small of my back with one hand. 'I'm the whore, the home wrecker, the other woman. That's me. Pleased to meet you.'

I felt short of breath. I reached up to try and detangle the chain at my neck, catching it in the threads of my scarf, to get some oxygen. 'Look, do you have a phone? Do you think you could get me a taxi? I really need ...'

'Did he give you that?' asked Eve in a voice that sounded as if she was the one being half-strangled or was speaking through a sewn-up mouth.

She pointed at the chain as it broke between my fingers. It was not robust, flimsy, really, a bit like Eliot and me as it turned out. It slipped from my grasp and slithered to the sand.

Eve bent down and picked it up. I waited for her to hand it back.

'Yes, indeed, though, come to think of it I suspect he actually bought it for her.' Because it occurred to me then, in a moment of mixed clarity, how well it would have suited bright and breezy Bella. Her feet were small and on the day Eliot had given it to me on the Langland cliffs, I'd rifled it from his pocket. 'It was probably meant for her birthday,' I sighed.

The look on Eve's face was a mixture of avarice and fury.

'Poor stupid cow,' I said, with a soft half laugh. I meant myself.

'You stupid bitch,' she muttered, her eyes glassing over, then, 'You stupid cow.' I realise now she was talking about herself.

A sound came out of her throat like nothing I've ever heard from a human. It was too dark, too deep, too impotent. She whirled around and stumbled away, back across the sand, clutching my chain.

And that was that, the last clip of video tape popped up and replayed in my mind as Eve held my gold chain, the one she thought Peter had bought for her and given to me, as she held it in her hand in front of the TV. Stunned, on the sofa, I started to wonder if it wasn't all a joke, if I wasn't being toyed with by something, or someone with a nasty taste in pranks. Why else was it taunting me by changing people's faces, and therefore the parameters, once again, just to watch

270

me squirm. As a player of games I knew sharp practice when I saw it but what could I do except keep watching, watch what happened next from inside Eve's head, as the TV news ended and the weather report came on.

In Eve's memory of that night, after she left me, she was stumbling away up the beach, running like she was on a deadline countdown, looking at her watch. I saw how, in the hour before our meeting, she'd visited her mum, sneaked out to Mumbles because of the pneumonia, because the doctor had come that morning and she'd been afraid Mum would take a turn for the worse. She'd known Peter would be at the council event at the other end of town, in The Gowerton Hotel, until ten at least so it was probably as safe as it would ever be.

He'd never have agreed to her seeing Mum, or not easily anyway, not without him being there too and rubbing it in, how he was trying to save her from a similar fate by looking after her interests and all that sanctimonious bullshit.

So she'd rung Mair, bright and breezy as could be, persuaded her to come over for an hour, to look after Adam while he slept. She'd borrowed Mair's car, pleading low petrol, that way there'd be no need to explain the extra mileage when Peter did his check with his bloody blue book.

Mum hadn't been too bad as it turned out, and had eaten some soup and bread and kept it down. Nora'd said the bout was breaking. Eve had hoped to be back in her own house, without Peter ever knowing she'd left, but driving home along the prom, because of the road works on the coast road and the promised snow, Eve had spotted something inexplicable. She'd seen Peter's people carrier parked near The Rose and Crown, not far from The Schooner.

271

In all the years they'd been married she'd never quite been able to convince herself that Peter didn't lie to her about where he went after work. She'd never been truly certain he was at the gym, like he said he was, or was putting in overtime on reports in the office. She knew only too well the way women looked at him, women who didn't know him. So she wasn't sure if she was surprised or vindicated when she'd swung the car back towards the pub to investigate, saw him walking down the steps to the beach with me.

At first she'd been gripped by panic, terrified of being spotted, caught breaking his rules, before she'd realised how absurd that sounded. *She* was afraid of *him* spotting her, when he was the one stepping on to the beach with some tart.

She'd pulled into the bus stop and watched us walking, arm in arm, Peter leaning in close, me wearing his gloves, the special gloves she'd given him for their anniversary, so friendly, so intimate. Looking at them, at the £100 hand-stitched, black calfskin gloves, something had torn open inside her. In a flash she saw herself creeping around like a spy, living every day with Peter's bloody rules and regulations and still smiling, with his expectations of what a perfect fucking family should be because it was best for her and best for Adam. After all his sanctimonious crap about being a good father and provider and head of their fucking perfect family, was he screwing that tart?

She'd crept out of the car, her heart striking out the seconds in her chest as she crouched in the grey slush by the salt bin, watching us walk down the shingle, losing line of sight when we went behind the rocks and groynes but unable to

272

move, frozen, furious. Clenching her fists she'd wished for the courage to tear down on to the sand and confront us, curses spitting from her mouth like rifle fire. But she took so long to find the spark that, before she could act, Peter was striding up the steps to the prom once more, brushing off his clothes, getting into his car.

She was afraid then, of what he might say, might do, if he got home before her. She should have jumped in her car, got ahead of him through the back streets. But instead, seven years of shoe regulation and pot roasts and boiled eggs and loose leaf tea created a whirlwind in her brain. Without any idea of what she was going to say or do her feet were hitting the steps. She had to find out the truth. Once she knew who I was she'd finally have the ammunition she needed to shoot Peter down in the flames of his own flagrant betrayal, topple him from his self-made pedestal.

I saw all this in her head, as we sat on the sofa together, how her moment of hot courage had burned so brightly, her righteous sword drawn, then how it had ebbed away at the sight of me, at what I had said to her, at the words, 'Maybe. I'm on the telly.' Whatever she'd been expecting she'd thought her competition would be an ordinary woman, not a real life TV news personality, such as that was.

I didn't know you were dying, she was saying to the TV then, in her head and out, to me, to my picture on the screen, angelic and soft-focused. 'I didn't know he'd hurt you so much. I mean, I saw your mouth. I knew he'd hit you, or you'd had a fight. But I didn't know he'd really hurt you. Or I did know and I just didn't care. Better you than me, I guess. I don't know. I'm sorry. I'm so sorry, Melanie. I should have helped you.'

That was the first time I'd heard her speak my name. As she said it I knew it had never crossed her mind that I wouldn't leave that beach. She hadn't seen how I'd really needed help. She couldn't see the wound in my back. She had never turned around to see me fall again and fail to get up. She'd had one thought only, to get home before Peter found Mair in the kitchen eating his lemon cake.

She'd had no real idea of what she was going to do when she got there, whether or not to confront Peter right away. As her anger cooled she'd realised she needed to be cleverer than that, to be smart and rational and make a plan. Peter's infidelity would give her a door to the outside world as long as she was organised. She could get a private investigator maybe, and legal advice, evidence of adultery to support a divorce.

The moment she got home she'd been relieved to see that Peter's car was not in the drive after all, that he wasn't standing, thunder-browed, in the hall demanding explanations. She hadn't needed to use the excuse she'd concocted on the way, that Mum had been taken into hospital and had needed a lift home. She had a little more time to think so she wound in and tied off for the time being, sent Mair home with profuse thanks. Then she tossed her sandy trainers under the stairs and rearranged her face into its usual greeting just in time for the sound of Peter's key in the door.

The next morning, the morning I'd arrived, she'd made her usual perfect breakfast. She'd seen Peter off to work then cleaned off her trainers, gummed with some sticky black stuff from the beach, while she started working out her plan of escape.

It wasn't until she'd heard the missing person's report on the news a few days later that it had become clear to her.

Something worse than she'd first imagined had started on the beach that night and Peter had been at the heart of it. He obviously hadn't hurried home after he'd got in his car. She realised that he could've gone back to the beach, restarted the argument with me, or followed me home and . . . things could have got out of control. She knew only too well how that could happen.

How could she come forward then, without revealing to Peter that she'd been there, too, and knew his secret? What might he do if cornered or accused of something worse than adultery? Would the police believe her word over his, with her history?

She'd started to hedge her bets a little then. It was a good job she hadn't had a chance to take that mackintosh of his to the cleaner's. That black stain on his coat sleeve suddenly assumed a new significance. She went through his pockets and kept the receipts from The Schooner she'd found there, in case she needed them.

She was more afraid of Peter after that, but she was also afraid for herself, that someone would find out she'd been on the beach too and hadn't helped me. That made her culpable, didn't it? What if she confronted Peter, or told the police and he turned the tables on her? He'd do that, to save his reputation, to make sure she didn't take Adam away from him.

I saw it all in her head, clear as a cinema screen, with sound and fear and all the frantic moments of panic she'd somehow balled up and packed away deep inside her in the months since. No wonder she'd resisted my attempts to show her what Peter had done that night, when I'd whispered to her. She hadn't wanted to go back there, to relive it, to acknowledge that Peter might have killed me and that she might've been part of it.

And I hadn't seen it, not in all the time I'd spent with her. I'd never stumbled across the last thing she'd been guarding, for the sake of her own self-preservation. She had wonderfully wrong-footed me, kept me in the dark.

'I'm sorry, I'm sorry, I'm so sorry,' said both Eves' voices, once more.

Then she got up, returned the necklace to its place of safety, switched off the news and got ready for Peter's eventual return.

The kitchen radio warned the South Wales world of another crisp and treacherous frost, snow on the way that night to add to the black ice, of roads becoming gridlocked from skids and prangs and train delays on the Swansea south line, following an incident on the track, but she wasn't listening. She was getting a cake out of the oven, letting great tears plop from her eyes, the words, *a baby, a baby*, humming on a loop in her head.

I cried then, too, for the first time in a long time, perhaps ever. After what I'd just done for her, what I'd just given her, this last truth was the hardest thing to swallow. She'd had a chance to help me but she'd walked away. Even if she hadn't understood what was in motion she could have stayed on the beach and acted differently. And since then, she hadn't come forward, not even when she'd seen Mum and Steve, blanched and broken on the news. She'd watched my life become the subject of scrutiny and speculation. She'd watched Eliot get arrested and all the while she'd kept on boiling Peter's eggs and baking him cakes. I didn't know if I could let her get away with that.

After a while I left her. I went upstairs to Adam's room and found him, as I'd expected, cross-legged on his bedroom floor bent over his Transformers. From the way their heads were together, whispering, it was clear that the Decepticons were hatching another devious plot of some kind.

'No, no, you are very bad robots,' boomed Adam, in a theatrical villain voice. 'You must pay for your bad ways!'

I sat down beside him, watching his little-boy fingers manipulating the toy, revealing the robot in its disguise. Children's fingers are surely miracles, aren't they, the little knuckles, the perfect nails? I laced my own fingers over my empty belly. After a while I started to sing.

Chapter Thirty-One

It was the end of October when the police officially declared Eliot no longer a suspect. It had taken a few weeks, for the effects of my work to trickle down, but I knew it would happen eventually. It was the only outcome possible once everything had been weighed and revisited in the light of events and the new information that surfaced. In the months that had passed I'd learned nothing if not patience, so I watched the news each day and waited, until Polly appeared with a statement, first as ever to break the news.

The press release had no doubt been received with professional relief by Bron. Though I imagine the rest of the newsroom crew had felt a twinge of regret, that the most promising story in their midst had ended with such an unsatisfying conclusion. Polly, in particular, must have been hoping for a nice, TV-friendly show-trial, lasting several weeks to seal the deal on her future London appointment, but *them's the breaks*, as Eliot used to say. I knew she'd find something else to occupy her pretty head soon enough. The next murder or scandal is never more than a few weeks away

from a newsroom door and Polly was appearing on the BBC
London network by February, so it hardly mattered.

Eve did it. She got Eliot off the hook. I helped her prepare
what she needed to say, of course. I told her pointedly and
clearly in the plainest language and this time my truths
took easy root, perhaps because, by then, there was nothing
left to hide. Inspector Murphy wasn't very happy about it
though. He made that clear when he interviewed her at the
house, drinking her tea but not touching the lemon cake she
offered. But she didn't flinch before his gaze. It seemed she
was actually starting to grow something of an iron spine.

It was so hard, you see, she told him, to make people
understand why she'd waited so long to come forward, to
explain what she'd suspected for a long time. At intervals
she dabbed her eyes with a paper tissue and added a sniff or
two for good measure.

She didn't watch TV that much, she explained. She vaguely
knew that Melanie Black, the reporter, had gone missing but
it wasn't until much later that she'd recognised the description
of the scarred man, of Peter, her husband, on the TV appeal.

She remembered how he'd been out so late, come home in
such an agitated state and wouldn't say why, but she hadn't
wanted to believe he could have been involved in anything
like that.

It was only later, when she'd remembered his coat, the
mackintosh she was supposed to have taken to the dry-
cleaner's she started to get really afraid. She'd forgotten
the coat was in the laundry room with some sports kit, the
receipts for The Schooner still in the pocket. And there was
that stain on the sleeve – so much like a blood stain. She'd
meant to call the incident room then, she really had. She'd

been trying to pluck up the courage. But Peter didn't let her have a phone, except for emergencies and he wouldn't let anyone call at the house. And, well, he could be aggressive, if he didn't have things the way he liked them. You understand what I mean, Inspector.

She was wearing her pink, short-sleeved shirt, as I'd told her to. Her fingers scratched absently at the cigarette butt-sized scar on the soft flesh of her inner arm. The Inspector's eyes fell upon it for a few seconds and his mouth tightened.

Eve gave a weak, pink smile.

Then, well . . . she continued, just as she was finally plucking up the courage to call the number and share her suspicions, it was too late. Peter . . . well, she got the call from the police after waiting for him to come home all night. Later when she'd sorted through his things, she'd found the gold locket, shoved in a drawer in his study, the old-fashioned one she'd seen on the news appeal. Melanie Black's necklace.

Peter had been prone to affairs, she admitted. Melanie Black wasn't the first. When she'd heard how that poor girl had been pregnant with his baby . . .

'That's actually not the case, Mrs Albright,' said Inspector Murphy, speaking finally, giving a professional smile fostered over years of listening to the sad stories of victims of domestic abuse.

'We've no reason to believe he was the father of her baby. In fact there's nothing to suggest he and Miss Black knew each other at all, or had even been having an affair. It's very odd really. It might just have been a case of wrong place, wrong time. We'll probably never really know what happened between them and why.'

So that was that. The police couldn't be certain that Peter was their murderer; the locket wasn't exactly a blood-caked murder weapon; a receipt for The Schooner wasn't exactly a smoking gun either; but Eve was able to confirm that the glove they'd found on Miss Black looked very much like the one she'd bought Peter for his birthday, from Frederick's Men's Retailers, though the one that would have borne his initials stitched inside the wrist was missing.

Circumstantially the CID had their culprit, their *stranger full of danger* off the streets, a man with a history of domestic abuse, the victim's blood on his sleeve, and, of course, Eliot Masters's identification of him in the photo. Eve provided it on request and collaboration was given by The Schooner barmaid, who confirmed that he was the man I'd left with.

The case technically remains open but what more is there to add?

Conclusion reached, sum up, sign off. End of story. Black screen.

Except that's not the case in real life, is it? Something always continues, even after the lights go out and the end credits roll. I'm proof of that, though not living proof exactly. So, all the players in my piece continue in their roles. I should know, I've been keeping an eye on them over the past few months. After Inspector Murphy left us for that last time, and everything began to settle down, I made a particular effort to get out of the house more, to try and be more independent. I wanted to test a theory I had developed about no longer needing a chaperone to leave Rosemary Close.

Sure enough, it was evident immediately that my travelling skills were greatly improved. I had to concentrate hard at first, to step away from the security of Eve and Adam, and the old familiar paths we'd worn together over the months, but before long I found there was no more sickness, no more weakness waiting for me at the front door if I ventured past the step alone. I think it comes down to determination really, to wanting it enough, now that I'm free to really focus on something other than Peter.

These days just thinking very hard about a place or person I know seems to be enough to place me at their side, whenever I wish. It's nice to be independent – to be able to drop in and see a few old friends. Who knows now, where my new boundaries might lie, if I just keep practising?

In the long run, perhaps I can explore much further. It's all a learning curve, isn't it? We come into our lives innocent and incapable, then spend years learning how we fit into our space with others, inside this crazy and alarming world. I'm still a child in this new life, there must be so many new things to discover and understand I haven't even imagined yet. My potential may be boundless.

For now, though, I've stayed close to home. I paid Steve a visit, at his flat, a few weeks ago and discovered he's met a girl. She was there, making cheese on toast in the kitchen, a pretty thing with curly red hair and a tattoo of a rose on her shoulder. She works for some environmental charity and he's moving her into his place. He hasn't actually asked her yet but it's more than an idle thought. I could hear it in his head. He thinks it's too soon, though. He misses me, he really does. I could feel it, something cold and sinking in his stomach, and that was nice. It's the sort of mourning I would expect as my due, for a little while at least.

I was able to go to Eliot's house, too, to see him with the

new baby. The boy, tucked into the nook of Bella's arm, was a cute little thing, dark black eyes and hair, more like his mum than his dad. I sat with her for a while as she fed him and Eliot made supper. I traced my fingers over the soft plates of the baby's skull, you know, the ones that don't fuse for a few months but stay soft and bruise-able. He cried when I touched him, a little mewling sound. Then I touched my own belly, feeling for what had been inside it once. I wondered if Eliot ever thinks of it when he touches baby Josh's head.

I didn't stay there long. The constant crying was annoying to be honest, even when you're, *you know* . . . and technically without ears, and I didn't really want to see the two of them smiling wistfully at each other all the time. Some part of me still loves Eliot, but it makes me more than a little angry that he clearly has no room left for my memory now. Bella is squashed up in there with the baby and Kyle and not even a little space for Melly? How can that be? Especially when I'm not all that far away? Just a hair's breadth, a heartbeat, a sound on the tip of his tongue, a glance over his shoulder. A shadow in the mirror. A voice in another room.

Perhaps he needs to know that I'm still here . . . I'm sure I can think of ways to make him understand.

And finally, Peter.

I know you're wondering what happened to Mr Perfect, as you rightly should. I've cheated a bit, haven't I? I've delayed the conclusion, changed the genre at the last minute because this isn't really a news story any more. It's an autobiographical note, a reminiscence, a memoir, or perhaps an urban myth. It's something to be retold and whispered on a thunderous winter night, when the curtains are pulled tight and the wind whips its wings through the dark and brittle night outside. It's a cautionary tale and, as such, isn't subject to the constraints of form and structure, just as I am not.

But every tale needs a conclusion.

Chapter Thirty-Two

When I last saw Peter it was 5.54 p.m. precisely. He was standing on the edge of the frosted tarmac, in his coat, carrying his briefcase, both his feet balanced calmly on the edge of the slippery strip of red paint.

I was with him, speaking quietly.

I was saying, 'Peter Albright, your throat is tight. Peter Albright, your head is light. Peter Albright, your head's not right. Not now, not ever. Albright by name but not by nature.

'Peter Piper, your peck is pickled. Feel my fingers tickle, tickle.

'Night, night, Mr Albright.'

I was smiling.

It was much easier than I'd thought it would be. He was already half way towards the point of no return by then, after that morning's meeting with Julienne, knowing he was being set up to be moved out, to take a fall. More than once that day he'd envisioned the outcome where he'd be forced to slink off and vacate his special parking space in disgrace, accepting a quiet payoff because the alternative was worse – a public tribunal, accusations and recriminations, suggestions of fraud, embezzlement, a nervous breakdown. Backstabbing and arse-covering. The newspapers. The TV, too, probably. The photos and the talk. He couldn't bear that. Not Perfect Peter. Not for one millisecond.

All the while Peter had known Eliot was out there, in his cottage on the coast, with his face in his head, the picture of the scarred man getting a little keener every day perhaps, until one day he would pop up in blazing digital colour and pixels followed by a knock on the door. And Peter knew there was a DC from Inspector Murphy's incident room team waiting to talk to him about the gloves, as soon as possible, (the black leather gloves, a murderer's mark if ever there was one) because Officer McCartney had left a message on his office phone that very morning because he hadn't been able to find a landline number for his house. Peter had deleted it but he'd known there'd be a call back.

So, by teatime that day, Peter's head was already wonderfully full of fear, barbed and prickling and spreading. He no longer had any resistance in the quiet night where there were no more interruptions and in the perfect place.

What was it that finally broke him?

'What would your mother say, Peter Perfect?' I asked, 'What would she think of her son now? What a failure. Oh the humiliation. How weak and snivelling you are – just like your father. If you were a real man you'd do it. You'd end it here and now. Save us the embarrassment.' I heard old Edith's voice, then, or thought I did, as if she were standing there with us, as did Peter. I might have imagined it of course. The dead continue to talk to us all, don't they, long after they've departed in one way or another? We're used to it. At that last moment, as I pulled back to let the inevitable happen, did I see the air on Peter's other shoulder shiver, tremble slightly?

Either way Peter no longer had any resistance left, not in the perfect place I'd chosen. We all know how important setting is.

At first I'd thought about taking him back to the beach to do it, of making him long for the cold suck of the water, the washing of the waves. I could have encouraged him to take off his clothes, put them in a neat pile and walk into the quiet, black sea that would open its arms and its memory for him. Maybe I would've held his hand as he stepped from the shore, drawn him in, shoeless, across the shingle as the waves closed in, higher and higher, knees, waist, chest, until they crept up to his mouth and nose and I led him into the halls of the dead.

'Breathe,' I could have said. 'One last breath, then under the waves, to sleep with the fishes.' There would've been a certain poetic justice in that – a nice sense of dramatic symmetry – but I decided it would have been risky. What if someone had intervened, someone immune to my whispers, someone who thought they were merely the hushings of wind on water? They might have broken his concentration and mine, pulled him from the shallows, breath smoking, trousers slopping on the shingle. Or, he might have drifted away across the channel like I had, lost in recriminations and appeals, for days and days. I hadn't wanted to give him that, the status, the importance, the quality of a tragic accident or unexplained enigma. That wouldn't have been a neat conclusion to my final piece. Simple and quick was best.

There was only one set of footsteps in the hard, crisp snow at the end of the railway platform, when I slipped away into the newly whitened streets, away from Eve and the TV for such a short time. Peter liked railway stations. Even with the modern diesel and the grime they brought back a child's memory, like the photo on the bedroom dresser, of a rush of steam and clanking, of a small hand in a large one. It seemed only proper to use this liking for my own ends.

The last words went in the most easily. 'Peter gonna cry? You know what they say about spilled milk, boy? You lost this game, you couldn't step up – it's time to step off, literally.' So he did.

Afterwards, when the police came, there was only one conclusion to draw; no one could have influenced him or issued instructions. If you'd been watching the CCTV at the exact moment you might have asked yourself what that man with the briefcase could be looking for exactly, walking right out to the edge like that, eyes fixed on the platform between his feet, slowly, methodically, glancing up the track to see in the distance the watery yellow eyes of the approaching train.

What caused him to stand like that? At the last minute to raise his hand to his forehead as if someone was sticking something sharp and cold right between his eyes? Was that wince anything to do with why he made a half-turn and then stepped off the platform into the air?

If you'd looked closely, if you'd known how to look, you might have seen a slight shimmer, something like interference around him, but that must have been distortion on the tape. He didn't slip, that was obvious, despite the frost and the possible black ice that everyone had been warned about. He just stepped off, casually, effortlessly like stepping into a swimming pool.

5.55 p.m. Thomas the Tank Engine is coming into the station. All aboard!

If you'd been close enough you would have heard the silence first, then felt the rush of warmth from the non-stop express meeting the warmth of his last breath. You'd have seen the bright scarlet splashing on to the pristine furring of snow as he impacted with the front of the engine. In the screeching, steaming aftermath of brakes and blood there were no screams. The platform was empty, save for that single lonely set of tracks and the graffiti-art splashes of red on white.

Peter's eyes were open for a second, as he lay crumpled at the side of the track, knocked over to the fence rail. I was beside him, looking into those black pools that were winking with final knowledge. I couldn't help myself. I had to ask:

'Do you see me, Peter? Do you see me, now? Do you hear me? Do you understand?'

I think he did. He blinked, though that might have been a reflex. He couldn't answer anyway because his lungs were full of blood . . .

Then I walked away, just as he had.

As it happened Peter hadn't ventured onwards into that icy night on his own. Two other people died in car accidents and there was one other suicide on that night during the unexpected, early start of winter, when the country became Blizzard Britain and other colourful clichés were coined and overused by the media. Gardens and houses, schools and supermarkets bowed before the debt and inflation of Credit Crunch Britain. On the coldest, sharpest November night for twenty-five years, families slept on obliviously while news reporters scrambled through studios and newsrooms to cut their footage into final nightly bulletins before the all-important weather slot.

Outlook? Forecast brightening. Fade music up, roll credits.

Chapter Thirty-Three

I honestly thought I'd be gone by now, now that all the loose ends have been gathered in and tied up; boxed away in the archive with the rest of yesterday's news. I was sure this predicament of mine would turn out to be one of those closure issues after all, that as soon as I'd meted out justice, punished the guilty and made peace with being plucked from this earthly realm in so untimely a fashion, my business here would be concluded.

I'd half-hoped for the appearance of a hazy light in the living room wall, seeping choral music and rustling sounds I'd feel compelled to enter, as a deep, resonant voice proclaimed, 'Come, Melanie, your work here is done.'

Or possibly I'd detect the sounds and odour of something more sulphurous and uninviting as the afternoon became suddenly darker . . .

Either way, *Flap, flap, off we go! Up above or . . .*

But it didn't happen.

Peter died. He was buried.

Eve cried briefly and the days kept on turning.

Here I am. No rest for the wicked?

If this is a test of some sort have I passed or failed? Is this a punishment or a reprieve? A chance to redeem myself? Or is it just what comes next?

Either way I'm thankful Peter hasn't reappeared at Rosemary Close, not on the night he died, or any other since. It crossed my mind it might happen but I had a feeling that wasn't how it would work for him, that he just didn't have the will to remain as I had, the necessary iron spine or any kind of spine when it came down to it.

If he had re-materialised we'd have had a lot to talk about. It would've been an epic battle no doubt, with lightning and thunderbolts enough to shake picture frames and rattle windows long into the night and the months to come. I might have enjoyed that. But, no, I think I know where he went – no reprieve for him. No grey area, not like mine, if that's even a factor. So many questions, so few answers.

I know I need to find someone to ask, so, one day soon, I intend to strike out and see if I can make sense of those tricks of the light, those whispers. I'm starting to see them more and more, now that I have the focus and energy to really look and listen. I've begun to feel as if I'm not alone after all. This knowledge comes in the night, in the sounds of the house and my stilled heart, somewhere in the spaces where I used to dream. My eyes flit around, almost catching sight of something, under human hearing, through the movement of the shadows. I would not be surprised if one day it thickens into a touch. I may not be the only one here, or out there, biding my time. I'm ready to grow up and make some new friends.

But for now, here we are, just the three of us, Eve, Adam and me.

Eve is doing well. I couldn't hurt her in the end. I decided not to, though I won't pretend I didn't think about it in that dark night, after I realised she'd left me at the beach. I wondered if I could let her get away with it, because it had lain with her at the last moment, the ability to save me, to have called for help. She failed me there and I thought about whispering to her, about taking my revenge, of saying, 'Walk in front of a bus, Eve, jump in the sea, pull that radio into the bath with you – come to me.' I could have taken a life for a life. My life.

But in the end enough was enough. I'd lost the stomach for it. We all make mistakes. I've decided that, for now at least, I'll just wait and see how things turn out. Once more I watch and wait and have all the time in the world, or so it seems. There's always another story on the way sooner or later. I just hope I don't get too bored in the meantime. The devil makes work for idle hands, and the same applies to memories of them, I suspect.

There are things I can do to keep busy. As I said, with Peter passed into the ether, the chain forged between us on that February night, shackling me to his side for so long, is gone. I have a kind of freedom, headed neither up nor down just onwards, so I might as well get out and about. A little visit to Eliot might be in order soon, to see what he's up to and if he's suitably sorry yet. I have a few things to say to him and perhaps to Bella.

It will be nice to be here for a while first, to see if Eve will make a go of it. She's different now, far more organised and driven than I would've expected of the woman who permitted her husband to lock up all her shoes. It's almost as if she had a plan all these years and was working on it deep down under her subservient smiles – a plush, new quilted life plan. With Peter gone she's unfurling it, piece by piece, square by square, the canvas of a new life.

She wears a lot of black and lace these days and bolder lipstick. She's bought chunky-heeled boots and a leather jacket. She's bought a CD player for the kitchen which belts out classic rock when she cooks and she smiles between stirring while Adam air-guitars around her.

Once Peter had been six feet under for three months she started working three afternoons a week as a nursery assistant. The letter had come yesterday to say she'd been accepted on a GNVQ course to train as an art therapist with a view to working with children with learning disabilities. That made her smile even more.

She has a pretty smile now, a warm rather than a tight one. Adam thinks it's pretty, too, and sometimes we both think it simultaneously so we tell her at the same moment and as she smiles ever wider so her confidence expands. That's good because she's going to need it in this life. Other men will want her and there are other Peters out there, who no doubt sense that Eve might still have some of the qualities of easy prey.

So, for now I stand guard, at the front door, lightning bolts at the ready, and the days keep turning on a falling leaf, through the dark days to come into another spring, the three of us tumbling forward.

Thank God Adam is still young enough to forget his father.

Only the years will tell how much of a seed Peter has left in him and what kind of tree it will grow into. I'll keep an eye on that, just in case in the future I have to act again, in case the sins of the fathers really are visited upon the sons.

I'll keep a close watch on him when he and other people are near flights of stairs – I'll listen for any whispers other than my own.

But for now I watch. I watch him play and sit beside him and Eve on the bed when they read bedtime stories. He's a smart little kid, thoughtful beyond his years and I've begun to wonder if he senses me sometimes, or even sees me.

Just yesterday, when Eve asked him who he was smiling at, in the bedroom door, at story time, he said, 'The lady with the golden hair like an angel.'

'Maybe it's your guardian angel,' said Eve with a grin at the empty doorway, tousling his hair.

Then without any prompting, Adam started to sing:

'There was a little girl, who had a little curl . . . right in the middle of her forehead . . . when she was good she was very, very good . . . '

He looked at the spot where I was standing and smiled.

I smiled back. I smiled as if I was alive again, with teeth and eye-crinkles and lips drawn back, what I hoped was a perfectly angelic smile. How sweet! A girl in a suit and red scarf, a girl *like an angel*. Bless him! In all my life I think I've never been called anything so inappropriate or so optimistic.

All I can do now is make a wish to be very, very good.